WITHDRAWN

the end of east

JEN SOOKFONG LEE

the end of east

thomas dunne books
st. martin's press ✹ new york

This is a work of fiction. All of the characters, organizations, and events portrayed in this novel are either products of the author's imagination or are used fictitiously.

THOMAS DUNNE BOOKS.
An imprint of St. Martin's Press.

www.thomasdunnebooks.com
www.stmartins.com

Library of Congress Cataloging-in-Publication Data

Lee, Jen Sookfong.
    The end of East / Jen Sookfong Lee.—1st U.S. ed.
        p. cm.
    ISBN-13: 978-0-312-37985-8
    ISBN-10: 0-312-37985-4
    1. Chinese—Canada—Fiction. 2. Immigrants—Fiction. 3. Family—Fiction. 4. Aging parents—Care—Fiction. 5. Chinatown (Vancouver, B.C.)—Fiction. 6. Vancouver (B.C.)—Fiction. I. Title.

PR9199.4.L438 E53 2008
813'.6—dc22

2008004747

First published in Canada by Alfred A. Knopf Canada

First U.S. Edition: May 2008

10 9 8 7 6 5 4 3 2 1

for my father

prologue

At first, what frightened her about this place was the drizzle—the omnipresent grey of morning, afternoon, nighttime too. She was afraid that she would slowly be leached of colour and that, one day, while she was combing her hair in the mirror, she would see that her reflection was as grey as the sky, sea and land that surrounded her. Everything she saw as she moved about the city was filtered through the mist—dampened, weighed down, burdened.

She would come home after a day in Chinatown and find her wool pants covered in tiny drops of water—cold, as if no human being had ever touched them before. If she didn't brush them off, they would seep into the fabric until they chilled her skin and she shivered into the night, long after the dishes were washed and everyone else had gone to bed.

In the summer, the sun finally emerged, dried up the puddles, opened flowers that had cowered in the rain. Buttercups shone in the light and multiplied in the lawn faster than she could dig them out. Children spat watermelon seeds over the porch railing, laughing at the squirrels who scurried across the lawn in fear. But every year, as winter returned, these days slipped from her memory. Too good to be true, perhaps. Too few to be important.

One morning, she woke and realized that she had come to accept the drizzle, that she had grown resigned to the squelch of rubber boots, the smell of damp wool on the bus. She walked around the park in the mornings, a film of fine water on her cheeks and eyelashes. Soon, she could not start her day without washing her face in the mist, letting the coolness do away with the bad dreams from the night.

And the half-light that lingered throughout the day let her believe that she was somewhere else, a dream-like netherworld in which anything might happen. Men could become lovers again. Women could be ageless. Children might even come back home.

But what she settled for was the cool, wet breeze that came in through the windows, the air that straightened her spine as she walked. The way the drizzle stayed with her, soaked into her hair, her clothes, her sheets. It pushed itself onto her skin, huddled with her when she cried, remained cool even as she cooked at a blazing stove. Unshakeable. Like family.

one

stanley park

"It is time," my mother says as she pulls me from the cab, "to run that old-man smell out of my house."

As I haul my luggage out of the trunk, the smell of smouldering dust and gas fills the air, burning my nose and mouth. I follow my mother's rapidly retreating body around the side of the house to the backyard, wondering if she has finally snapped and set one my sisters ablaze.

In the driveway off the lane, she pokes angrily at a crackling fire with a metal garden rake; I catch my breath, holding my suitcase in front of me like a shield. Piles of my grandfather's old, woolly clothes line the backyard and spill into the gravel alley, waiting to be tossed into the gassy flames. A light rain begins to fall, generating puffs of smoke that blow into my face. I cough, but she doesn't seem to hear me above the snap and sizzle.

Waving the rake in my direction, she shouts, "Take your suitcase upstairs and go help your sister." As I turn back toward the house, she slaps down a stray spark that has landed in her permed, greying hair.

Once inside, I scan the front hall. The same rubber plant behind the door. My old slippers by the stairs. I breathe out, and cobwebs (suspiciously familiar) sway in the corners.

My mother steps through the door after me, her hands on her wide hips. "What's taking you so long? I thought I told you to run upstairs."

"I'm jet-lagged," I mutter, kicking off my shoes.

She inspects my face closely, staring at me through her thick glasses. "Jet-lagged? Montreal is only three hours ahead. Go. Penny is waiting." She spins me around with a little push and pokes me in the back with one sharp fingernail.

I trudge up the stairs to my grandfather's bedroom, where my sister is on her hands and knees, ripping out the nubby red carpet he brought over from his small apartment in Chinatown. Her long black hair drags on the sub-floor.

"Samantha," Penny says, pushing her bangs out of her eyes. "I feel like I've been waiting for you forever."

My hands shake. I try to tell myself that it's only the dampness in the air that's causing this deep bone shiver. But, really, I am simply afraid. When I was sitting in the airplane, the idea of coming home didn't seem so real or so final, and I could pretend that I wasn't passing over province after province. Standing here, in my grandfather's old room, with my mother's footsteps coming up quickly behind me, I know that I have irrevocably returned.

"We have to get rid of your grandfather's junk before the wedding. We'll need his bedroom for the tea ceremony," my mother says, pushing me aside to inspect the closet. She turns to Penny: "I don't know why you have to get married so fast. I'm too old to run around like this. Inconsiderate girl." She lets out a loud breath, punctuating her rapid, angry Chinese with a huff.

"Grandfather's been dead for ten years, Mother," Penny says quietly in English, as usual. "And we've been engaged for almost a month. You've had plenty of time."

She waves her hand. "Why do I think you'll understand? I've had other things to do, like look after all you girls by myself."

Penny looks at me with her round, seemingly innocent eyes and shrugs.

I walk to the window and open it even wider. A prickly wind starts to blow out the thickness of my grandfather's mysterious balms, the slight mouldiness of his tweed. Sharp chemical smoke wafts in. My mother walks briskly out of the room with as many of my grandfather's possessions as she can carry—old books, a grey knitted scarf, a faded wooden apple crate with its lid nailed shut. The fear of bad luck and death hangs over her like a storm cloud, and her face is set.

"Sammy," she snaps as she disappears down the hall, "clean out the dresser." Penny starts to follow, dragging the rolled-up carpet behind her. As she passes, she whispers to me, "Your hair looks nice." I put my hands on my bangs as she hurries away.

My grandfather left this room intending, perhaps, to come back one day. We kept it undisturbed, as we thought he wanted us to, but then he died and the door just stayed shut until my sisters and I forgot it was even there. I suppose my mother never thought his long life was as important, or as unlucky, as my father's. It took her only one week to burn everything of his.

Listlessly, I open my grandfather's dresser. In the top drawer is a cigarette tin stuffed with papers and photographs, all of them yellow around the edges. As I pull documents out one by one, I can hear his cough, the chime on the radio signalling the end of a hockey game, the click of his false teeth.

If my grandfather was ever young, I never knew. He was quiet, eating his daily bacon and eggs and reading newspapers in his brown upholstered chair. Now, I unearth a folded and yellowed piece of paper. His head tax certificate. A thin neck balancing an irregular head. Bulging eyes. The date stamped near the bottom tells me he is not quite eighteen.

I read quickly, my ears turned toward the back door and the sound of my mother returning. "Chan Seid Quan," it says, "whose photograph is attached hereto on June 27, 1913, arrived or landed at Vancouver, BC, on the *Empress of India*." His arrival is stamped and duly noted by G.L. Milne, Controller of Chinese Immigration.

The old cigarette tin, with its aging photos and cracked papers, suggests that my grandfather, in all his silence, never wanted to forget. In these pictures, his right leg is always shorter than his left. His bow tie is never straight. His face is bony. But what did it mean that he wanted to remember these things?

Perhaps my grandfather wanted to think of his flaws so he could say, "I am not perfect, forgive me."

I hear my mother and sister coming through the back door for more things to burn. I thrust the tin under the bed and feel something sharp cut my thumb—one of my grandfather's old straight razors, its blade protruding from its crumbling leather sleeve. I never saw his barbershop, never walked through Chinatown with him, meeting all the men he knew. He was eighty when I was born, his shop long since sold, his customers long since dead.

When I turn around, sucking the blood off my hand, it's only Penny standing in the doorway, brushing the dirt and ash off her baggy T-shirt. She looks up at me, meets my gaze and drops her eyes again.

"Find anything else to burn?" she asks, staring at the ends of her hair.

"Not much." I sit down on the bare mattress, facing the window. "Where is everyone?"

"Oh, you know how it is. Wendy is busy at work. Jackie can't leave the kids. Daisy is off on some business trip." Penny pulls an old stray sock from the closet. "It's not you they don't want to see." She gestures toward the kitchen, where I can hear my mother muttering to herself.

"Of course." I wipe my thumb on my jeans. "How's the wedding coming along?"

"You know, it's all just flowers and food and dresses." She puts a hand on her stomach. "Wait—that reminds me. I have to make a quick phone call to the hotel. You can finish all this by yourself, right?"

I nod and see the relief on her round face—the loosening of the muscles around her eyes and mouth. I wonder if I looked the same when I left Vancouver for Montreal six years ago, delirious with the kind of happiness only escape can bring. My hands begin to shake again, and this time they will not stop.

As she steps back into the hall, Penny turns her head. "Sammy? Thanks for coming back. Adam really wanted to get married quickly, and I knew I just couldn't live with her anymore. And someone has to."

We hear my mother walking toward us, the slap of her slippers on the floor. Penny looks suddenly afraid. I stare at her T-shirt, at the completely obscured belly inside it, and wonder what she has been hiding. She shifts on her wide feet.

"I have to go," she says quickly as she backs out of the room.

I haul the rest of Grandfather's clothes out to the fire. The smoke begins to form a dark grey layer over my face and arms as I throw hats and vests and belts into the flames. I look over at my mother, and she stands perfectly still, staring fixedly at the burning pile in front of her.

Later, after hiding the cigarette tin on the top shelf of my closet, I return to my grandfather's bedroom one more time. There is nothing left but a sub-floor, a bed and his empty dresser, yet his smell remains, embedded so deeply into the walls that nothing, not even the tornado-like energy of my deceptively small and shrinking mother, will ever erase it. I am looking at a beginning and an end, and a myriad of possibilities for the body in between.

For once, the curtains are open. I am six years old and lie on the floor in my favourite teal blue tracksuit as the sunlight pools around me, warming my closed eyelids. I see yellow, dots of white, the faint shadows of movement from the television. I open one eye and push my glasses back into place to see how Laura Ingalls Wilder, newly married, is faring on *Little House on the Prairie*.

"I need a haircut," my father announces, walking in the back door from the garden. He stands between me and the television. "Sammy, be a good girl and tell your grandfather to bring out his scissors."

I pull myself up and run into my grandfather's room, rubbing my eyes as I go. "Dad wants a haircut," I shout, just to make sure he can hear me. "Can I see your barber's pole?"

Grandfather smiles and stands up slowly from his dusty brocade chair. "Of course. You just sit here and watch while I get my things." He pulls an old wooden apple crate from the closet and unwraps the pole from its layers of newspapers.

The barber's pole seems to spin endlessly—red, then blue, then white and red again. I wonder if it somehow turns inward on itself, pulling its own striped skin into a hidden and perpetually hungry mouth. My father, passing by on his way to the basement, sniffs. "An optical illusion," he says.

"Why did you become a barber?" I look away from the pole just long enough to squint at my grandfather's lined, thin face. "I want to be an interior designer."

He turns off the pole then, and passes his hand over the scissors and combs in his haircutting kit. "After I married your grandmother, the man who used to own my shop wanted to retire and go back to China, so I took over, simple as that."

He picks up his barber's kit and, with one foot, shoves the apple crate back into his closet.

While I stand in the corner, half-hidden by our yellow fridge, my grandfather slowly lines the kitchen floor with a blue plastic tarp and arranges his small broom, scissors and shaver on the table. My father brings up the bar stool from the basement, and my grandfather, his hands trembling just slightly, goes to work, the silence between them an invisible, unbroken wall.

These haircuts were the only times I saw them touch, those brief moments when my grandfather awkwardly placed his hand on my father's shoulder for support, or when his long, delicate fingers brushed my father's neck clean—gently, carefully. As they both grew older and thinner (mirrors of each other, yet also somehow not), my grandfather would linger over my father's head, the expression on his face, as always, impassive.

I creep through the basement door as quietly as possible, hoping that my entrance won't wake my mother. As I walk toward the stairs, I can hear Penny snoring through her open bedroom door. I climb upward, passing the doilies my mother has draped over the banister, my body dull and heavy with wine and cigarettes. *Such a long evening,* I keep thinking, *like a boring foreign movie with no subtitles.* The whole time, even as I was sitting on a bar stool with my old friends from high school, nodding along to the beat (monotonous, cold), I could only think, *Fuck you, Matt.* I push open my bedroom door, throw my shoes on the floor beside my bed and put on my pyjamas. *I just don't know how to finish things, that's all.*

I stumble my way to the bathroom. My mother mumbles in her sleep. I turn on the light and look in the mirror. Red eyes, flat hair, makeup rubbed off a long time ago. I suck in my thin cheeks.

"What's up, Dollface?" I say to my reflection, realizing too late that I have just mimicked the way Matt used to greet me in the mornings. Our last day together, he placed his hands on either side of my face, holding my head just so, daring me, it seemed, to move. I did move, but only when he let me, after he kissed me and asked, "How about just one more time?"

I shake my head, rub the smokiness of the night out of my eyes. *At least I have all this.* I wave my hand around my mother's pink and peach bathroom, knock over the crocheted toilet paper doll, and laugh. *Memories can go fuck themselves.*

I walk through the hallway and look up at the family portrait hanging on the wall. My own younger face looks back at me from within the heavy wooden frame. Shadows play across the picture, making the faces of my parents and my four older sisters jump out—three-dimensional, gargoyle-like. My eyes pass over their faces until they come to my father, sitting in a tall leather chair, a rolled-up newspaper in his hands. I walk a little farther, and his eyes follow me, the irises moving with every step I make. I think I see him breathe.

I stop moving and close my eyes, hoping that this living, breathing version of my father will go away, disappear into the night. "Are you watching me?" I whisper. "I thought you had left us a long time ago." I open one eye. My father's photographed face, usually so benign, sneers.

I run forward and shut my bedroom door, feeling the resistance of the darkness without.

The next morning, I walk into the kitchen for breakfast and blink at the bright sunshine pouring in through the window. Outside, the back garden is tangled with weeds, but even so, through the tangled blackberry branches and dandelions, I can see the beginnings of returning chives, the buds on the branches of the neighbour's cherry tree.

Penny stands in the driveway, slowly digging at the huge pile of ash with a snow shovel. She places a hand on her belly, rubs it counter-clockwise. Still wearing my flannel pyjamas and slippers, I step outside and join her.

"We have to get rid of this somehow," she says, kicking at the ash with her shoe. "Are people even allowed to burn garbage in their yards anymore?"

"Of course not. But do you think Mom cares about bylaws?" We giggle, hands over our mouths just in case. "We'll put it in bags and drive it down to the dump. No one will ever know." I take the shovel from her and start working.

Penny stands to the side, watching me dig through the black, dusty pile and holding her sleeve up to her face. My pants are streaked with ash. I start to wonder what this looks like to the neighbours. My unwashed hair and skinny arms. My dirty pink pyjamas. The remains of my grandfather's life floating through the air and into our noses and mouths, no heavier than useless flakes of skin. I look up the unpaved alley at the decrepit garages and dangerously leaning fences. Nothing, it seems, ever really changes.

I can feel my sister behind me, unmoving. I turn.

"Are you going to help, or are you just going to stand there?"

"Don't be a bitch, Sammy. If you want to complain, then I have six years' worth to get off my chest."

I turn back to the garbage bags.

"You didn't have to come back," Penny says suddenly. "You could have stayed in school forever. Don't blame me for this."

I try to think of something to say, because she's right, but she's also wrong. Walking down Ste-Catherine or St-Denis, past the well-dressed Montrealers, I had become convinced that they could smell the stink of Vancouver's Chinatown—durian and rain-soaked cardboard boxes—leaking out of my pores. I had tried to let the city absorb me completely, envelop me in its own particular smells of poutine and river water, but it was no use. Leaving Vancouver was like leaving myself.

When I fled Montreal, everything was unfinished: my thesis, my feelings about my boyfriend, the unpainted walls in our apartment. I had run away once before, and I did it again, fear and duty propelling me back to the place I had once escaped. I kept telling myself that, after all, it was my turn to be the good daughter. What I didn't know was that my spot in the family had been ready for me for a long time, carved out like a cast made from my body.

My contact lenses itch; a tear drops off the end of my chin. I wonder if Penny can hear me sniffling. I take a deep breath and turn around, but she's gone. I squint through the ash toward the house, but all the doors and windows are closed tight against the sun.

Chinatown shows its ghosts on every surface. They appear and disappear in the shifting light, hiding and re-hiding in the uneven concrete. In the brightness of day, homeless people fight by the Carnegie Centre on the corner of Main and Hastings. The produce merchants pace up and down the sidewalks outside their shops with their rubber aprons and boxes of vegetables and shout, "Very fine bok choy! Only ninety-nine cents a pound!" And the few surviving old men without families congregate around stoops and doorways, smoking their cigarettes, saying hello to everyone who walks by. When I was a child, my mother walked me quickly past these men, and threw away the candy they gave me.

"Nothing but a tourist trap. A dumping ground for human trash," my father always said, his eyes darting left to right as we hurriedly made our way through the markets on Keefer and Pender. The inevitable smell of rotting produce and piss only angered him more. "These old buildings should be torn down. Probably full of rats; squatters, too." Even now, I am still faintly scared of the alleys, the sides of buildings with their mysterious downward steps that don't seem to go anywhere, the cloudy purple glass bricks embedded in the sidewalks that seem to hide yet reveal something both underground and sinister.

I avoid the roasted pigs hanging in the butchers' windows and the pungent smells rising from the ragged corners and, instead, propel myself westward, where the ocean salts the air, where I can pretend that those old Chinatown sidewalks aren't so deeply lodged in my body that they tilt my walk just so, shift my eyes left and right.

The photo from my grandfather's head tax certificate feels stuck to the inside of my head as I trudge along the seawall in Stanley Park (gulls and hot dogs, sand and flesh; here, this strip of sand and high-rise apartments makes me forget the stubby lawns and cracked driveways of our neighbourhood in East Vancouver, where cats mate behind garbage cans and old women try to grow squash in the thin, acidic soil). I imagine him walking beside me, a little off-balance, dressed, even in this unseasonable, early spring heat, in a well-pressed grey suit. He would ask me why I walk here, why I've grown so thin. Why I am unable to finish school or hold on to a boyfriend. Why I spend so much time away from my mother.

I imagine he understands.

At a concession on the beach at English Bay, I buy an orange Popsicle. My grandfather shakes his head.

"You'll get a headache."

I ignore him, but he follows me anyway, staying a few feet back so that he is out of sight. He says nothing, only treads softly behind me, his hands behind his back as he leans forward into the sea wind. I do not turn, knowing that once I look directly at him, his gaze will hold me until he is ready to let me go, until I've done exactly what he wants and he rests, allowing me to do the same.

I'm not ready for him, not ready to understand what he needs. I would rather rush ahead, let my body do the thinking so that I am only following the urges of my own flesh.

I stare ahead, feel a gust on my back.

That old man smell, I think. *Not again.* I turn to look.

arrival

Seid Quan knows he is dirty; he can smell the boat on his skin, the salty, rancid odour of cured fish, other men's hair oils, rotting wood. It is windy, and the water is nothingness: grey, bottomless, incomprehensible. The roof of his mouth is crackling dry, and his hands shake as he smoothes down the front of his only jacket. He wants his mother.

Only one thought runs through his head: *I cannot imagine that this will be all right.*

He looks out toward the city and sees the mountains, dark blue and hazy behind the wood frame buildings, which appear dirty and brown, larger manifestations of the smell on his skin. He fears that the stink will be mistaken for the smell of China, but he does not know how to say that there would be no smell if Canada never was, if the boats were not so full of desperation, men trading one kind of poverty for another. Mud pools around the wooden sidewalks, indistinguishable from horse dung or something worse. He hears the water crashing, changing shape as it hits the shore and the wooden docks. He wonders if the ocean (so close, so savage) will consume him and sweep everything else away. He shifts his small bag from one hand to the other.

He does not know where to start, which lineup he needs to be in, which direction to walk in to find the part of the city where all the Chinamen live. He had hoped someone would be able to guide him, but when he was on the boat, while they were talking and eating their watery soup and salt-cured, fatty pork, he found that everyone knew as little as he did. Like him, they had read the letters that other men from their villages sent home describing the beautiful land, the generosity of the white men, the fortunes they were making. And like him, they saw how much richer those men's wives and children became.

The first afternoon at sea, an older man shuffled past him on the deck, his thin hips only partially hidden by his oversized Western-style pants. He turned to Seid Quan and looked him over from head to shoes.

"You must be new."

Seid Quan nodded.

"I am the only one on this boat returning to Canada. My wife begged me to stay home—I must be crazy."

"Don't say that, Uncle."

The old man pointed a finger at Seid Quan's nose. "You'll go crazy too one day. And by then, it won't matter if you say it out loud or not."

That exchange, Seid Quan now reflects, was not very helpful.

He joins one of six lines, each with a white man at its head, sitting at a desk. He hopes he is in the right one.

No one on the boat had been worried. A golden mountain it couldn't be, of course, but there would be jobs, good paying jobs, jobs with which you could feed your whole family for a year with only two months' pay. And in a place with that kind of opportunity, the going could only be easy. However, Seid Quan still isn't so sure.

The line moves, and he pushes his suitcase two feet forward. He peers ahead and sees that a policeman is leading one of the men to a building on the left, a building with bars over its tiny windows. He hears someone say, "They are going to put us in that jailhouse for a couple of days, so they can fully check our papers. I didn't come here to be thrown in prison!"

Just before they disembarked, he told one of the other men he was worried that the stories couldn't be as good as they sounded. The man laughed and said, "Well, why do we keep coming, then?"

Seid Quan responded, "Do you see any rich men on this boat?"

The other man laughed again and, as he walked away, the loose soles of his worn-out shoes slapping against the floor, he turned around. "You can doubt all you want, brother, but remember how much money the people in your village saved to send you to this gold mountain. So, for their sake, it had better be as good as everyone says."

The white man peers at him over the rim of his glasses. "Your papers," he says, with his hand stretched out. Seid Quan swallows. It is his turn.

He is one of the lucky ones. He spends only one night in the jail cell at the dock and manages not to cry, as some of the other young men do. They beg the guards to let them out, snot and tears running down their faces for everyone to see. The guards turn away and pretend they don't understand.

Really, thinks Seid Quan, *what else could these young men possibly be asking for?*

When Seid Quan is released, he follows the rest of the Chinese men who are leaving the docks from various boats. Some of them are coming back after having visited their families. Some are like him: gangly, open-mouthed, eyes squinting in the morning sun. Like a line of ants, they walk east. He sniffs the air, smells rotting fish and freshly cut wood.

One of the older men asks Seid Quan what his family name is. "Chan? Why, that's my name too! Good to meet you, little brother! You should come with me to our clan association. The men there, they'll help you find a place to sleep, maybe a job, too. It's always good to have family in a strange place, eh?"

At the clan association's offices, which turn out to be in the storage room behind a restaurant, the men quickly find Seid Quan a just-vacated room in a boarding house and arrange for him to begin English lessons at the church every morning for two hours, starting immediately. The next afternoon, he finds a note slipped under his door from the clan association president, telling him to report for work at Yip Tailors at five. There, he discovers that several businesses in Chinatown have hired him to clean their offices and front rooms after they close. They dare not hire white cleaning women, so it is Seid Quan who begins sweeping up the loose threads at the tailor's shop, cleaning windows at the laundries and washing out towels for the barber. *Women's work,* he thinks, looking down at his thin, chapped hands, *but better than nothing.*

He doesn't start until the evening, and spends most of his days walking through the city, although he stays away from the richer neighbourhoods. Stanley Park lies just beyond the tall houses and manicured gardens of the West End. He has heard that it is like a forest within the city, a place where trees the size of buildings dwarf even the brawniest white men. Seid Quan wants to breathe in the tang of the trees every morning and feel the moss with his hands, but he dares to walk only as far as the entrance, where he stands and stares at the white families strolling along the water. One morning, a photographer, who had set up his camera opposite a large tree stump, turns to him and asks, "Brother, do you need a picture to send home?" Seid Quan fishes in his pockets for some change, poses for the photo and scurries off.

A few weeks later, he walks along Pender Street, nodding at the laundrymen who call out to him from their front steps. "Lucky brother," one shouts. "My shop is like an oven, it's so hot, and here you are, walking in the fresh air without a care in the world. How about we trade places?" The frail, wood-sided tailor and laundry shops begin to disappear, and Seid Quan finds himself among tall brick and limestone buildings. He shrinks into his jacket and keeps his head down, avoiding the glances of the well-dressed white men walking around and toward him. Some, walking in pairs, whisper to each other, and Seid Quan can only guess what they are saying.

"Another one, did you see, Robert? I wonder if they simply cut off their fingers to grow more Chinamen and breed themselves that way."

He turns south to the Granville Bridge. He cannot keep his eyes off the teeming grey-tinged water below, swollen with floating logs. Somehow, he had expected the water here to be clean, reflective of the sky and the faces of people surrounding it, not this brown and grey mess, not much cleaner than the Pearl River, which Seid Quan had never liked to visit. *All that shit smell,* he remembers. *Made my eyes water.*

He steps off onto the shores of False Creek; even here, more Chinamen. Their shacks are built with scraps from the lumberyards and whatever else they can find—hammered-out biscuit tins, aluminium wrappers. Seid Quan notices the gaping holes in the walls, the small plots of limp vegetables growing in the muck. He feels the failure in the air, almost as thick as the smell of the human waste being used as manure. *How can they keep on like this? Doing nothing, making the rest of us look so bad and lazy?* An old man peeks through his open doorway and smiles when he sees Seid Quan.

"Young man! Come in and have some tea with me." He waves his skinny arms.

"Thank you, Uncle, but I need to go back to Chinatown very soon to start work."

"Ah, you young fellows, always working. I used to work hard too, laying down tracks for those godforsaken trains." He shakes his head. "Some other time, then. I'm always here."

Seid Quan, back on the bridge, sighs with relief.

That night, Seid Quan washes the floors in the front room of Mr. Yip's shop on Carrall Street. There are rat droppings everywhere, and some of the cloth used for winter suits has been chewed through, probably for nests. This close to the waterfront, the rats seem to outnumber the people. Seid Quan carefully kicks a trap into the corner, where the white business-men who come in to get their shirts made cheaply won't see it. The high windows above the door are open for the fresh night air—clear and, as Seid Quan thinks, blue to the eye if it weren't invisible. The streets are mostly empty, and even the sounds of gambling that sometimes float out into the night—the tapping of mah-jong tiles, the shouts of men losing the money they have

just made, whisky-rough singing—are absent. *It's eerie tonight,*
Seid Quan thinks. *I don't like being alone when it's like this.*

He hears footsteps, several of them, running. He puts out
his kerosene lamp and steps back into the shadows of the dark
shop, behind a dressmaker's dummy.

A man is shouting in English, "There, over there! All these
places are owned by them!"

Just as Seid Quan begins to understand what it is they're
shouting, the front window of the shop shatters. Seid Quan
ducks, covering his head and face with his arms. Someone outside laughs and the running footsteps continue. He can hear
other windows breaking in the distance.

He walks to the front, glass cracking under his feet. A brick
lies on the floor, and he sees that there are English words written on it. Just then, Mr. Yip, who lives upstairs, comes down in
his nightshirt. He walks over to the window and shakes his head,
murmuring, "It's been a long time since someone broke my
window, ten years, maybe. I thought this wouldn't happen anymore." He looks at Seid Quan. "You okay, little brother? Not
cut anywhere?"

"I'm all right. I found this." Seid Quan hands over the brick
to the older man. "What does it say?"

Mr. Yip takes a look at the writing and drops the brick on
the floor. Glass fragments bounce up. "It says 'Die, Chinaman,
die.'" He turns away and starts heading to the back. "I'll get a
broom and help you clean this up."

After they are done, Mr. Yip sits down heavily on the stool
behind his sewing machine. "Such anger," he says, shaking his
head again. "They are only afraid of us, you know. Afraid
that we will take jobs they think are theirs, afraid that we will
one day be their next-door neighbours and turn their children

into lazy opium addicts." He looks up at Seid Quan. "Look at that long face. Come. We'll have to do something to forget about this mess."

Forgetting. Seid Quan puts a hand on his stomach to try to quell the rising guilt. *They think we are all lazy and shouldn't live here, and I thought the same.* Forgetting is the very thing he needs.

Mr. Yip won't tell Seid Quan where they're going, only that they must pick up Mr. Lam, the barber, on their way. Seid Quan looks suspiciously at the tailor's finely fitted shirt and pants and wonders whom he is dressing up for.

Mr. Lam opens the door to his apartment. As soon as he sees them, he hoots loudly. "Coming to get me in the middle of the night," he laughs as he pulls on his trousers, "can only mean one thing!"

Ten minutes later, Seid Quan sits in a small living room. He perches awkwardly on the edge of a red and purple velour sofa and does not speak to the other men. His friends slap each other on the back, make lewd jokes and take sips from a flask Mr. Lam pulls out of one of his pockets. Seid Quan fixes his eyes on the gold-painted ceiling.

A fat woman with red lips and ratty hair waddles into the room. Her blue eyes are small and almost invisible in her puffy face. She breathes heavily and winks. "All right, who's next?"

Mr. Yip pushes Seid Quan in the back until he stands up uncertainly and wavers slightly in place.

"C'mon, fella. Up the stairs, second door on the left. Enjoy." The fat woman laughs wickedly and waddles back to her desk by the front door.

He goes up the stairs slowly, one foot in front of the other.

The plush carpet silences his approach, and the sweat on his hands leaves the banisters sticky and wet.

He stands in front of the door and breathes deeply. He knocks.

"Come on in!"

He opens the door—slowly, creakily—and pokes his head through the small crack.

On the enormous bed sits a woman. She wears a black satin robe and high-heeled slippers, her toes glinting red in the yellow light. Her hair is an impossible brassy orange colour, and her eyes are long, serpentine and lined in kohl. She pats the spot on the bed beside her.

"Have a seat, lovey."

He sits on her bed, his hands steadying his body on the satin spread. She talks rapidly, giggling about her job and the other girls and what she tells her parents she is doing out west in her letters home. He listens carefully, trying to understand as much as he can.

"They're such *nice* people," she trills. "Dad practically kills himself working in that mine like he does, and Mum, she just raises her chickens and takes in washing, kind of like you people. So I tell them I work at the telegraph office, copying messages down and things like that. Mum would die if she thought I did *this*." She drapes her arm around his waist and whispers, "What are you gonna tell your family?"

"Nothing," he mutters.

"Gosh, your English is pretty good compared to some of the others I see around here. I tell you, if I had ten dollars for every mute Chinaman I had to keep company with, I'd be a rich woman and not doing this anymore."

He looks at her face covered in white powder, smells her

perfume of lilies and musk. He closes his eyes and tries not to think about who else has been on this bed, inside this whore.

It is as if he is sitting on his marriage bed, and he sees the red-veiled face of his future bride looking down at her shoes. He can smell her freshly washed skin—lye and rosewater—and hear her breath. He imagines her hair, how it might feel, how blackly it might shine in the light. In his mind he reaches for her hand.

The whore giggles and thrusts her tongue in his ear.

Seid Quan's long arms and legs have become tangled in the slippery sheets, in the long, dry clumps of her hair. He can smell sweat (his or hers or that of the man who was here before, he does not know, and does not want to find out), the heady odour of what he thinks must be gin. Her bony chest and ribs are pressed up against him, her white, white skin stretching so much he is sure it will be torn in two, revealing her bird-like skeleton, her blackened and diseased lungs. He places his hand over her face and lets out one high-pitched, razor-sharp cry.

"My God," she whispers. "I thought you were going to snap my neck."

The quiet of dawn helps Seid Quan forget the scratchiness in his throat, the fuzzy coating on the inside of his mouth. As he walks up the stairs of his rooming house, he rubs the back of his aching head. He wonders how badly he smells of whisky.

"I've been looking for you."

Seid Quan jumps at the sound of an unexpected voice. He shoves his room key back into his pocket before he turns around. Leaning up against the window at the end of the hall is a young man, dressed stylishly in pleated trousers and suspenders. As Seid Quan squints in the early morning light, he notices that the man's hems trail loose threads on the floor and the knees are worn shiny and thin.

"Lim? Is that you?"

The young man walks over to Seid Quan, his arm outstretched. "It's me, all right. Come and shake the hand of an old friend."

"Is this your room, then?" Lim asks after Seid Quan has opened the door and offered him his only chair.

"Yes. It's not much, but it's dry and cheap." Seid Quan smiles. "I should take you out to the café for some coffee and a doughnut, but first you must tell me how everyone is doing in the village. Have you seen my mother?"

Lim nods. "Yes. She wants you to know that she's looking for a wife for you." Lim laughs loudly. "I don't know how you could manage a woman, old friend, when you can't even say boo to a cat."

Seid Quan blushes. "And how are all the others? Kam? How about Hon?"

"Kam went to Hong Kong, started working in a restaurant. Wants to find a lady to marry." Lim snorts. "Hon, he went to America, lives in California. Doing laundry." He brushes a piece of lint off his pants.

"All our friends gone," mutters Seid Quan.

"Are you still cleaning shops?"

Seid Quan nods.

"Degrading jobs, all of them. I'm not going to stoop, though. If anyone is going to suck everything out of this country, it's going to be me."

Seid Quan raises his eyebrows. "What do you mean?"

"I'm going to be the richest Chinaman in Canada, you wait and see."

"How are you going to do that?"

"I'll figure something out. I always do." He grins widely, showing all his long teeth.

Seid Quan sighs. "You should go to the church, like I do, and start taking the English lessons. I can read some now, and I'm working on writing next."

Lim laughs loudly. "I didn't come all this way to go to school." He stands up, adjusts his suspenders. "How about that coffee? Your treat." He saunters out the door and down the hall, not even looking to see if Seid Quan is keeping up.

Mr. Lam watches Seid Quan as he mops the floor and manoeuvres around the empty barber chairs. Outside, the light is fading. The fish peddler dumps his cart of melted ice onto the street, leaving behind a slick, fishy puddle.

"How long did you stay at the gambling den last night, little brother?"

Seid Quan grins. "Just until nine. I don't have much money to gamble."

He nods. "No, I suppose not. You know how to save your money, don't you?"

"Don't we all? I don't think anyone really has much of a choice."

"No, this is true. How long have you been here now?"

Seid Quan looks up. "About a year."

"How is your family? Your mother?"

"She's doing well. Always busy, you know. My sisters keep her on her toes."

Mr. Lam laughs. "Yes, I bet. Have you been looking for steadier work?"

Seid Quan shrugs. "I suppose. But finding good work is

harder than it sounds." He looks down at the wet floor and the scuff marks on his shoes.

Lim had come to him three weeks ago, early in the morning, dried blood like a snake down the side of his head. He had lain on Seid Quan's bed, wheezing. It was only after he had slept for an hour that he had said anything.

"I went to the sawmill to look for work, and the boss, he said I could start the next day, but only at Chinaman wages. When I left, some of the white men working there followed me and asked if I needed a ride." He stopped and covered his face with his hands.

"What did they do to you? Tell me."

Lim swallowed hard. "I tried to get away, but they pushed me into the foreman's truck and drove me out of town. They said if I ever came back, they would beat me even worse. Then they left me out in a bog, and I think I passed out."

"Where were you?"

"I don't even know. I woke up and just started to walk toward the mountains on the side of a road. Seid Quan, I walked for six hours."

Seid Quan drops the mop head into the bucket and bends down to wring it out.

"How about coming to work for me?" asks Mr. Lam.

Seid Quan stands back up. "Here? In the shop?"

"Sure. You have steady hands. I'll train you to cut hair and shave."

"Really? But can you afford to pay me?"

Mr. Lam stands up, runs his hands over his pants. "You shouldn't worry about that. I want to retire one day, go back to China and see my wife again. I would like someone I trust to buy the shop, run it like it should be run. In a few years, maybe that will be you. But only if you think it's a good idea. So, yes or no?"

"Yes, of course." Seid Quan reaches out and grabs the barber's hand. "Thank you."

Mr. Lam reaches into a cabinet and pulls out a bottle of whisky. "You're too serious, Seid Quan. This will lighten you up."

Later that night, sitting on his single bed in the rooming house, Seid Quan sips at one more glass of whisky from the bottle he keeps hidden in one of his boots. *My own shop*, he thinks. *That's more than I ever thought.* He imagines his mother's face as she opens the letter announcing the news, her voice as she shouts to his sisters, the speed with which the gossip will travel through the village.

The village. He rests his face on his sharp knees. *How will I ever pay back the village?* He calculates how much money he will be able to save working as a barber and how much he will need to buy the shop. He shakes his head. *I will have to keep on cleaning at night as well, for as long as it takes.*

He turns to his small desk and the long scrolls, brushes and inks he keeps on its surface. He walks to it, leans over his calligraphy and squints. He thinks of the hours he spent as a boy on the floor of his mother's kitchen, crouched over old newspapers. He drew character after character with a dull pencil, imitating the grand strokes of the calligraphist he once saw in Guangzhou on a trip with his mother.

His mother, sighing, would always say, "If only your father were alive, then maybe we could afford a tutor."

Now, he stares at his own, self-taught work. The mistakes are obvious. Seid Quan rubs at the foot of one character until the paper's top layer comes away in small brown and black pills.

Smudged, he thinks. *Of course.*

He bundles up his papers and places them in an empty apple crate. He pushes it under his bed with his foot; clouds of dust puff up on the opposite side. Sighing, he reaches into his closet for a small broom.

"I am still a cleaner, after all," he says to himself. When he turns back to his desk, he pulls out his English exercise book from the drawer and places it on the surface, so he won't forget.

After three years in Canada, Seid Quan must return to China to marry. His mother has chosen his wife, and he has to consummate the marriage and impregnate the girl, all in the six weeks before he returns to Canada. His mother, in the letters she dictated to the local scribe, never asked what kind of girl he wanted and never mentioned whether the girl she eventually settled on was pretty. Seid Quan was afraid to ask. He reasoned that, since he hadn't seen a Chinese girl in two years, anyone would look pretty to him.

The night before he leaves, Lim takes him to the Bamboo Terrace for dinner. He orders shot after shot of whisky and tells Seid Quan grandly that he can order anything he likes because money is no object.

"Where is all this money from, brother?"

Lim places his hand on the pocket of his jacket. "None of your business. I told you I'd make it. I'm going to buy a car before the year is out."

"But how? The last time I saw you, you were driving the Canada Produce truck."

Lim drums his fingers on the red tablecloth. "You don't need to know, Seid Quan. Just eat your dinner and drink your whisky. It's all taken care of." Lim pats Seid Quan on the shoulder and grins.

Four weeks later, Seid Quan is back in the village. Everything looks just as it did when he left it: dusty roads, children everywhere, squat little houses filled with noise, the voices of women. He walks past the houses and waves at the people inside. Everyone asks him about Canada. They all want to know if it is as wonderful as it seems, if it is true that no one goes hungry because there are jobs for everyone, if the trees are so tall they are like mountains, if the mountains are so tall you can't see the peaks, if people are happier there.

Seid Quan only says, "As long as I can send money home, that's enough for me."

The villagers are amazed by his humility and say that he is remarkably down-to-earth, even with all his success.

The night before the wedding, he realizes that the only men left in the village are old men. Seid Quan brings out a bottle of Canadian whisky; he had meant to have a party with all the young men left in the village, but instead, he finds himself sitting around his mother's kitchen table with his great-uncle and all his friends, men with no teeth and stooped shoulders. His great-uncle says to him, "I'd go to Canada or America or even Hong Kong myself if it weren't for my bad hip. I suppose I'm forty years too late now."

It doesn't take much to get them drunk, and by nine o'clock, everyone but his great-uncle has fallen asleep at the table, their heads cradled on brown, bony arms.

"So, young man, how do you feel about getting married tomorrow?"

Seid Quan shrugs. "It feels good, I guess. I have to leave in a few weeks, though, so I'm not sure that I'll really feel married even after it's all over."

His great-uncle looks at him out of the corner of his eye.

"Yes, I can see how that would be difficult. But you've done well with what you have. Why, you speak English now, even better than those snobs in the city. You know, your mother has been able to buy a lot more things since you left. She's started dowries for your sisters already. Widows always have the hardest time, don't you think?"

"Yes. My mother has always worked hard for us. I just wish there was a way that I could stay home and make the same money here." Seid Quan taps his glass on the table, and the old man on his right raises his head for a moment before sleepily dropping it again.

"The children are so much healthier here since the young men started going away and sending money home," his great-uncle continues, as if Seid Quan hasn't spoken. "No more bony knees, no more sunken bellies! Our village has waited a long time to be healthy, I'll say. You must have seen that new water pump in the square. The village owes a lot to its young men overseas. But, as I'm sure you'd be the first to admit, the young men owe a lot to the village too."

"Of course we do, Uncle."

"All the money we saved to send you boys to Canada and America in the first place—the amounts can keep me up at night. It brightens my day just to think of you all working so hard so far away—I know you do it for us, for the money you send home to make everything better here."

Seid Quan sighs and stands up. "I should take the others home now. Are you going to stay here, or should I take you home first?"

The old man stands up and pats his great-nephew on the shoulder. "Oh, I think I can go home by myself. Without any young men, the village has never been safer."

That night, just before he falls asleep, Seid Quan imagines that he is king of his village. Fruits, vegetables and game are laid at his feet, and he says grandly, "Pass this food out equally among the villagers and let the men serve the women and children, so that these men may also know what it's like to find joy in domestic rituals." He is called the Magnanimous King, and he parades around the village, magically living without food and watching his subjects grow fat.

When Seid Quan wakes up, the insubstantial light of dawn has seeped into his room. He sees his trunk and his wedding clothes gleaming redly on the hook by the door. Through the wall, he hears his mother, her steps slow and heavy, as if she is dragging something behind her. He runs out of the room in his nightclothes to help her because he cannot bear the sound.

He wanders on the deck, his hands clasped behind his back as he makes his way around piles of rope and other Chinese men. *Another boat,* he thinks, *but exactly the same.*

It has been only twenty hours since he left his new wife standing in the doorway of their new home, where she will be its only permanent occupant. That morning, she was wearing a jacket and pants, her hands held behind her back as if she had something to surprise him with, or as if she were afraid he would see her shaking hands. Her eyes, small and sharp, darted left and right. He placed his suitcase in the yard and put his hand on her head.

"Will you be lonely?"

Shew Lin snorted, the nostrils in her broad nose flaring. "No, silly. I'm still in the village, aren't I? I should be asking *you* if you will be lonely."

He kissed her on the forehead. "No more than usual."

But this, he now knows, is a lie, because he did not have her to miss before. He stares at the ocean—limitless, forever moving men away from their places of birth. *I haven't known her for very long,* he reasons to himself. *Really, I've only just met her.* But in those five weeks they lived together in their little house (the only thing, he reflects, that he actually owns), they conducted a marriage in miniature—shopping together, cooking together, eating and sleeping together.

"I feel so old," he whispers to himself. And then he laughs, his twenty-one-year-old self amused.

He watches the young men and boys around him, some no older than fourteen or fifteen. They are dressed in the working clothes of their villages: pants rolled up well above their ankles, ropes as belts, long-sleeved jackets unbuttoned to show bare chests. As Seid Quan knows, each boy will have only one good Western suit in his bag and will not waste it on the boat. But Seid Quan, like the others who are returning to Canada, wears his Western suits all day, every day. He can feel the envy boring into the back of his jacket from the newcomers, who must suppose that he thinks nothing of ruining his good clothes on this dirty boat. But he doesn't care—he has done well so far, and the jealousy only makes him shrug.

Only four more weeks of this boat, he thinks. *But then it will be years before I see her again.*

He pushes his hands into his empty pockets, feels the cotton muslin, the loose threads he never bothers to cut. If he could, he would strip off all his clothes and jump off this boat, swim back to the Guangzhou port and walk on the river's shore all the way back to the village. But there is no money there, no wool to make Western suits, no one who could pay for a straight razor shave. The house would have to be sold. He would have to repay the village elders somehow, but there would be no way to do it.

He looks out at the ocean again, knowing that his only destination is to the end of east, where the west begins.

The smoke is almost solid, forming transparent walls between Seid Quan and the next man. He squints, but that does not help. He can hear men shouting and the jingle of coins. He steps forward and bumps into someone else's back.

It's not often that Seid Quan goes to the gambling dens, rooms hidden between floors or underneath cellars in almost every building in Chinatown. There's the danger, of course, that the police might come, or that he might lose all his money. But really, these places always make him feel sick. Perhaps it's the trapped smells of cigarette smoke, stale whisky and dozens of men crammed into a windowless room. Or perhaps, like Lim always says, he's just not man enough to play real stakes with real gamblers.

Midnight, and the action shows no sign of slowing down.

The mah-jong table is surrounded by men, all crowding around to peek at each player's hand and whisper to each other about who is most likely to win. The players have been sitting for six hours already, having rushed here as soon as the work-day ended. One of them, a short, fat man whose butchering apron is still draped on the back of his chair, is sweating so much that his shirt is soaked through. Dozens of beads sit glistening on his forehead. The crowd murmurs that he has not even gotten up to relieve himself. Someone makes a loud joke about wet bottoms, but the butcher still does not move. His eyes are fixed on the tiles.

Seid Quan is scanning the room, looking for anyone he knows, when he feels a gnarled hand on his shoulder.

"How are you, young man?"

"Mr. Yip. I'm very well. How about you?"

The tailor grunts. "Not so great. The arthritis is getting worse, and I haven't been working as much as I used to. I'm sorry I haven't been around to see you when you come in to clean. I've been relying on my brother to do most of the work." He smiles. "But I hear you've been busy. Your wife had a baby?"

He blushes. "Yes. A girl—Yun Wo. Everybody is healthy."

"Good. Good." Mr. Yip cranes his neck for a look around the room. "Ah, it's old Mr. Wong. I should say hello before he decides to get his shirts made somewhere else."

Seid Quan walks over to the mah-jong table and peers at the players' tiles. He hears a familiar voice behind him and turns around.

"I can get you anything you want, brother!" Lim waves his arms at a man standing in front of him. He blinks his eyes twice and shakes his head before continuing. "You and me and these useless drunks, we're family. You just need to ask. How do you think I can afford all this?" He gestures down at his shiny black shoes, the perfectly sewn cuff of his glen plaid trousers. "I can get you fellows everything you want: women, Scotch whisky, even some of the good stuff." He pauses as he looks into the stony eyes of his companion. "You know," he whispers loudly, "*dope*. Don't ever sell anything you don't use yourself, that's my motto."

Seid Quan looks around, wonders if anyone else has heard Lim's speech. He hurries over and grasps his friend by the elbow.

"Lim. Good to see you. Let's go for a walk, get some fresh air."

"I don't want to leave. This is a great party. Just great." Lim smiles widely at the room.

"Maybe you just need some sleep, maybe something to—"

The butcher has overturned the mah-jong table, sending tiles sailing through the air and skittering across the floor. Someone pushes someone else, and men start shouting obscenities, throwing glasses, shoes, anything at each other. Other men push past and pour into the street.

"All this noise, the police will surely come now," someone shouts as Seid Quan runs down the stairs, losing his grip on Lim's sleeve. He slips into an alley, pokes his head around the corner to see if Lim is anywhere in sight. Men are running into every alley and street, but in this dark, it is impossible to see if one of them is Lim. He turns to walk home and breathes the night air. Into the blue light.

He has come to understand the movements of the boats, the sway that means a storm is coming from the west, the rocking that means another ship, miles away, is slicing through the water at the same time. He lies on his bunk, listens to the breathing of the three other men in his cabin. He places his hand on a pocket in his pants, feels for the wad of papers he will need to re-enter Canada. At the port, they will look him over, ask him questions about where he has been and why. They will mark his return on a piece of paper— one more little check mark on a list of comings and goings.

This last trip, he played with Yun Wo, a serious-faced three-year-old who asked him alarmingly adult questions about his life in Vancouver. "Do white men treat you badly? How many hours a week do you work? Why do you stay?"

He helped his wife cook meals (she laughed at the clumsy way he chopped vegetables and claimed she could do better with her bare hands), poked around in their garden. He showed her the pile of bills he had brought back, and she went with him to his great-uncle's house to pay the rest of his debt to the village. As they left, he whispered in her ear, "It's all going to be better now. You'll see."

He held her at night, his hand resting on her solid hip. He watched her sleep, noted the way her mouth fell open as she exhaled, the movement of her eyeballs beneath the lids. It was warm, as he remembered, and he shed layers of wool, relishing the lightness of linen and cotton, sun on skin.

He sits up in his bunk, hitting his head on the low ceiling. He feels around in his bag until he pulls out a knitted grey scarf—Shew Lin's goodbye present. He wraps it around his neck and over his chin and lies back down, noting the tilt of the boat to the left and wondering what it means.

"Congratulations, little brother! This surely predicts a long, lucky life for you!"

"You're a good man."

"I'll never get my hair cut anywhere else again."

"Hey, he gives a good shave, too!"

Seid Quan stands in the middle of a crowd of men at the clan association offices, now located in a newly purchased house on Keefer north of Gore, shakily holding a glass of rye. He knew before he arrived that everyone had heard about his new ownership of the barbershop and that even more knew about the birth of his second daughter in China, but he did not know they would hold a party for him, complete with food supplied from the Bamboo Terrace.

"Seid Quan, we need a speech!"

He blinks rapidly, wonders what he will say when, usually, he says so little. Perhaps, *I fear I will forget what my wife looks like* or *I am so lonely that I stay in my barbershop after closing until late at night, pretending that I am still cutting hair.* He walks to the front of the room, turns and faces the crowd of eager, half-drunk men staring at him, waiting for the words that mean time here is not wasted and their lifetimes spent chasing success will count for something in the end. Seid Quan opens his mouth to speak.

"I am only a man. I don't feel successful, and I'm not sure I ever will. This," and he waves his hand around the room, at the streets of Chinatown beyond the windows, "is what I'm living. I make the best of it, as you do, and I don't think I deserve a party all to myself just for that."

He looks around him. The men are crestfallen, so disappointed with his speech that their mouths are gaping open. Some shift uneasily from foot to foot. Others cough.

"But," he begins again, loudly, "here we are, together despite all the bad things we have experienced in this country: washing dirty laundry, poor wages, living with these white ghosts." The crowd snickers. "And yet we still succeed. We have improved our villages, fed our families and helped tame this wild place. We will go on and conquer anything in our paths, brothers, I promise you that. Thank you."

The applause crashes over Seid Quan, and he steps backward, as if pushed by the sounds of clapping hands and uninhibited hoots. The men surround him until he can see nothing more than their blurred faces, the movement of their hands slapping him, shaking his hands, like birds. He begins to laugh. He sucks his stomach in, stands up straight and plunges forward

into the crowd, allowing the pull of the party to lead him farther into the throng.

A weathered wood house. Five small bedrooms, three up and
two down. A fireplace in the living room, where the men gather
and burn newspapers, scrap wood from construction sites,
pieces of things they find and do not need.

Seid Quan's room is upstairs, in the back, its window facing
the vegetable garden they once tried so hard to keep going. When
Jimmy, a younger man from the clan association, told Seid Quan
about the empty room in his rented house, Seid Quan immediately thought it was an extravagance. But then, he realized that
he needed to leave his room in the boarding house on Pender
Street (a room where he had tried to accumulate nothing, where
he only slept and, sometimes, when he couldn't help it, thought).
This place, even though the floors are bare and the siding is
beginning to rot, is still a house where he can do as he pleases and
where no strangers peer at him as he moves down the hallways.
It is more expensive here, but he can still save some money, as the
profits from the shop are growing. He splits expenses with Jimmy
and the others, each shopping and cooking in turn.

None of the men have had much time, and the yard has
grown over with weeds and grass. The vegetables are still
there, lurking, half-unseen, among a riot of plants that no one
knows the names of. Five old kitchen chairs are set out in a
circle, and a full ashtray sits on a tree stump in the middle. Seid
Quan's chair is the farthest from the house.

Even on sunny days, the ground squelches underfoot, and
their trouser hems are always wet.

Seid Quan has just received a letter from his mother. Without
wasting words, she suggests that he might want to plan on

coming back once more, or perhaps twice, to see if he can conceive a son before his wife grows too old. "Shew Lin is twenty-five now," his mother writes, "and you must come back soon, for she will have only so many chances before she becomes dried up." She writes about Shew Lin as if she were a breeding pig.

He counts his money and writes back. "I cannot afford the trip home for a long time, Mother. I would have to close the store while I'm gone, and we would all lose money. Coming back cannot be my first priority."

He smells the odour of preserved dace and rice, hears the sound of a crowd of men cooking together in one kitchen, on one coal-burning stove. He steps into his slippers and places the letter into the pocket of his work pants so he will not forget to take it to the post office in the morning. He glances out the window, sees a red-haired child in a striped sweater cycling slowly up and down the dirt alley.

"Brother, come eat!"

He pulls his chair up to the table and sits down. His roommates are laughing, teasing each other, making faces behind each others' backs. *Another trip*, he thinks, *and another child I will never see.*

Seid Quan wonders if he will ever go home for good, or if he will always be stuck in this land that shimmers with rain and is not quite dream, not quite day. He looks behind him at his empty shop and then out the big front window at the sheets of almost opaque rain.

"No one will be out today," he says to himself. He listens for the echo of his own voice bouncing off the walls. "Not even to go to the barber." A stray dog lopes across the street, pausing to sniff the wet air with its even wetter muzzle.

He thinks he will count the combs, maybe dig out the old hairballs that collect in the corners and between the tiles. As he turns to walk to the back, he hears the bell on the front door.

A tall white man, dressed in a dark grey raincoat and hat, stands in the doorway, water streaming off his shoulders and pooling around his rubber boots. He shakes his head, and tiny drops spray across the room, hitting the mirrors and Seid Quan right between the eyes. All Seid Quan can see of his face is his jutting and pointy chin, clean-shaven.

In English, Seid Quan says, "Here for a cut, sir? Have a seat." He gestures to the chair closest to the door.

The man stands still and breathes heavily.

"What can I help you with, sir? I do a good shave, too. But I don't think you need one."

The dripping man steps forward and holds out his hand. "You should leave now, lock up and go home," he whispers. "There's no point in boarding up the windows. Don't even try to warn the others. There's no time."

Seid Quan steps backward. "What do you mean?"

"A mob is coming. They want to scare you and make you leave. Get out. Hide in your cellar. Just run away." He backs out, pushing the door open with his hip. He walks out into the waterlogged street, turns the corner and is gone.

Seid Quan blinks nervously. He has heard stories of the 1907 riot many times and wonders if this could be something just as destructive. However, this warning from a stranger could be a joke, or a way of luring him out of his shop so that goons can drag him into the alley and beat him. But he's not sure, so he runs to the safe in the back room and stuffs his trouser pockets with cash. He throws his barber's coat on a chair and leaves, turning the lock as far as it can go. He runs down the wet street, thinking that all the others who can see him through their windows must think he's mad. He slows to a walk, his face flushed with embarrassment, until he hears the sound of breaking glass. Not daring to look behind, he throws himself through puddles until he arrives at the rented house. He locks the front door carefully behind him and stands in the corner by the window, hidden by the curtains from the street.

It starts so quickly that Seid Quan does not even have a chance to take off his wet trousers. He stares down the hill through a crack in the curtains, his arms wrapped around his body as if he is afraid that he will crumble. He holds his breath.

Outside, a dozen white men are throwing bricks and stones through the windows of all the shops, dragging boxes of produce and bags of laundry out onto the sidewalk, where they overturn them into the mud. Seid Quan can see Chinese men running away, ducking into the alleys only they know so well, disappearing into skinny gaps between buildings. Some of the white men chase them, but the Chinese always manage to slip away from the crowd and vanish. Seid Quan sighs with relief.

He cannot see his barbershop from here, only the storefronts of Canada Produce and Yip Tailors. Seid Quan has never seen such violence first-hand and is afraid that Chinatown will fall, be flattened to its very foundations. The windows are all broken, and the white men have started to laugh and pound each other on the backs. Seid Quan closes his eyes and slides down the wall until he is sitting on the unfinished wooden floor. There's no point in watching anymore.

When the white men leave, chests puffed out, he and the others run into the streets. Seid Quan searches for any hurt men, poking his head into doorways and alleys. He can see overturned furniture and graffiti through broken windows.

Rain falls steadily, soaking the men who are returning to their shops. Seid Quan wipes off his dripping face with his sleeve and looks up at the grey sky, now somehow greyer than it's ever been before. No one speaks.

An hour later, when Seid Quan and the others have determined that there are no casualties, he finally walks down the street. He is afraid to see what has happened to the shop. Mr. Yip weeps on the sidewalk at the sight of his smashed sewing machine. Seid Quan turns away. Better to pretend he has not seen.

He stares at the barbershop. The big front window is smashed. One of the chairs has been wrenched from the screws holding it to the floor, and the front of his safe in the back has been dented. The money is safely hidden in his room at the house, and all his razors and scissors are unharmed. He leans against the counter and sighs. *It could have been worse*, he thinks. *But why should I be thankful for that?*

Mr. Mah, who owns the café across the street, pokes his head through the broken window. "Is it bad?"

"Just the windows and this chair."

"Good. They took my whole cash register and tried to get into the apartment."

"I'm sorry."

"Yes, me too. Listen, we're going to have a meeting in the morning at church. This isn't even half as bad as the last big riot, but still. Old Mr. Wong says we should lobby the city to pay for the damage. The others will need you if we have to write a letter."

Seid Quan nods. "I'll come."

"Good. I'm going to the lumberyard to see if there are any boards. I'll grab you some."

Mr. Mah hurries off. Seid Quan begins to sweep up. He can hear the fall of hammers and the sawing of wood. *No one will even notice,* he thinks, *because they just want Chinatown to disappear.*

He sits in the Hong Kong Café, drinking his coffee and looking at the cracked mirror behind the counter. *One month after the riot,* he thinks, *everything made of glass remains broken, even now.* He sees himself, a man with large ears and thin, upright shoulders. He sips his coffee and takes a bite of his apple tart. When he looks up again, he sees that his face looks different, but right then, amid the noise and commotion of the café, he cannot put his finger on it. He finishes his snack, nods to Mr. Mah behind the counter, and returns to his barbershop.

Later that night, as he is sweeping up the last of the hairs on the floor, he looks up into one of his own mirrors. He suddenly sees what has been confusing him all day: his eyes, once dark brown, have begun to turn grey.

The rumours start as whispers that snake their way through the streets of Chinatown, bouncing off the walls of buildings and ending as suspicions, not quite groundless, in the heads of men who have learned to fear the worst.

They're sending us all back.

The illegal ones are going to be thrown in jail.

There are spies everywhere.

Seid Quan is not immune. He has heard many rumblings over the years, but this time, it is getting worse. There is no labour shortage anymore, and the whites want the jobs they once rejected and threw to the hungry masses of Chinamen, who still work for half-price. The Chinese men, sitting in his customers' chairs, their heads tilted precariously back as he shaves them, ask him for information, ask him what the newspapers are printing, what the radio declares. To them, he seems to hold a golden key that unlocks the long words, the sounds that seem to flow into one another with no pause for breath.

Men mobilize, hold protests and march down Pender Street. The grocers strike, and the wives of the West End and Shaughnessy find themselves without lettuce and onions. But this, as Seid Quan knows, is futile, for none of these Chinamen is of any consequence to anyone. They are not citizens and they do not vote, so, like the generation before them who died, weathered and forgotten, on the cold rail lines, their suffering is barely noticed. The Chinamen have families—mothers, wives, children—but they are unseen, hidden away in small houses in China, where politicians can ignore them and disregard their well-being. Seid Quan writes letters to the mayor, the prime minister, even the papers.

"If only you could live as we do for one whole day," he writes, "you would see what we suffer. After the riot in 1907, the government promised us protection. Now is the time for that protection. Let us live as freely as white men."

No one writes back.

One week later, he reaches for his newspaper, stares at the headline and blinks to clear his eyes, hoping that what he sees is a mistake. He looks again. His eyes have not tricked him.

"NO MORE CHINESE TO ENTER CANADA," it shouts.

Seid Quan reads through the article slowly, poring over each word so that there can be no confusion. He knows he will be asked about this later, when fear will spread through Chinatown like a fast-moving and vicious epidemic. The men will swarm him, push their newspapers in his face so that Seid Quan can tell them what is really happening, even though he would rather lie and say that nothing has changed or has only changed for the better.

"The Parliament of Canada has passed the amended Chinese Immigration Act of 1923, which limits the class of Chinese that will be allowed to enter Canada. It is hoped that this exclusion will curtail the number of Chinese now living in our cities and towns and slow down the waves of immigrants, which have not abated despite efforts such as the federal Head Tax. Chinese will be allowed to leave the country only for a maximum of two years before they will be denied re-entry to Canada. All departures and returns will be closely monitored by immigration officials."

Seid Quan pushes his hair off his forehead and clenches his teeth. This is no surprise, although for months he had hoped that it wouldn't happen, that all their lobbying work after the riot would change something, that the number of sympathetic politicians would grow and overwhelm the others. But change, he knows, isn't popular with the rest of Canada. Still, his hands shake as he folds the paper up, the other articles unread.

In his mind, he sees Shew Lin and their two daughters, one of whom he has never even met. They are small, almost indistinguishable from each other. He had not yet decided whether he would return to China to retire or whether he would bring his family here. Few men have been able to bring women over at all, most preferring to save the passage and head tax money to bring young men and boys who can work and repay the debts they owe. Women are money-losers. *Still*, he thinks, *we could have built something here, lived in a house, walked through Stanley Park together.*

He hears someone running up the stairs, heavy shoes hitting the wooden steps with force great enough to shake the walls.

"Seid Quan! We must go. They're calling for you at the clan association to read the papers out loud! Come!" Jimmy pounds on the door.

He stands up. Already, he can hear an elevated buzz coming through the windows from the streets of Chinatown. He follows his roommate and walks toward it.

As Seid Quan unfolds the letter, written on thin, tissue-like paper, he sees that Shew Lin's writing, despite his hints to her that she should practise, has not improved. Her characters are big and open, like the eyes of a child seeing cotton candy for the first time. She writes deliberately, one character after another, each painstakingly drawn, thought in every stroke.

"Dear Seid Quan," she writes. "There isn't any point in waiting, so I will tell you now. I would like it very much if all of us could come to you. I know this isn't possible, but still I wish it. The other women are saying the Japanese are in the north, although I do not know how this will affect us. I do not like to be a woman alone with female children in such times, especially now that Yun Wo will be turning fifteen. If we cannot come to you, you should come to us."

Seid Quan folds up the letter, stuffs it back into its envelope. He stares at the photograph of Shew Lin and his two daughters in the garden of their home. If he looks carefully, he can see the dying vines of the winter melon curling around his wife's feet. He stands up, scraping the chair along the unfinished floor.

He walks the streets of Strathcona, just east of the produce markets and butcher shops that line Keefer Street. He thinks about going to the barbershop, but it is seven o'clock already, and if he were to go in now, he would simply be standing around or cleaning something that doesn't need to be cleaned again. Instead, he walks along the residential streets, looks at the front porches and gardens, the children playing in the street after dinner.

Men have been going back to China in droves, scared that the Japanese will soon begin a war and this will be their last chance to visit before the borders are closed. Some stay with their families, forgoing the money they make in Canada that keeps their wives and children well fed and well clothed. Seid Quan stuffs his hands into his empty pockets and continues walking.

A few days ago, he heard a young white man who, for some reason, was waiting for Seid Quan to give him a haircut, say that this was a ghetto, a place where the city lets all the poor and unwanted live so that they don't contaminate the nice neighbourhoods. The young man had snorted mightily. "I'd rather live with you lot than be rattling around in one of those new stone mansions in Shaughnessy. A whole lot of rich snobs there, if you ask me."

Seid Quan had only murmured a noncommittal agreement, nodding like the good Chinaman this white man expected him to be.

As he walks, he can identify each house by the family who lives there. There is the Jewish house. The Italian family who shouts all the time lives in the yellow house with the red trim. And here is where the Gins live, complete with wife and daughters. There aren't many Chinese children, but the ones who do live here are now out playing in the streets, chasing balls, skipping rope. Seid Quan watches the little boys with their short Western pants and unruly hair. He would like to join in on their games but does not have the least idea how to play them, so he marches on, the setting sun on his back.

A young boy with hair the colour of sand and freckles all over his broad, pale face, stands in front of Seid Quan. His smile is crooked, and Seid Quan can see that there are chips broken off his front teeth.

"Hey, mister," he says. "Are you Peter Wong's dad? He still has my set of jacks, and I need them back for Saturday."

Seid Quan stops and smiles. "No, I'm Mr. Chan. I run the barbershop down there."

The little boy looks disappointed. "Oh. I'm Pat. I thought you looked like Peter." He puts his hand on his hair. "But I'll tell my dad about you, and maybe you can cut his hair. Maybe mine too, one day."

Seid Quan hears a woman's voice from down the street.

"That's my mom. She's calling me in because today is bath day. Yuck. I'd better go though. Nice meeting you, Mr. Chan." He runs down the sidewalk just as Seid Quan reaches out.

He draws his hand back to his side, not knowing what he is reaching for, but knowing that he shouldn't; the boy could have been embarrassed or angry or both. Then what would Seid Quan do? He turns around and walks back to his rented house to write a letter to his wife as the sun disappears behind a line of steeply angled roofs. *We must have a son,* he thinks, *so I will go back, maybe for the last time, no matter how long it takes or how much it costs.* He blinks, cursing under his breath.

As usual, he walks to work, his three-piece suit carefully pressed and cleaned. A misting winter rain has just started and is dotting his fedora with tiny drops of water. He holds his face up and feels the water graze his forehead. He passes a house shaking from the noise of a mah-jong party still raging from the night before. He glances in and sees several men he knows, all now in their undershirts, swearing furiously at each other as tiles move swiftly back and forth. One man walks out and stands on the front porch with a cigarette.

"Seid Quan! You're out early."

"Hello, Jimmy. Still going at it, eh? You didn't come home last night."

"Well, I can't bear to lose. Listen, I was just listening to the radio in the kitchen for a break. They say the Communists and Nationalists are united against the Japanese. Nothing about occupation, other than in the far north, so the south and the villages by the Pearl River are probably safe. But still."

"I hope no war breaks out."

"Yes." Jimmy lowers his voice. "I'm thinking of going back and fighting with the United Front. I don't know how yet, but I can't stand it here anymore. They could still use me, I think. I'm only twenty-eight."

"We're raising money, you know, with the penny drives and that banquet tonight. Let me see if I can talk to the treasurer—we might be able to pay for your passage back."

Jimmy grins. "You're a good man. Never an obstacle for you, is there? Well, I'd better get back inside. You never know—the food might run out, and then they might start eating each other."

Seid Quan unlocks the door to his barbershop and changes his jacket for his white barber's coat. He sets up his shaving kit, boils some water for hot towels and checks to make sure all the disinfectant jars are topped up. The doorbell tinkles and, not even turning around, Seid Quan says,

"Mr. Mah, you're right on time. Every week, like clock-work."

He hears a strange voice behind him. "A telegram for you, sir."

He sees a young white man with a sneer on his face staring at the instruments. *Probably wondering if he'll get an infection just from standing here,* Seid Quan thinks. He hands the messenger a few coins and watches him leave and carefully wipe his hands on his pants as he walks out of the shop.

Seid Quan tears open the envelope carefully. When has anyone ever sent him a telegram? He feels his stomach drop.

"CHO LAI HERE STOP SON BORN DECEMBER 14 NO NAME YET STOP EVERYONE WELL STOP NO JAPANESE IN SOUTH."

He sits down in one of the customer chairs, the telegram crumpled in his hand. It took him over two years to save the money to visit his family all those months ago. Cho Lai, one of his sisters' husbands and a tea merchant in Guangzhou, must have worked for hours to send this message in English. Seid Quan can feel the corners of his eyes start to sting. He dabs at his face with a corner of the telegraph.

Mr. Mah pokes his head through the doorway. "You open for business?"

Pon Man, he thinks, *that will be his name.*

"Come on in, Mr. Mah. You're always right on time."

The letters are intermittent. No one is sure if the money they're sending back home is arriving. Their wives may claim to be fine, but many of the men are suspicious that the Japanese have taken control of the post and are now censoring or doctoring every letter that is sent out. The accounts of how badly the war is going change every day, and no one knows what to believe. Old Mr. Wong's three sons have left to fight for Canada, and others sign up daily. They pour into Seid Quan's shop to have their heads shaved.

He touches their heads gently, as if they are as breakable as eggshells, knowing that they will not be touched with care again for a long, long time. He listens to them talk, sometimes shout, in excitement, their hands fluttering under their smocks.

"It'll feel good to shoot up those Japs."

"My father doesn't want me to go, but you understand, don't you, Uncle?"

"They say we'll be used for special assignments, like spies."

"I can't just sit here and wait. I have to do something."

He nods, brushes the hair off their necks and shoulders, gives them coffee if he sees that their hands are shaking. When they leave, their white scalps show through the stubble, a vulnerable white—the white of baby skin, the white of raw nerves and new bodies.

Seid Quan scours the newspapers every day for news about the occupations, asks every customer in his shop if they've heard anything from family in China and Hong Kong. Walking down the street every morning to work and every afternoon home, he is beset by images of Japanese soldiers raping his wife and stealing his children, sleeping in his home in the village, torturing the old men. Months pass. The Japanese occupy Guangzhou and the rest of the province. He receives a single letter from his wife.

"The children are fine. I am afraid that someone is intercepting the mail and taking the money you send home. But I have been poorer than this, so we are managing. Yun Wo will be marrying a young man whose family name is Gin. He has consented to live with us here, as protection. We are being like mice—quiet and unseen. Do not worry."

And so he cuts hair, glued to the radio, glad, at least, that he has had practice in waiting.

He runs through the crowd. People shout and throw things—hats, gloves, pieces of paper—in the air. He pushes his way through, steps on newspapers with the headline "VICTORY! JAPAN SURRENDERS!" Men slap him on the back as he goes by. He hears old Mr. Wong yelling, "I knew that our sons and friends leaving to fight for Canada wouldn't be for nothing! The government can't deny our citizenship anymore. We're going to get the vote now, brothers! And then we'll see change. Our wives will come, our children too!"

Seid Quan reaches the doors of his barbershop and stumbles in. He closes the door behind him and collapses on the low windowsill. Outside, the celebration rages on, and Seid Quan is sure he will find broken and empty whisky bottles on his front stoop in the morning. He catches his breath and walks to his office in the back room.

He opens the safe quietly (his habit even if no one is there—you never know who might be listening) and pushes the papers and legal documents aside. He reaches into the very back and takes out a pile of money, carefully organized into stacks bound by rubber bands. And he starts to count.

When he finishes and each stack is snug in the back of the safe, he sits at his small, yellow-varnished desk. He writes a list.

Shew Lin

Pon Man

Min Lai

He stares at the list. His wife, well into her middle age, his young son and his unmarried daughter. He calculates their passage money in his head, the cost of a house to fit them all, the head tax if the government continues with it. It is far more than the amount in the safe.

He sits back in his chair, his eyes closed. There are nights when he is so hungry for his wife that he thinks he will crack in two. During the day, he thinks of buying her a house and giving her the kind of garden she always wanted. The idea that he might soon see her makes him catch his breath; he inhales slowly, holding the air in his chest until his head and heartbeat settle.

By the time he opens his eyes again and stands up, he knows that it is his son—the boy he has never even seen—who must come first.

He walks up the courthouse steps, reaches with his hand to touch the cool, stone-grey columns. His heart is beating faster and faster with every breath he takes. He stops, rummages in his jacket pocket and pulls out a piece of paper.

> You are hereby notified that, in pursuance of your petition for a decision, you are qualified and fit to become a Canadian citizen, delivered to me dated the 22nd day of December 1949.
>
> His Honour Judge Boyd will hold a sitting at the Court House of Vancouver on the 25th day of March 1950, at the hour of 11:00 in the forenoon for the purpose of considering such petition, and you are required to be present at my office, together with two sponsors, on that date to be examined by the presiding judge with respect to the matter set out in your petition.

Seid Quan touches the Canadian shield of arms at the top of his letter. It seems cruel, somehow, to read everything he has wished for on a piece of paper, as if his life and the years stretching before him are nothing but words that can be contained in a notice. He has not been back to China since his wife conceived their son thirteen years ago, and now, it seems, they will come to him. He swallows, folds the letter up and straightens his back. Eyes fixed on the door in front of him, he walks through the columns and inside.

He hurries down the street, unshaven, wearing only a pair of trousers and a thin cotton shirt. He looks up at the perfect mid-blue sky, the sun reflecting off the high windows of the three-storey buildings. *How appropriate,* he thinks and plunges on.

He turns into an alley and knocks on a dark grey unmarked door. Silence. He coughs and then knocks again. The door opens slowly and smoke floats out, wrapping itself like fingers around Seid Quan's chest.

"Lim. It's me. Let me in."

A thin man (so thin that his hands hang like weights from his stringy arms, his sharply angled shoulders) squints through the gloom. "Seid Quan," he whispers. "Yes, of course. My old friend."

The room is tiny, with only one window, like a wound cut out of the cinder block. Seid Quan steps over bottles—mostly empty—and piles of mud-coloured clothes. He hopes the smell won't cling to him and follow him home.

Lim waves at a small chair in the corner and lies down slowly. Seid Quan swears he hears his friend's bones creak on the bare mattress. Lim pulls a wool coat over his body and stares at Seid Quan, waiting.

"I came to tell you that Pon Man is coming. The government

has granted me citizenship and is allowing me to bring him over, just like any other immigrant."

Lim smiles, nods. "Good news."

"Yes. He'll grow up here, have all the advantages. Things are changing, I can feel it." Seid Quan stands up in his excitement and begins to pace, weaving his way around piles of garbage. "Things will only get better."

"An optimist, eh? I never would have thought it of you. You were always too practical for hope, my friend." He pulls a mug toward him and spits in it. "I once thought things would be better too."

Seid Quan walks over to the mattress and kneels down. "It can be, Lim. You just have to work hard. There's still time."

"You silly fucker. You've worked in this country for almost forty years and this is the first time you've felt hope. Once in forty years. We have no time left, Seid Quan. We're old men."

"You're not old. Let's get up right now and get some food. I'll help you find a better room. You can work with me."

Lim's laugh emerges as if it has been trapped in his dusty chest for months and has only now been let out. "Doing what? Cutting hair? Sweeping up? I made a lot of money doing things that good men would never do. And then I lost it smoking and whoring and drinking. I don't need a new, pious life. If things are going to get better for me, then they're going to get better the way I know how." He stares at Seid Quan until the intimacy forces Seid Quan to look away. "Why do you come to me now? You could have come two years ago, ten years ago."

"I didn't know it was like this, or where you were. I hadn't seen you in years. I had to ask four different men this morning to find out where you were living."

Lim waves his hand. "It doesn't matter. I don't want your help now, and I wouldn't have taken it then. Just go away. I'm glad your son is coming. Make sure he works hard." He turns to the wall, offering Seid Quan only a view of his pimpled and skinny back.

When Seid Quan returns to his rented house, Mr. Yip, waiting just behind the front door, hands him a glass of whisky. Immediately, men pour into the living room from the kitchen. "Surprise, brother! Consider this an early welcome-home party for your son."

It has been many years in this place, trees brilliant and green against a summer sky low against the mountains. This is what it is: a man grown old (who seemed to go from eighteen to fifty-six in a matter of weeks) waiting to see his son, a man who has been back to his village three times, one visit for every child he has fathered, a man standing at the docks, looking with tired eyes at a large boat fresh from China.

He spots his son immediately even though he has never seen him in person before, a small, slight boy with slicked hair and blush red lips. *He is so pretty,* he thinks, *like a little girl.* He calls his name, and Pon Man looks over, an insolent expression on his face.

Seid Quan reaches out to him and Pon Man steps back. *He is smelling the old-man odour on me,* he thinks. *Like the odour of this huge and unfathomable country.* Seid Quan is desperate to touch him, and Pon Man looks scared, as if his fifteen-year-old self is completely unable to cope with his father's tangible and enormous emotional need. He sneers instead, turning his head to avoid the smells and sights of despair and pathetic happiness.

Seid Quan's hands shake as he puts them in his pockets, his son still untouched.

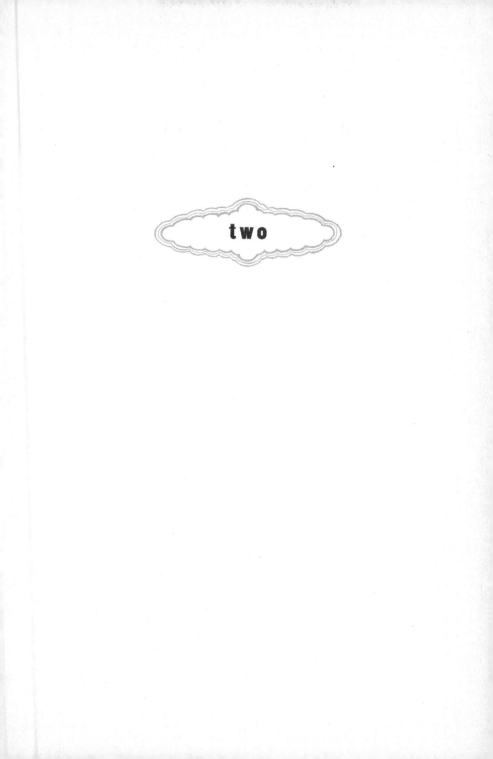

two

the port

When I was a child, the house was never quiet. Even if everyone was sleeping, the collective sound of our heavy breathing and body shifts during the night reassured me when I woke up from a bad dream.

In the day, my mother called out for all of us, "Wendy-Daisy-Jackie-Penny-*Samantha!*" even if she only wanted one, her mind seemingly unable to make the distinction. And we ran, jostling into each other in the hallways, pushing against the walls that barely contained us. As the youngest, I was always last and out of breath, my thick glasses fogged over from the heat of my own exertion.

Now, the night before Penny's wedding, it really is just my mother and me. Penny is staying in her complimentary hotel suite tonight, and her room is empty. Everything has been moved to her new apartment in a low-rise building across town.

I walk past my mother on my way to bed. The living room, so large with its heavy stone fireplace (the hearth covered in plastic, of course, for fear of bone-chilling drafts and way-ward squirrels), and my mother, so small in her red cardigan. The dimness pools around her as if threatening to absorb her.

"Going to sleep?" she asks.

"Yes, what about you?"

"I won't be able to sleep tonight, not with the wedding tomorrow. At least the TV keeps me company."

I take a breath, step toward the couch and sit down beside her. "Mom, when Dad was young, what was he like?"

"I don't know. He was like a lot of boys." She pauses. "Except your father always did like the lounge singers. Not so much into the rock and roll."

"What else, Mom? Did he play poker? Was he a good dancer?"

"So many questions," she mutters in Chinese as she picks a ball of lint off her sweater. "He was angry sometimes, your father. Always trying to prove himself, as if other people thought he was dirt. No one thought he was dirt. He was very popular, especially in Chinatown." She looks at me. "I don't remember much these days, you know, only little things here and there."

I stand up. "Yes, I know. Thanks anyway."

She nods. "He hated cutting hair. I don't think I ever even saw him in the barbershop." She stands up and heads to the kitchen. "I don't like talking about the past—who knows how much bad luck we're stirring up? Why don't you ask yourself why you can't finish school instead?"

I stare at her retreating back, wondering if I should say something, explain that school means nothing, dispute her ideas on good and bad luck, yell at her for being the only, faulty link I have left to my father as a young man.

She pulls a package of tea from the cupboard and turns to look at me one more time. "I burned everything a long time ago, except for his tools and the gardening things. They wouldn't have burned and, besides, they were expensive." As soon as she looks away, I run downstairs.

When I reach the garage (old oil stains on the concrete, the emptiness of a garage without a car) and open the door, a cold rush of air pours out, and I pull the sleeves of my sweatshirt over my balled fists. The flickering light bulb reveals shadows and then hides them, over and over again. Finally, through the appearing and disappearing light, I see my father's toolbox.

The latch has rusted and pieces of decayed metal chip off onto my hands and the floor. I push my open palm against the lid, and it finally snaps open. Old finishing nails fly through the air.

I half expect the contents to smell of my father (that smell I can no longer remember but am sure I would know if I ever encountered it again), but they simply smell of metal and rust. As I rifle my way through the first layer of screws and bolts, small metal bits fall and skitter across the concrete. Frustrated, I pull the top tray out and begin to dig through the screwdrivers and wrenches in the very bottom of the toolbox.

A piece of paper tickles my palm. I squint and see the corner of a book buried underneath the hammer and mallet. A sketchbook. My father's name, in Chinese and English, is scrawled on the cover. I hold it gingerly, afraid it will crumble to dust at the touch of my oily, spastic fingers. I walk quickly back through the house to my room, leaving the scattered tools behind.

I turn the first few pages and find sketches of his parents, the noses and hands passed over quickly, some of the mouths crossed out in frustration—signs of an artist impatient to finish. As I look further, I see pictures of towering trees as seen from below, angular and rough mountains, fantastic clouds. The landscapes are both real and imagined—Canada as he saw it, or Canada as he feared it was. These are not drawings of love; the monstrous outgrowths of wilderness are frightening or possibly challenging, but not endearing. I find nothing lovely or precious here.

At the very back of the book is a sketch of my mother. She is naked, lying on her side, her features unmistakable in my father's quick, light pencil lines. Her legs, arms and breasts are drawn deliberately; she is beautiful. He made her fecund, a rounded symbol of fertility; her hips swell.

My father's landscapes thrust upward, rip open the sky. His picture of my mother is light, smooth, floral in its homage. "My love," I imagine him saying, "you are all the earth to me."

I trace the lines with my fingers, feeling the marks my father made in the paper. The light cast by the side lamp shines yellow, and the forty-year-old paper is a soft, pliable gold. *This is so much about them and their beginning,* I think. *Lives framed by love—think of that.* I can't imagine anything more tragic.

I look up from the sketchbook and listen for the sounds of my mother lurking outside my door. Nothing. The confinement of my bedroom walls keeps the voices at bay—both my mother's and those girly voices from the past, the ones that rise and drop with the sounds of tinkling earrings and the smacking of lipsticked mouths. Even though silence unnerves me, the echo of sounds that have come and gone is worse. Sometimes, silence is better.

I hold the book in my hands, wishing one of my sisters would come barging in so that we could turn these pages together and both be embarrassed by our parents' young, naked love. But they all left, gradually, one after the other. Somehow, it never occurred to me that, in the end, I would be the only one still here.

The clouds overhead make it a grey evening, and the ocean sounds weak, as if it has lost its purpose for being. Hundreds of people mill about the port as they wait for their cruises to Alaska or Mexico. Vancouver is a kind of oceanside attraction, a pretty place on the way to somewhere else.

I can hear the sounds of Penny's wedding behind me: the shouts of my drunken uncle, the tinkling of chopsticks against rice bowls, the giggling of my sister and her other bridesmaids. My mother comes out to see what I'm doing, takes one look at me and hurries back into the hotel ballroom. I'm alone except for the old man in a dirty apron squatting in the corner—and he silently smokes Marlboros, one after the other. It's a nice view from this balcony, a hotel builder's dream. The cruise ships sit, massive, like bloated whales, white on grey-black water. I look down at my bridesmaid dress; the big skirt reminds me of a porcelain doll one of my childhood friends kept propped up on her dresser. I feel almost as stiff, but not quite so virginal. I laugh to myself (the smoky old man doesn't seem to notice); Matt would find this whole charade screamingly funny.

On our last day together, he pulled me toward him on our unmade bed. The harsh afternoon light pushed its way through half-closed blinds. His eyes were shadowed, but his mouth remained flesh pink, his teeth bright. He licked his lips, his tongue flicking in and out like a small lizard tasting the air for the next fly. He moved out of the dark, back into the light. Black, white. Black, white. My hand lay flat on his chest— graphic, tattoo-like, a dark stain.

"Small breasts," he said, "are the most sensitive."

He preferred the daylight, and it made me want to hide; I don't like seeing myself naked, watching my own breasts move up and down, my thighs open wide. Everything with him was revealed: the fleshiness, the soft give and take of skin, the glitter of sweat, shades of pink, peach and brown. And he talked, his voice absurd against the sound of our bodies coming together, the slapping of fornication. Like an actor raising his voice above the crowd, Matt made sure I could hear him, and he spoke clearly, slowly—a little public speaking.

It was the feeling of his body on mine that made me wish these moments could last and last—the feeling of him holding me completely. My hands, my face, everything. I could look up and see nothing but him, count the differences between his features and mine. I could forget that I was naked, sweaty, thin; I could forget that I existed at all.

Afterward, he stroked my breasts and looked up at the ceiling. "When we're together, everything goes away. I don't have to think when I'm with you." Matt rolled over and looked me in the face, his blue eyes blinding. He kissed my forehead. "But you have to leave, don't you?"

I opened my mouth to say, *No, I don't. I could stay here forever.* But then I closed my lips tight and swallowed. Through the crack in the blinds, I could see the hazy sun poking its way through the smog. The atmosphere in the room was heavy with the smell of our bodies, but I knew the air wouldn't be much better outside. I shut my eyes and imagined rain.

I shake my head, trying to empty it of all thoughts not related to Penny's wedding. Walking back into the ballroom, I weave my way through the tightly packed tables of mostly drunk middle-aged Chinese couples. The best man has started his toast to my sister, who sits with her arm around our mother.

"He's a lucky guy, folks. Doesn't she look beautiful tonight?"

Penny's face is a deep red, and she giggles into her new husband's shoulder. My mother laughs loudly. *The theatre of marriage*, I think, *makes everyone get along.* I make it to the bar and sit heavily on a stool, facing away from the head table, and rearrange the lavender layers of my bridesmaid dress. I order a double gin and tonic.

The bartender passes me my drink and then leans with his elbows on the bar. "So, how do you know the happy couple? From the look on your face, I'd say you hardly know them at all or you know them too well."

I laugh and look up at his face. Blue eyes, red, purposely messy hair. Smooth, white skin, so pale he's almost blue. Sly smile.

"The bride is my sister, so I guess I know them too well. See that big white dress? Well, everyone thinks she's pregnant, but no one wants to ask her."

"Ah, you're the black sheep, aren't you? That's a good thing, because I don't think I could talk to anyone who would voluntarily wear this dress." He touches the ruffle on my sleeve. "Listen, I saw you standing outside just now and you didn't look very happy. I think you need some fun."

His eyes glimmer in the dim; the tea lights on the bar cast moving shadows on his face. He seems not quite there, a phantom bartender on a dark and stormy night. The noise of the room disappears, and it's just him and me, lit from below by candles.

"I get off shift in ten minutes. I think you and I should take a little walk and get a drink somewhere."

As I walk out of the cloakroom with my jacket and purse, Jackie, dragging her sniffling son along with one hand, stops me. "Where are you going? You have to come back in time for the bouquet toss, especially now that you're the only single sister left."

"I'm just going out to grab some gum."

"Oh good. You don't want to miss the cake cutting either. All *right*, Tyler, I know you have to pee. Let's go, then."

As Jackie turns toward the hallway, her carefully set hair sitting in unmoving curls on the top of her head, she touches my shoulder. "Penny just told me this morning how happy she is you're living with Mom right now. So, thanks."

I look at her narrow face and stiffly sprayed hair. I shrug. "I had nothing else to do," I mutter.

At the exit from the ballroom, I turn around. My sisters move quickly, like sparrows, quivering, grouping together and then moving apart. My mother stands behind Wendy, her nose on level with my sister's straight shoulders. I see her move as if to touch her, pick a piece of dust off her dress, but then my mother thinks better of it and lets her hand fall to her side. She turns and looks at me, sees my jacket and purse and then turns away again. If she knows I'm leaving, she isn't asking any questions.

Fifteen minutes later, I'm in the bar down the street, crushed up against strangers in a sweaty, boozy crowd. He shouts over the noise and orders a double gin and tonic for me before looking me in the eye. "I hope this isn't weird for you."

His head is bent over, and his breath is hot on my ear. "Because I know I'm just what you need."

"We were going to name you Christopher," says Wendy as she paints her fingernails. "But, you know, you came out a girl, so we had to turf that idea." She blows on her long fingers, carefully moving them back and forth so that the polish will dry evenly.

I sit cross-legged on the floor of her bedroom, breathing in the nail polish and the dry, dusty smell of the potpourri packets she has placed on every surface. Her wedding dress hangs on a hook on the back of her door, its white satin shining in the dim light. Her veil lies on her dresser, covered in plastic. I touched it once the day before, when my sister had left the house to buy more wrappers for the fruitcake party favours. It felt stiff, wiry, completely opposite to the way I had expected (lighter even than air, white froth made solid). Weddings are a disappointing business when you are only seven years old.

"And then, you know, Mom was sick, so no one really took care of you. I mean, we all did, but we were just kids then, and we didn't know what to do." She looks at me through her asymmetrical bangs and reaches over to tousle my hair. "I actually melted your baby bottles once. How was I supposed to know that water boils away so fast?"

Daisy, her highlighted hair in curlers, runs into the room with her bright pink bridesmaid dress in her hands. "Listen, can you help me iron out this pucker right by the zipper? How did I not notice this earlier?" She looks at me, surprised. "Aren't you in bed yet? You're too little to stay up this late." She runs out of the room again, leaving behind a curler that has dropped out of her hair.

Wendy sighs. "Well, Sammy, I'll be out of the house for-ever by tomorrow. Can't say that I'm too sad about it either." She pats me on the head. "You have a big day tomorrow too. Go to bed. I still have a lot to do."

I sit on the stairs for a long time, watching my sisters break in their shoes, run out to the twenty-four-hour drugstore for last-minute makeup and hairspray. Penny joins me briefly. "They're going to play Christopher Cross at the reception, you know. How sappy. I'm going to see if I can request something better, maybe some New Order or something, like they played at the school dance." She punches me in the arm. "I'll get my own bedroom now that Wendy's leaving. I can't wait, because you're the biggest pain in the butt when you snore."

Upstairs, my parents play mah-jong with the out-of-town relatives, the moving tiles like little footsteps, dozens of tap shoes on a wooden floor. I rest my head on a banister and fall asleep. When I wake up, the house vibrates with suppressed energy, full to the rafters with back satin, boutonnieres. Expectations.

At the airport, my father, thinner than he has ever been before, stands in line with Daisy as she checks her luggage and requests an aisle seat. He hoists her suitcase up onto the scale, his scraggly hair falling over his forehead and into his eyes. He straightens up again, sighing.

I stand to the side with everyone else: my mother, Jackie and Penny, even Wendy and her nervous husband, who fidgets and rubs the top of his head until his straight black hair sticks up on end. He stands on one foot and then the other, twisting his hands together and whistling. My grandfather is at home. No one has bothered to tell him that Daisy is leaving to live in Hong Kong.

"I guess I have to go to the gate now. Goodbye, Sammy. Remember to write." Daisy stands tall, unwilling to go anywhere without her heels, even when travelling.

I look at the floor, dig the toe of my dirty sneaker into the concrete. Daisy laughs.

"You don't have to hug me if you don't want to, but I wouldn't mind if you don't mind."

I push my face into the side of her body, feel her arm wrap around my shoulders.

She whispers, "I'll miss you too, Sammy. But I have to leave. I'll be back someday—just think of that. I'll phone you on your birthday. Turning ten is a big deal, and I don't want to miss it."

She turns to my mother. "I'll call when I get in."

My mother sniffs. "Remember what I said. Hong Kong isn't like Canada, you know. Men will rip the necklace right off your body. And don't let anyone charge you more just because you're Canadian."

Daisy waves her hand dismissively and nods along. "I don't want to fight, Mom. Last night wasn't any fun for either of us."

"Who's fighting?" Her lips are stretched thin over her uneven teeth. "Don't accuse me of fighting when all I ever wanted was to teach you right from wrong. You'll come to a bad end in Hong Kong, I just know it. It's only what you deserve for leaving your father at a time like this—no good daughter would go off alone just for a career. Who will marry you now?"

Daisy pushes her face closer to my mother's. "I'm surprised anyone married you."

My mother steps back and spits in Daisy's face. Wendy's husband giggles nervously. Then my mother, her entire body quivering with rage, walks away, out the doors and toward the parking lot. No one follows.

My father sighs, then half-heartedly punches Daisy on the shoulder as she wipes off her cheek with her hand. "Ten percent of your paycheque in the bank. Always. No exceptions."

"Of course, Dad." Daisy pauses. "If you need anything, I'll come home right away."

"Don't worry. We'll be all right. Hey, how do you avoid falling hair?"

Daisy smiles. "How?"

"Jump out of the way! That one always kills me." He coughs into his hand and then grimaces. Daisy rubs her eyes.

And then she is gone.

Somehow, her empty place grew over, like a bald patch of grass that slowly fills in. We started to use her room for sewing and soon her old bed was covered with fabric remnants and half-pinned dresses, most of them in pink taffeta, Jackie's favourite.

In the end, she did come back for good, but by then, everything had changed.

Jackie is posing, the heavy white silk of her mermaid wedding dress pooled around her feet. The crowd gathered around the church murmurs, "So beautiful, isn't she?" She smiles, puts her hand on her hip and tilts her elaborately styled head for the camera.

Penny stands beside me. "It's just us now, Sammy." She looks behind her, waves at her boyfriend, who is leaning against his silver sports car. "I don't know how we'll ever stand it. At least Dad was around before."

I stare forlornly at my pink bubble skirt, designed to give

my prepubescent body the shape it doesn't yet have. "You won't leave, will you?"

She sighs. "One day, I'll have to. But not right now, Sammy. Not right now."

That night, I dance with my brothers-in-law, with Penny's boyfriend, too. At midnight, Jackie changes into the going-away outfit that Daisy brought back from Hong Kong (a purple silk suit, nipped at the waist with a peplum on the jacket) and poses for a picture with all of us: Wendy, Daisy, Penny and me.

"Penny, there's a run in your pantyhose."

"Come on, Sammy, stand in front of me, like this."

"I don't know, Daisy, maybe it would have been better without the earrings."

"Okay, okay. Let's just smile."

It's not until everything is all over (Jackie rides off with her new husband in a white limousine, her head sticking out of the sunroof; one of our uncles throws up on the dance floor, his right hand still firmly grasping his glass of whisky; Wendy walks around the dance floor for ten minutes before realizing that the back of her designer knock-off dress is tucked into her pantyhose), that I speak even one word to my mother. She sits at the messy head table, her head resting in her hands. Her red dress looks limp, as if it is hanging on a hook, empty.

"How are you feeling, Mom? Did you have fun?"

She doesn't even open her eyes. "A little. The food was good."

"Wendy's coming around with the car. We should go."

"All right. Take my purse, will you?"

Aunt Min Lai's husband, his breath smelling of vomit and the mints he must have eaten to hide it, lurches toward us. "Siu Sang, how are you?"

"I'm fine. Weddings are happy business, after all."

"No, I mean, how are you *really?* Pon Man's not here any-more. You're all alone. Tell me honestly."

My mother smiles tightly. "As I said, I'm fine. Daisy is back now to help out, at least until she finds an apartment."

My uncle starts to cry. Giant tears like golf balls roll down his thin cheeks. "This isn't fair, is it? Nothing about any of this is fair. Some wedding, huh?"

His daughter swoops toward us, her hands fluttering like anxious birds. "Daddy. Daddy! I'm so sorry, Auntie, he just needs a good sleep." And she drags him away, his head slumped over her shoulder, his body folded over like a garment bag.

My mother wipes her hands on her skirt. "Close call. I was afraid he would try to hug me." She laughs, an empty, trilling sound that dies abruptly as if the air is slicing it in half.

The bartender laughs and moves closer. I close my eyes, won-dering if that red hair will burn my fingers when I touch it.

It's strange, the feeling that everything you're thinking is in plain view, that your thoughts are being anticipated by someone you've only just met. When he says, "This is what you want," you think, "Yes, that's it!" You wonder if he's reading the expression on your face or your body language. Maybe he's hearing the subtext, the unsaid things running like shadows underneath your conversation. Maybe he has a mys-tical gift. Maybe you and he are just the pawns of fate. Or maybe you're just imagining all of it. But the origins don't really matter, because the strange feeling is still there—unnerving, sexy.

It's a relief, too, not having to think about what you want all the time, especially when everything you thought you wanted has gone to shit. You thought critically at school, but now, when the analytical eye turns inward, it meets a murky, gelatinous mess, opaque enough that it's impossible to see through, but not so opaque that you lose hope of catching a glimpse of that one thing that will explain who you really are. Even if what he's telling you about yourself is untrue, it's better than looking inside your messy head one more time. Whatever. Coming up with your own words is sometimes the hardest thing of all.

When his hand finally touches yours, you realize, right then, that you have been waiting for this all night, this sting from his fingertips on your palm. Your eyes close for just a second, just so you can turn off everything else except this touch, the touch that means he knows the darkest wishes of your being and is not scared, the touch that means you will never feel like this again unless you're with him, the touch that means you have come this far and there is no turning back now.

reception

Pon Man stands in his father's room, looks at the small cot pushed up against the closet door, the slightly larger bed opposite. The bare window is open, and a breeze smelling of moss and mud floats in. Pon Man edges up against a wall, fits his back into a corner. Seid Quan walks in and drops his suitcase on the floor.

"All right." He nods to the cot. "Your bed is that one over there. Do you want to have a nap now? Are you tired from the trip?"

Pon Man looks down at his shoes. "No."

"Are you hungry? I could make some sandwiches."

"No." He is still looking at his shoes. "Do we have to sleep in the same room?"

"Yes, for now. I'm saving to buy a house so that your mother and sister can join us."

"Min Lai might get married soon. Some guy named Ng has been hanging around."

Seid Quan sighs. "Oh. Is there any other news I should know?"

"I don't know. Mother and Yun Wo both like this Ng guy, say he has relatives in Canada too, so Min Lai can come here without costing you too much if they get married. And Mother told me to tell you to take good care of me because of those nosebleeds I get."

"Right. Of course."

Pon Man shoves his hands into his pockets, shakes his head as if he is trying to get rid of something. "I don't like this place."

"What do you mean? You've only been here for two hours."

"It's wet." Pon Man flicks at the damp cuffs of his pants. "I don't like feeling cold all the time." He stares defiantly into his father's eyes. His strange, ghost-grey eyes.

"Once you get used to it, it's not so bad. There's no money to be made in the village, just remember that." Seid Quan lets out a long breath as if he is unused to explaining himself, or talking at all.

"I don't see anything worth money here, just a room we have to share. Our house in the village was nicer, and it didn't smell so mouldy." Pon Man wrinkles his nose.

Seid Quan falls silent for a moment before he begins to speak again, his voice deliberately even. "It's not about expensive things. It's about hard work and saving and supporting a family. I've seen men ruined by chasing expensive cars and clothes, taking shortcuts to look big around their friends. That's not going to happen to us. Do you understand?"

Pon Man watches as his father leans forward and chops at the air with his hands for emphasis. He can see the emotion like snakes under Seid Quan's skin—sinister, squirming. He is suddenly afraid, so he shrugs. "I guess." He pushes himself farther into the wall.

"All right. Let's go to the café and order something to eat. We'll have some real Western food. How about that?"

Pon Man almost whispers, "Okay."

He is, finally, out of Chinatown and wandering down Hastings Street. He is a small boy, and slight, but he walks with confidence in his basketball shoes, the swagger of a man who has been to many places and found them wanting. Hidden inside his jacket is a brand new sketchbook, his going-away present from his mother. He reaches inside and caresses its spine, then zips up his jacket again before anyone can see.

He has been in Canada for eight days, and had begun to think that Chinatown was Vancouver in its entirety. During the day, he stayed with Seid Quan in the barbershop, cleaning up the cut hair, washing out the towels. Pon Man gagged whenever he had to touch the wet clumps of hair that gathered in the corners of the shop and collected in the sinks. When the last customer had left, newly shorn, Pon Man could feel a thick layer of other men's skin over his own, as if the flakes had flown up into the air while his father was cutting hair or shaving beards, and then settled down again on Pon Man's face, arms and shoulders. Even after he washed himself down in the back room, he could still smell the oil of other men. He thought he would rather be at home with his mother, helping her rinse the dirt off vegetables, counting the money in the family jar.

He asked his father, over and over again, when he could start school. Seid Quan always shrugged and said, "In the fall, when everyone else goes."

When they closed up, they walked together up and down Pender Street and looked into the windows of the shops, the dark windows of the nightclubs. The older men on the street nodded to them and gave Pon Man candy. He didn't like it, but he ate it anyway. The night before, a thin man wearing a tattered wool overcoat had lurched toward Pon Man from the shadows.

"You must be the boy," he slurred in Chinese.

Pon Man looked at his father, who held his hands out, palms up. His face was so pale and thin it looked as if it were made of paper. "You must leave him alone, brother. He's still just a child."

The thin man pulled himself up straight and stood facing Seid Quan, their chins almost touching. "He won't catch anything from me, old friend," he said in English. "He will learn the truth about this fucking country on his own. Even you cannot protect him."

And the thin man backed away, disappearing into the dark alley as if he had never emerged. Seid Quan sighed. "Someone I used to know, I'm afraid," he said. Pon Man did not dare to ask his name.

This morning, as Seid Quan was busy shaving a customer, Pon Man slipped out the back door and headed west on Hastings, dizzy with adventure. Now, he sees downtown ahead of him and, if he looks behind, he can see Chinatown retreating, a picture postcard growing smaller and smaller. A bus trundles toward him and he steps on, determined to stay on for as long as he can.

The bus rolls past Granville Street, and Pon Man stares, open-mouthed, at the fancy shops lined up, one next to the other, all along the street. Jewellery, furs, shoes. Everything. Women in high heels walk with shopping bags, alone and without men. As the bus travels farther west, he looks up and sees the tall office buildings, grey, carved with lions and gargoyles, constructed from stone, sixteen, maybe twenty storeys high. *This is nothing like Chinatown,* he thinks. *This is like the magazines Mother gets from the city.*

When the bus finally stops, the driver shouts, "Last stop! Stanley Park!" Pon Man steps off and walks straight into the thick green of the trees.

The park is empty in the middle of the day, and the only people he sees are old ladies walking their dogs, old ladies who look at him once and edge farther away from him on the trails as they walk past. He does not notice and gapes at everything else around him. A goose flies out over Lost Lagoon and honks loudly, and somewhere, invisible in the trees, another goose honks in response. Pon Man thinks they must be related.

He walks off on the horse trails and, suddenly, the summer sky disappears. He stops to look up and sees nothing but trees, their dark green tops meeting overhead, obscuring the sun. Here, the ground is wet, soaked through as if it has never been dry, and pools of water collect in his footprints. The smell is sharp and medicinal. *It's like being in a pit,* he thinks. *Nowhere to go, and so far away from the top you can hardly see it.* It is so quiet that Pon Man can hear only his own sharp breathing. His fear at being lost stops him from pulling out his sketchbook to draw this dripping, fantastic landscape. Instead, he turns around, trying to remember which direction he came from. He stumbles forward, hoping that the trail he is on leads somewhere. He shivers in his short-sleeved shirt.

He sees a break in the trees and runs through it, cracking branches and pushing aside leaves as he goes. Just ahead in a clearing, a photographer focuses his camera on a family standing beside a giant hollow tree. He rushes forward and stops directly behind the photographer, happy to be so close to another human being.

The mother of the family, wearing a pink sweater and a white skirt, screams.

The father runs forward and says, "Watch out, there's a Chinaman behind you!"

The photographer turns around and looks at Pon Man. His eyes narrow and he hisses, "Get out of here, kid. Chinamen are no good for business." He gives him a little push.

As the photographer tries to calm down the hysterical mother and outraged father, Pon Man walks north, on a different trail. He did not understand what those people said, but he knows what they meant. His head hurts and his legs feel like rubber. He carefully places one foot in front of the other, one step at a time, until he reaches the seawall. He sits on the stones for a few minutes before walking back to the bus stop. His father will be angry, and then he will want to feed him, but Pon Man just wants to sleep somewhere, a room of his own where he does not have to face anyone.

"I bought something for you." Seid Quan places a lumpy brown paper package on the table between them at the Ovaltine Café.

Pon Man takes the package in his hands, turns it around and around. "What is it?"

Seid Quan smiles. "Well, I can't tell you that. Just open it."

Pon Man peels away the paper slowly, placing each torn piece on the table beside his plate of steak and eggs. It was not his mother's way to wrap presents for him. She only passed him the sketchbook with a grunt and then smiled at his happiness, turning her head as if she thought she was hiding her pleasure from him, even though he could see it anyway.

"A radio!" Pon Man smiles broadly. "Thank you, Father."

He fiddles with the controls, trying to find a station. Seid Quan leans forward. "You see, if you turn this one, that changes the frequency. That's what this word means. And this one makes it louder or quieter. The word here means 'volume.' Here, just let me show you how to do it." He takes the radio out of Pon Man's hands.

Pon Man stares at his father, drums his finger on the table. He watches his father's forehead, the lines deep in the skin, the muscles around his eyebrows, the brown spots around his hairline. Pon Man feels sick.

"Seid Quan! Is that your son?" An old man leans toward them and pushes his cane behind his back.

"Mr. Wong, how are you?"

"Fine, fine." He waves his hand dismissively. "Is this Pon Man, then?"

"Yes, of course. Pon Man, this is an old friend of mine, Mr. Wong. Say hello."

"Hello, Uncle Wong."

Old Mr. Wong chuckles. "A nice, polite boy too. Well, Pon Man, you must come to my house and meet my grandson. He's about your age, I think. He started a basketball team with his friends, you know. Maybe you would enjoy it."

Pon Man nods and opens his mouth to speak.

Seid Quan says quickly, "Oh, he wouldn't want to barge in like that. They probably don't have a spot for him anyway."

Mr. Wong looks confused. "I'm sure they could always use extras."

"Yes, but he helps me in the shop all day, and then I want him to rest up before school starts. You know how it is."

Mr. Wong nods absently. "Yes, I suppose. Well, whatever you think, Seid Quan. I suppose I'll see you at the funeral for Mr. Yip?"

"Yes, I'll be there."

"All right. Well, it was nice meeting you, young man. I'm sure I'll see you around." Mr. Wong walks slowly out of the café.

Pon Man looks at his father. "I want to play basketball."

Seid Quan shakes his head. "No, you don't. Those Wong boys, they're trouble. All they do is smoke cigarettes and chase white girls all day. You're better off staying away from them and working in the shop."

"I don't want to work in the shop."

"What?"

Pon Man sits up straight. "I don't want to work in the shop. It smells funny."

"You can go to school in the fall. You are going to work in the shop for the rest of the summer. I won't have you running around the streets of Chinatown like one of those thugs."

Pon Man stares at the speckled table, imagines he can see his own reflection in one of the tiny embedded sparkles. *I wouldn't mind being that small,* he thinks. He looks up at his father, at his set face, which seems as if it might crack and let out tears or laughter or maybe rage. *You don't know me. No one here knows me.* He remembers his mother's gruff voice the day before he left her. "You must do what your father tells you, even if you don't like it or don't want to do it. It doesn't matter. He's your father and he deserves your obedience. He works hard for you and the rest of us."

Pon Man twists his mouth. "Yes, Father. Of course."

In the hall, there are hundreds of voices, and Pon Man cannot understand one.

He is in the New Canadian class, and the teacher is smiling toothily. She speaks loudly, her mouth exaggerating every sound she makes. She points at herself and the writing on the board, saying, "Teeeacherrrrr." Pon Man snarls and looks out the window at the cars speeding past on Broadway, the seagulls flying in low to the wet pavement. Soggy brown paper lunch bags litter the school's front lawn. *Rain,* he thinks, *always the rain.*

Later, he stands outside at recess. Other Chinese boys his age stand around in twos or alone like him. He tries to look cool and leans against a pillar, his eyes focused directly on the wide cuff of his jeans.

A boy saunters up, his shoulders slouched and his head cocked at an angle. He stops in front of Pon Man and jerks his chin at his face. "You wanna smoke?"

Pon Man looks at the cigarette in the boy's outstretched hand. He glances away coolly and back again, taking in the other boy's pockmarked face. He nods.

That afternoon, in B block, Pon Man sits in a ditch and smokes cigarettes with four other boys. They are laughing, pointing at the students in the windows above them who are reading, looking bored or falling asleep.

His English is still not good, even after a summer of instruction from his father, but his new friends are easygoing and correct his speech tactfully. They are Chinese boys like him, and they know what it's like.

"Pon, you gotta learn better English. They'll eat you alive if you don't understand. You gotta be like them."

He squints into the afternoon sun, wrinkling his smooth, pretty boy forehead. He has no idea how to say what he thinks (which is, *I left everything I know, so why should I be like them, when they could try just as hard to be like me, but even I know they would never do that, only force me to forget where I come from and the places I love, even now*) without seeming weird.

He takes another drag and says, "Yes, this I know."

He walks back to the house from the post office, his first Canadian letter in his hand. He hurries along Hastings and then turns onto Princess, the thin brown envelope burning like a smouldering coal in his tight fist. He is afraid to look at it again, afraid that his name in English ("Pon Man Chan," how odd) will have disappeared and that he will be left with a worthless envelope and a blank piece of paper. He wants to hold the letter up to his face and smell it, breathe in his mother's house, the oil she rubs on her ankles when it rains. But he tells himself he must be patient, for if he lets himself consume it as he would like, he might end up destroying the letter in his frenzy.

He pushes into the house and runs up the stairs, ignoring his father's roommate, who yells, "What's the hurry, you crazy boy?" He butts open the bedroom door with his shoulder and stumbles in, collapsing face first on his father's bed. Only then does he open his fist.

Dear Son,

I am not very good at writing letters, as I am sure your father has said to you already. But I guessed that you would rather read a tiresome letter from me than read nothing at all. Your father did say I should begin taking

English lessons and writing letters for practise, but I cannot imagine writing in a foreign language to my boy. It does not matter, because this is just between us. Your father need never see it.

Min Lai is getting married next month to that Ng boy. I have arranged it all. I hope he will be able to bring her to Canada soon, as his older brother is living there now. It will be nice to be in the same country, although young Ng tells me his brother lives across the country from Vancouver in a city called Toronto. But Canada cannot possibly be as big as China, so I am sure you will see her often. You must tell your father for me.

Your father writes that he will be looking for a house soon. You must go with him, because you will know the things I like better than he will. He means well, Pon Man, and wants only the best for us, even if he does not say so. He is not like me, with my big mouth that seems to let words fall out no matter what my intention, so you cannot expect to be comfortable right away.

I sometimes look east, which is the direction your father once told me the boat sails to reach the west, although I still don't see how. I feel you all the way over there, my gentle boy. I know you are lonely and I know that your father is a stranger to you. Just be patient. He will learn. Remember that I will be coming to Canada very soon. That is what we are all saving for.

Be careful and always think twice before you say or do anything. I am looking forward to seeing your new Canadian drawings when your father finally sends for me.

Mother

He stuffs the letter back into its envelope and looks around the room for a hiding place. There is nothing much, only their beds and a small desk, so Pon Man kneels down and reaches under his father's bed. He feels a wooden box and pulls it out, surprised. It is covered in a thick, even layer of dust that doesn't quite obscure the drawings of apples on all of its sides. Carefully, he pulls open the lid and peers inside.

One by one, Pon Man draws out scrolls covered in Chinese calligraphy, each stamped with his father's seal. He sees the brushes and inks at the bottom, practice sheets with penciled words carefully drawn out. They are all the same. "Friends come from far away, isn't it a happy thing?" Pon Man remembers it as a quote from Confucius, one they had to practise writing in school over and over again. He counts the scrolls. There are seventy-two.

He repacks the box, slides it back under the bed. He collects the dislodged dust balls in his hands and throws them out the window. Still unsure of what to do, he rolls his letter into a tube and slips it into the lining of the empty suitcase under his cot. He quickly looks in the small mirror to make sure there is no dust in his slick black hair.

As he runs back to the barbershop (his father will ask him where he was, and Pon Man will know what Seid Quan suspects but rarely says: that he was out smoking with his friends, stealing penny candies and listening to no-good music), he thinks about what he will write back to his mother. He will tell her that he understands, that he knows Seid Quan only wants the best. Pon Man will promise his mother that he will do everything he can to help the family, that he will carry on his father's success and build on it, so that everyone is proud. *Yes,* he thinks, *if I cannot tell him, then I can, at least, tell her.*

Pon Man and his friends ride the trolley down Granville Street in a pulsing knot at the back of the bus. They are shouting over the heads of other passengers, swinging from the hand grips and singing "O Canada" as loud as they can.

An older man turns in his seat, glares and mutters, "Damned chink kids."

And it doesn't matter what this old coot thinks, because today is today and the sun is shining. They laugh and make faces behind the old man's back. Pon Man leans forward, pushes his body in the direction the bus is travelling. He feels its mechanical pull all around him—a buzz that travels to his physical core from north, south, east and west, through his fingers, his heels, the tips of his hair. He laughs again, though he hardly knows why.

The bus hurtles down the Granville Bridge, rushing headlong into downtown. Pon Man pushes his hand into his pocket, feels the coins with his fingers and counts them in his head. *Enough for a movie*, he thinks, *but not for a snack*. His father has cut his allowance in half and is hoarding their money, waiting for the right house to turn up. Pon Man accompanies him to every viewing and claims he knows if a house is wrong just by looking at it from the sidewalk. Nothing pushes Seid Quan into silence more than a surly Pon Man scowling at a house and refusing to enter. Pon Man shrugs when Seid Quan lets out a big sigh before he walks in by himself; he knows what his mother likes, so why should he bother if he knows it's wrong? The houses in Chinatown and Strathcona, where Seid Quan wants to stay, feel like a punch in the face to him—the rotting porches, the chipped siding. He tells Seid Quan to broaden the search, saying Shew Lin would never want a house so close to the busy city core.

"Hey, Pon Man, stick your head out the window and see if you can spit on the cars beside us." His friends hang half their bodies out the open windows as other passengers try not to look, hoping, Pon Man imagines, that one of these Chinese boys will fall out and be crushed by traffic. A tragedy, but then they would all learn, wouldn't they?

Pon Man checks his watch, sees that he has four hours until the barbershop closes. He will have to run back to Chinatown and help his father clean up. Even here, with the wind blasting past his head through the bus windows, Pon Man can smell the dead hair and cloying shaving cream, can see the disappointment on Seid Quan's face as he watches Pon Man angrily sweep the floor and rinse the combs. The bus lurches, and he starts to gag.

The old coot mutters to himself again, shaking his head. *Fuck you,* Pon Man thinks, but he does not say it.

Later that afternoon, Pon Man runs down the street toward the barbershop, already fifteen minutes late. Seid Quan stands at the window, waiting for him.

The bell on the door rings loudly. "I'm sorry I'm late, Father. The bus didn't come for the longest time. Honest."

His father holds up Pon Man's sketchbook and opens it to one of the first pages.

Pon Man jumps forward. "That's mine."

Seid Quan looks at one of the drawings, his face expressionless. He looks at his son. "I didn't think I looked so old."

Pon Man pulls the sketchbook away and holds it close to his chest. "You're not supposed to look at that."

He shrugs. "I couldn't help it, could I? Why did you hide it in the shop, of all places?"

"I'm the only one who washes the towels around here, so I thought the linen closet was safe."

Seid Quan sits down in one of the barber chairs. "But you were late, and I had to start your work for you." He shakes his head. "What am I going to do with you?"

"They're just drawings." Pon Man feels as if he is shouting, even though he can hear his own quiet voice floating in the high-ceilinged room.

"You scratched lines all over my mouth. Why would you do that?"

"I don't know. That's my private book. It has nothing to do with you."

Seid Quan stands up. "That's where you're wrong. It has everything to do with me. Everything you do involves me, whether you like it or not. This drawing is a waste of time, time that could be spent on working hard and helping me save. If I don't know what you're doing, how can I protect you?"

Pon Man frowns. "Protect me from what?"

Seid Quan starts to walk toward the back room. "There is still sweeping to be done. And make sure you polish the mirrors." He stops for a moment, as if he has forgotten something, then continues walking. "And do something with that book. I don't want to see it ever again."

A teenage girl stands in the doorway of the barbershop, nervously looking left and right. Her shiny black hair is rolled into thick curls that sit, like a nest, on top of her head. She wipes the palms of her hands on her green plaid skirt. Her eyes scan the men until they fall on Pon Man, washing off combs in a glass cylinder filled with transparent blue liquid.

"Pon Man," she calls, waving.

"Wanda." Pon Man steps away from the combs.

"Gee, this is some shop. My dad gets his hair cut here, but I don't think I've ever come in." She giggles.

Pon Man shrugs. "Yeah, it's all right, I guess." He looks behind him and sees his father standing behind Mr. Mah's head, his scissors held still as he watches.

"I just wanted to ask you if you're coming to the roller skating party tonight. May and Bill and me are all going together. There's an extra seat." She looks at the floor, scrapes at the black and white tile with her saddle shoe.

"Yeah, sure. That sounds good."

Wanda claps her hands together. "Oh, I'm so happy! Meet us at Oppenheimer Park at seven. We'll be in Bill's father's car, you know, the blue Chrysler."

Pon Man nods, and Wanda skips out the door, clasping her hands in front of her chest as she goes. He turns back to the combs, dunking his hand in the disinfectant.

Seid Quan walks over and leans in close. "Is that Mr. Chow's daughter?"

Pon Man can barely hear him. "I don't know. I think so."

"I don't want you going around with a Chinatown girl."

Pon Man almost laughs. "What's that supposed to mean? Aren't I a Chinatown boy?"

Seid Quan shakes his head. "Those girls, they're too forward. There are only so many girls here, and many more boys. Who knows how many they go around with? They get too much attention."

"That's the dumbest thing I've ever heard."

Seid Quan begins to walk back toward Mr. Mah. "We'll find you a girl when the time is right. A nice girl from the village. Maybe Hong Kong, if you want someone stylish."

Pon Man stares after his father. He wants to punch him in the back of the head or yell at him until he crumples into a ball of splintered bones. He takes in a lungful of air; he can still smell Wanda's perfume (peony, apple, bubble gum). He shrugs as he walks to the back room and lights a cigarette.

Later that night, he sits in Bill's car with his hand up Wanda's skirt while the others are skating around in circles inside the gym. She giggles into his ear, licks the side of his neck with her small, pink tongue.

"You're a bad Chinatown boy, Pon Man," she says as she wriggles out of her bra. "It's a good thing I like the bad ones."

They stand by the water, their hands on the railing, which Pon Man thinks is there only to keep the masses from plunging headfirst into Burrard Inlet. He can't help thinking that everyone, like him, wants to escape this city, for despite the trees and mountains and pure water, Vancouver is as cold and hard at its core as anywhere else in Canada.

He looks up at the clouded sky. He will never figure out exactly what it is about this place that attracts men from everywhere. The women follow, lie sick in boats that slice through the ocean, thick with fish and kelp and the leftovers of humankind (floating glass balls, lost buoys, the remains of fishing nets).

The boat sits on the water, floating as if it has been there forever, an organic growth of the ocean that supports it. Pon Man leans forward, scans the line of people leaving the deck, wondering if he will be able to spot her from this far or if she will need to be closer first. He rubs his chin, not as smooth as it once was, and pats the creamed dome of his hair. He looks across and down at Seid Quan, now two inches shorter than his son.

"It has been three years, after all," Seid Quan says suddenly. "You are not the little boy who left her."

"No, I'm not."

"If you are not able to recognize her, how will I?"

Pon Man tries to look into his father's eyes, but Seid Quan turns away. He isn't sure if his father's question needs an answer, so he says nothing, as he often does. *I always think he doesn't understand me,* he thinks, *but I don't understand him either. The only difference is that it is strange only for him.*

From the crowd, a short woman in a grey coat steps forward, her hands firmly gripping a brown and black suitcase. Her jaw is tight, but her eyes dart from face to face to face, staying on one man for only a second before moving to the next. "Mother," he whispers. He steps forward and holds out his hands. As soon as he touches her (her hands, rough and smooth at the same time, as if parts of her have weathered away, like river stones polished by age and water), he wants to push his head under her arm, breathe in her smell, fall asleep. But he stands straight, a young man now, and lets her embrace him.

"So tall," she says, "so handsome. Must be the cold Canadian air."

It is Pon Man who leads Shew Lin through the house, who takes her hand and shows her the kitchen, the closets, the backyard where anything might be able to grow. As they walk through the front hall, he says to her, "See, it is tall and narrow, exactly opposite to the house in the village. It is like it has grown up from the ground, like grass. And you can hardly hear the traffic on this street, not like in Chinatown."

Shew Lin sighs happily. "Yes, it is perfect. Only my boy knows me so well."

Pon Man feels a ripple work its way through his father's body, a prolonged twitch that pulses like electricity under the skin. Pon Man tightens his grip on his mother's arm.

"I knew you would like it," he says.

After twenty minutes in her new house, Shew Lin, already wearing a housedress, reorders the furniture and brings out some of the odds and ends she brought with her from the house in the village. Pon Man runs around, placing things where she instructs him, laughing at the silly calendar from 1938 she has kept all this time ("To remember the worst year of the war," she says, "and to remember that we are all still alive"), the little teapot in which she steeped Pon Man's tea so that he would feel special.

"Are you still drawing, my son?"

Pon Man looks nervously at his father. "Sometimes. I mean, only when I have a chance, on little bits of scrap paper, here and there. I hardly draw at all anymore, really."

Shew Lin looks skeptical. "You must show me later," she says, her hands still rummaging in her suitcase. "Remember this?" She pulls out a stuffed grey mouse with pink felt lining its ears.

"It's Bobo." Pon Man holds the mouse up to his face, inspects its fur with his fingers. "He has the same hole, right here." He pokes a finger into a seam by the armpit.

"Born in the year of the rat," says Seid Quan, speaking for the first time. "I see."

Shew Lin and Pon Man look up, surprised that someone else has spoken, is standing with them in a square of sunshine in the living room. Their laughter stops abruptly, and Shew Lin turns back to her suitcase, fiddling with the clothes left inside. Pon Man thinks that he is the one who must speak.

"Yes, that's right. The year of the rat. Mother sewed that for me herself while she was pregnant, even though she knew it might be bad luck to make things for a baby who was not yet born. Isn't that right?"

Shew Lin nods, looks briefly into Seid Quan's eyes, clasps her hands over her thick stomach. "I brought some of the old things we bought together from the house in the village. I just need to find them."

Seid Quan looks at both of them, his eyes travelling slowly from one face to the other. Pon Man watches as his father puts his hands in his pockets. He backs out of the room and disappears into the hallway.

Pon Man wants to run after him, allow all those words he wants to speak into the air, but Seid Quan is not that kind of father. *So I am the one who understands my mother,* he thinks. *I knew her first, and she knew me last. He only knows how to leave.*

He sits in the living room, waiting for his father to return home. He watches his mother in the kitchen as she nervously prepares dinner. Shew Lin peeks through the doorway, nods at her son. When he winks, she shakes her head and continues chopping.

The door opens, and Pon Man stands up to take a small step forward. He stares at the report card in his hand. As soon as Seid Quan enters the room, the smell of disinfectant and man oil following him, Pon Man sits down again.

He has been planning this moment for months: the talk, the understanding, the nodding of heads. He imagined the two of them, father and son, speaking quietly, heads close together, conferring in ways they never had before. And then his father would sit up suddenly, eyes beaming with pride and hope for the future. Pon Man wouldn't even notice the barbershop smell. It was all so clear.

Seid Quan sits down in his chair and sighs, nodding slightly to his son. He picks up the newspaper and leans back.

Pon Man sucks in his breath. "Father," he starts, his voice catching, "do you want to see my report card?"

Seid Quan puts his paper down and silently takes the card. He looks briefly and turns to give it back. "Very good, son."

Pon Man sees his mother peering at them from the kitchen. She looks once into his eyes and her head disappears again. He says, quickly, "I want to go to university."

Seid Quan folds his paper and stares at his son, a pretty boy sitting on the edge of the sofa, fearful. He rubs the back of his neck. "Well, that's just something you want, then. There's a difference between wanting and needing. I need you to help me pay for this house. I need you to work. You haven't been in the shop much lately. After you graduate from high school, you could come and work with me."

Pon Man hears Shew Lin cough and then immediately bang a pot lid to cover up the sound.

"If I go to university, I can learn something that will help me make more money later. I don't want to cut hair or sell vegetables. I want something else. Mother wants something else for me too."

Seid Quan looks at his son coldly, his eyes narrowing. "Do you know how many times I've heard that before? Don't you think I wanted more than this house, cutting hair, living here? Do you think a degree will change how people see you? You'll

93

just be a Chinaman who can read, that's all. And your mother knows nothing of these things."

Pon Man sits up straighter. "Aren't you the one who moved us all here so we could do better? Isn't that the point of living here instead of the village?"

"If you are not working for four years, how are we supposed to feed you? How are we going to pay for university? No one will give you a job. Do you know how many men I know who tried to compete with the whites? Do you know what happened to them?" Seid Quan smacks his fist on the arm of his chair. "Horrible things, that's what. Things I can't even talk about."

"It's not 1913 anymore, Father. Things have changed; Chinese people are moving up, leaving Chinatown. How will I be Canadian unless I go to school like Canadians do?"

Seid Quan says nothing, only stares at Pon Man's moving lips.

"Just because you weren't able to become a calligrapher, what does that have to do with me?" Pon Man sees the surprise on his father's face, the rise and fall of his eyebrows.

"If that's what you think this is about, then you're dead wrong, more wrong than you could ever know." Seid Quan folds his paper up and walks out of the room.

Pon Man fingers his report card. He looks into the kitchen, at his mother standing in the doorway holding a wooden spoon in her right hand. She shakes her head again and steps back, turning toward her hissing wok. Crumpling it into a ball, Pon Man throws the report card out the window.

the dream

A basement bedroom. There are dark stains on the walls that could be water, could be cat piss. A tiny window the size of a shoebox. A laminate and chrome desk, covered by an old pink sheet and pushed up against a wall of cinder blocks. I'm lying on my back on a fold-out couch, breathing in a mixture of mould, sweat and beer. He's undressing and he almost glows—a white, lean body, red, red hair. He sees me watching him. His blue eyes are like a kerosene fire in this half-darkness.

For the first time, I am aware that I am naked, that this bartender I've only just met will soon touch me, use his entire body to push us together. I can hear my mother's voice in my head: "Leaving your sister's wedding like that." I make up my mind to forget her.

He kneels over me, looks at my body, slowly, from my head to my feet, as if there is a map pointing to hidden treasure printed on my skin. His gaze feels like a touch, a tongue.

He lowers himself and licks my nipples. I put my hand on the top of his head, and his hair is damp, thick, soft. I can smell my own sweat, bitter like gin, tart like tonic. He looks up at me for one moment, his forehead wrinkled, and quickly looks down again.

It begins, and I can feel myself opening up to him, a dull ache, warm and waiting. He pushes himself inside me, as far as he can, as quickly as he can. It feels like razors, like a knife with a curved blade is sawing through my insides with deliberate, regular movements. I try to push myself away from him, but he's too heavy and does not notice.

"I can't do this," I say. "Please."

He looks up at me finally, places his hand against the side of my face and turns my head so that I'm looking directly into his eyes, into his black pupils. "It'll get better. Trust me."

"Really, I can't do this. I don't want to."

He kisses me on the mouth, gently. "I know you want this. Don't fight me."

And I stop fighting him. But it doesn't get any better.

In his car on the way home, we don't talk. I rest my head on the window, look straight ahead and try to ignore the sounds that mean he's sitting right beside me. His breath, the click of changing gears, the squeak of his hands on the steering wheel. He stops in front of my house and turns toward me, but I'm already halfway out of the car. He drives off without waving.

As I walk up to our front door, I check my watch to see how late it is, to gauge the possibility that my mother has not yet returned from the wedding. I feel wrung out, like a dish-cloth so thin with wear that it is being held together with only one thread. The last face I want to see is my mother's.

I walk through the hallway to the bathroom, and my mother's thin voice calls out, says, "Did you lock the front door?" I tell her I did. She doesn't ask me anything else, and for the first time since my return, I'm glad she's my mother.

I sit on the toilet and stare at my thighs. They're red and chafed with long scratches that stretch from my pelvis to my knees. I touch them and wince; they're soft and pulpy, like raw meat. The skin is already starting to turn blue. I pee, and it stings.

Lying in bed, I can hear my mother snoring, a low, soft hum, more nose than throat. A dog barks. The sun starts to come up, and I finally fall asleep.

In my dream I am helping my mother put away the groceries, my body half in the fridge, plastic bags littering the floor at my feet. As usual, she tells me I am putting the food away all wrong and that, as per her system, only beverages should be placed on the top shelf and only soft fruits belong in the crisper. I straighten up, intending to say that her system doesn't make any difference in the relative quality of the food, when I see a dark shape step into the kitchen.

My mother turns, says, "Pon Man, what are you doing here?" My father, wearing his dark red bathrobe, takes a step toward us. His skin is white, almost blue, and I can see that his pupils are so large that both eyes appear entirely black.

"I want to hold you," he says, extending his thin, sinewy arms.

I whisper to my mother, "We have to run."

Holding hands, we run out the back door and down the porch steps. I feel as if I am dragging her, pulling her shorter legs after me as she pants and whimpers. I turn around to yell at her, impress on her the importance of running as fast as possible. Instead, I see my father floating effortlessly down the stairs, his arms still extended, his mouth tucked into a strange, half-satisfied smile.

At the side of the house, my mother hangs back and stops, bent over double as she gasps for air. "Please," she says, "go without me. I can't run anymore."

I can see the street in front of us, and I know that if we make it there I can yell for help and our neighbours will come and help us beat back this version of my father who is not my father at all, but some kind of vampiric apparition.

"Mom, please run. Please don't make me leave you." But she will not move, and I can see my father closing in on her, his long, bony hand just inches away from grasping her shoulder.

I wake up, hearing my own raw breathing echo off the walls of my bedroom. I stand up and walk down the hall. I can hear that my mother is not sleeping; her breath sounds alert, as if she, too, has just woken up from a bad dream. As I step into her room, a floorboard creaks.

"Sammy? Is something the matter?" Her voice cracks on the air.

"No. I just thought I heard a noise, that's all. Are you all right?"

"I'm fine. I have some heartburn—it hurts right here, below my lungs. It feels jagged and sharp, you know, but you can go back to sleep. It must have been the crab."

I almost reach out and touch her cheek. I want her to realize that something is wrong, that my head and my body hurt. I suppose I could tell her myself, but I cannot open my mouth again. My hand stays where it is, glued to my side. I turn and walk back down the hall.

Back in my bed, the sheets cling to me like remnants of my bad dream made tangible. I know that if I close my eyes my father will come back for me, so I stay awake until the daylight burns away the rest of the night.

In the morning, I can hear her shuffling through the house, pink knitted vest puffy over her pyjamas. She is more than what she appears, this small, aging, slightly dotty woman. She is part of me, and I pretend to be asleep.

I have my father's bones—thin and frail, bird-like. My mother stands rooted to the earth, compact like a miniature bomb, wide hands grasping hot pans, impossible jar lids, bleach. Her apron says "Kiss the Cook," but no one dares.

She smells of soup, work, wool and spinach.

She told me once of a boy who stood outside her bedroom window, shouting, "Leung Siu Sang, please come out! Leung Siu Sang, marry me!" I imagine her, sixteen years old, calves covered in seamless nude stockings, hiding behind drapes as her younger sister makes faces through the glass.

Three years later, my mother came to Vancouver and married a handsome man she did not know.

Now, my mother stands solidly, her body in contrast to the sliver of thin light she's standing in. With one eye open, I can see her peering at me through the crack in my bedroom door. I hold my breath and watch her close the door slowly and silently, her face disappearing inch by inch until I am left with the greyness of early morning light and the smell of myself in the sheets.

departure

Her mother always said that Siu Sang was a dreamer.

Unlike her older sister, who attends school to learn accounting and business, Siu Sang stays at home, looking out the window with her small, round eyes at the busy Hong Kong streets below, or lying on a stone bench in the central courtyard, staring for as long as she can at the hot sun in the hazy sky. She reads romance novels and listens to the radio, dancing only if no one is around. Her mother once tried to insist that Siu Sang learn to cook or sew or do something useful, but she soon came to the conclusion that her middle daughter was stupid, or simply destined to be a rich man's wife.

But she is not a socialite like her cousins. Instead, she stays at home, content to nibble on snacks or try on her mother's wedding jewellery. She walks slowly, her movement confined by the walls of their house and its courtyard. No one knows what she is thinking, but her mind is clearly elsewhere.

Her brothers call her the Absent-Minded Princess.

One evening, her older sister, Yen Mei, begs her to attend a dance at the university. "Please come. One of the girls can't make it, so if you don't come with me, everything will be uneven."

Siu Sang agrees, sighing as she pulls herself out of her chair to get dressed. The night is sticky, and it is impossible for her to move quickly. Yen Mei is ready to go while Siu Sang is still brushing the lint off her pink dress.

As they are being driven to the dance in their father's big silver car, Siu Sang imagines that she is gliding across a ballroom, a martini in her hand. Couples spin in perfect time with the full orchestra behind them, and she can hear the murmur of appreciation as she walks through the crowd. Her long skirt with marabou trim barely touches the floor while she gazes at herself in the mirrors lining the long gilt wall. A moustached man steps in front of her and wordlessly offers her his arm. She dances with him, and the glitter of the room dims. They trail romance and glamour behind them.

Twenty minutes later, Siu Sang finds herself standing against a whitewashed cinder-block wall. A tinny record player plays warbled Artie Shaw in the far corner, and a card table has been set up with paper cups and a bowl of faintly purple punch. Her sister's friends surround her, talking quickly and laughing. The record skips.

"He's coming over here."

"No, don't look! Pretend you don't see him."

"All this waiting. Why don't you ask him to dance yourself?"

"What? I'm not that kind of girl."

At seventeen, Siu Sang has never been to a dance before. Whenever her mother showed her an invitation that had arrived in the mail, Siu Sang simply shrugged and stayed home.

She is unsure of what to do, whether she should sit or stand, dance in place by herself like some of the other girls or just hide in the washroom. She cannot look at the bank of boys standing against the wall opposite her.

One by one, each of the girls is asked to dance. Siu Sang sinks her insubstantial body closer to the wall and stares at the ceiling, noticing its bubbled paint and peeling plaster. The music sounds like a loop to her, each song indistinguishable from the rest, each chord like the one that came before. She looks back at the couples in front of her—awkward boys with their hands on red-faced girls. *They're messing up the steps,* she thinks, but then realizes that nobody cares. They are touching, and that is all that matters.

When the music stops, she finally moves from her spot in the corner and leaves the dance, nodding along silently as her sister talks and talks, filling the stale air of the chauffeured car. As they pull up to their house—grey stone with red columns, a gated archway made of black wrought iron—one of the maids throws a bucket of dirty water from the side kitchen door. When she sees Siu Sang and Yen Mei, she retreats into the shadows.

Later that night, their mother appears in the doorway to the room they share with their younger sister. The air hangs thickly; all the smells from the day's activities (cooking, laundry, bathing) have settled into a damp cloud that sits just below the ceiling. Siu Sang's upper lip is sweaty.

She lies on the top bunk. Her younger sister is on the bottom, snoring loudly. Yen Mei sleeps noiselessly on a bed across the room. Siu Sang can feel the silk sheets growing slimy with sweat underneath her. The window is open and the street din has not stopped.

Their mother stands in her spot for a long time. Siu Sang imagines that she is looking at each girl's face, judging what kind of wives and daughters-in-law they will become, speculating on how many sons lie dormant in their bodies. Her mother breathes heavily, her open lips wetly smacking together with every exhale. Siu Sang moves her eyes to look at her older sister. She will be leaving soon to be married to a man in Canada, but she lies there exactly as she always has, her left leg hanging down off the side of the bed, her eyelids slightly open, as if she is afraid she will miss something. Siu Sang watches her mother as she wipes her forehead with the silk handkerchief she keeps tucked in her belt. She shuts the door and turns to walk slowly back to her own bedroom.

Siu Sang waits for the sound of her mother's door closing before she raises her head. From her bed, she can look straight out into the street and see the lights of Kowloon district. It is close to midnight, and she can still hear the shopkeepers selling chickens, noodles and paper money for offerings to household gods. She can see people moving about in the building across the street, their house lights flickering and weak. She fidgets underneath her sheet.

A girl laughs outside, her giggle skipping through the streets like a pebble. Siu Sang wonders if she is on a date, if she has slipped out of her bedroom to secretly meet a young man, if she is, like her, a teenager dreaming of love.

Tonight, Siu Sang transforms Hong Kong into something else, creates in her mind a mannered, well-dressed city where she and the laughing girl skip along the clean sidewalks carelessly. There are no just-slaughtered chickens hanging on hooks at the street market, no dirty old women selling cheap jewellery displayed on threadbare blankets at every corner, no men spitting on the sidewalk as the girls pass. Here, in this different Hong Kong, the air is pure and no one ever sweats. The only vendors on the street are clean, polite men who offer trinkets and novelties: paper fans, cookies wrapped in red paper, pet birds in gold cages.

Siu Sang and the laughing girl walk into a café, order a Western soda, sit in the window and watch the people walk by. Women in pastel day suits, men in hats, children with candy. As they walk home in the evening, the windows in the tall buildings of the financial district begin to light up, one by one, like thousands of little eyes, winking.

A man shouts outside Siu Sang's window, and she looks out, blinking to clear her head. Across the street, on the side-walk, a couple argues. The man has grabbed the woman's arm and her body is half-turned, as if she is trying to run away. She wears only one high-heeled shoe, and even from this distance, Siu Sang can see that the heavy makeup around her eyes is running and her face is covered in black streaks. The man shouts, "You will do what I say!" The woman sobs and her body goes limp. She allows the man to walk her down the street, and they disappear around a corner.

Siu Sang lies back down on her damp pillows and turns on her side to face the room. Nothing ever changes here: the same rosewood chairs and table, the same scrolls hanging on the wall. She touches a bruise on her hip, the purple stain the exact shape of a table corner.

She watches as Yen Mei directs the driver how to pack her trunk and suitcases into the car. "Do you understand that soft luggage always goes on top? If you ruin my makeup bag, I'll have nothing on the boat and I'll look like a peasant girl."

Everyone else said goodbye in the house. When Siu Sang asked her sister if she could follow her to the car and say goodbye in the street, Yen Mei just shrugged and said, "Whatever you want."

She stands on one foot, enjoying the feeling of being slightly off balance yet strangely rooted to the concrete at the same time. The street in front of her is a blur.

"Well, I'm leaving." Yen Mei stands in front of her, staring.

Siu Sang puts her foot down and pats Yen Mei on the shoulder. "Goodbye."

"Is that it? I thought you had something special to tell me." She looks annoyed.

"No. I just wanted to see you drive away, that's all."

Yen Mei shakes her head. "You're a funny one. Well, goodbye."

Siu Sang watches the long silver car pull into traffic and slowly make its way down the congested street. She wonders if Yen Mei really knows what Canada is like, or if she has only been making things up as she goes along, preferring to provide an answer than say nothing at all. When their younger sister asked Yen Mei if it might be a good idea to bring clothes besides all her silk dresses, Yen Mei had snorted and said, "My new husband and I will be so rich so fast, I'll have no need for anything else. Besides, all the women in Canada wear silk all the time." Listening, Siu Sang wasn't so sure.

She watches until the car disappears and joins the traffic blur. As she turns to walk up the stairs, she looks back one more time and sees that Yen Mei has dropped one of her earrings on the street. It sits there, gleaming gold, its jade stone winking in the sunlight. A ragged woman, her pants held up with rope, bends to pick it up and laughs—a high, piercing cackle. Siu

Sang thinks she should say something, but then decides that the earring will make this poor woman happy, at least for a while, and that Yen Mei will only blame the driver for the loss and then forget about it altogether.

Siu Sang sits quietly on an ottoman at her mother's feet, staring straight ahead at her dimpled, well-fed knees. Her brothers have warned her, and she has been waiting for this talk.

"Siu Sang," her mother says, "we have had another offer from a young man and his family."

Her mind reels back to the boy with the big bum who has been following her around the city since she left school two years ago. Her stomach turns.

"Yen Mei's husband has a friend. He lives in Canada."

All her life she has been picturing herself the wife of a wealthy businessman, a man who will not expect her to do anything, a man who takes over his father's shops and land in filial duty, only adding to the money and prestige that her father spent his whole life pursuing. It has never occurred to her to wish for anything else, to conceive of anything off the coast of Hong Kong. Canada has always been a foreign concept, and became even more so when she received her sister's letters describing infinitely high trees, snow-covered mountains and a small, wild city.

In the time it takes Siu Sang to shift her mind over to this new possibility, her mother has finished telling her all the details: his family and hers have origins in neighbouring villages; he has great prospects in that vast and open country; he is handsome. She makes it clear that Siu Sang has a choice: she can marry one of the boys who have already approached the family and stay in Hong Kong, or she can go to Canada to begin something new, where her children will grow up never worried about China's occupation and far away from the possibility of a new, energized Japan.

"He is not rich, but the family is prominent. When China takes over, who knows what will happen? You will be almost sixty then and could lose everything in your old age, when you need your money most. Canada is a free country with unlimited opportunity, as I often hear your brothers say. There is reason to hope that this boy will be rich one day." She leans forward and touches Siu Sang on the cheek. "It is up to you."

She reaches to her left, picks up an envelope from the polished teak side table and withdraws a small photograph. She hands it to her daughter. Siu Sang, still dizzy, takes the picture and looks at it, blinking furiously to clear her mind.

The young man is smiling, his lips full. His teeth are shining white, and his hair is slicked back in a way that is almost tough, but at the same time not. His eyes are big, limpid, full of naughty humour. He is sitting on a floral sofa with his arm draped along the back as if to say, "You would fit right here and we would laugh at this ugly sofa together."

Siu Sang looks and looks. She puts her hand up to the back of her long neck to make sure that she is really here, that this is not one of her daydreams turned frighteningly real. She thinks to herself, *Remain calm. This is only a photo. This is not the real man.* But still.

It is in these thirty seconds that Siu Sang, with all her eighteen years, falls in love.

After all the arrangements have been made, her mother tells her she must not expect anything. When Siu Sang asks what she means, thinking she is, perhaps, talking about money or servants, her mother replies, "No one treats a daughter-in-law well."

Siu Sang doesn't quite understand and does not know what *not well* entails. Will she have to eat the last piece of chicken that no one wants? Will her mother-in-law insist on having her feet washed in scented water? Will someone beat her?

Her mother looks at Siu Sang with narrowed eyes and says, "They will expect things from you, and if you do not deliver, no one will protect you."

Surrounded by piles of silk and linen, Siu Sang packs for her move to Canada and is having a hard time. In her letters to Yen Mei, she asked what she should prepare herself for. But her questions went unanswered. Instead, Yen Mei wrote on and on about how wonderful her new husband is, how nicely he treats her, how he has promised her a maid by the following year. Soon, Siu Sang stopped reading her letters altogether.

She is sure that her party dresses and thin jackets will be of little use, that there will likely be no servants. This confuses her. After all, she owns nothing else. Her mother has told her that there is no point in buying clothes in Hong Kong when she will not know what she needs until she arrives in Vancouver. She sifts through her slippery silks blankly. She begins to pack randomly; after all, no one can tell her otherwise. She will carry only one trunk with her on the boat; the rest will be shipped ahead and will wait, like ghosts of herself, in Yen Mei's apartment.

Her younger sister has refused to help with the packing and has instead taken to spending all her time at the library and, as their mother says, "meeting who knows what." Siu Sang misses her and wishes her dry humour and wicked grins were close by to temper all the seriousness. Her brothers are little help and only smile at her sheepishly and silently, as if they feel sorry for her but cannot say it.

She pulls her clothes out of her drawers and closet blindly, pushing things into her trunk in clumps. A gecko stares at her from his perch on the wall.

She plucks one novel from her shelf and places it carefully between layers of silk. On the cover is a beautiful young woman sitting at a precise angle that shows off her impressive bustline and tiny waist. She wears a tweed pencil skirt and blouse and looks lovely, but normal. A girl to fall in love with, a girl you wish you were.

Her mother has told her she will have no time for dreaming or reading, but Siu Sang doesn't quite believe her. Surely washing dishes and serving her mother-in-law medicinal soups won't take up all her time. She will steal a few moments: before sleep, in the tub, in the morning. *Just one book, only one.* She is sure it will be fine.

The night before she leaves, she lies in her bed and peers out her window. There, in the street, is the scene she knows, has fallen asleep to her whole life. She has always changed it in her dreams, made it pretty. But tonight is her last one here, so she stares at the street as it is, lets its roughness and dirt and movement impress itself on her brain. *It hurts,* she thinks, but she continues, letting the bright hotness and dirt and noise assault her. She watches until dawn and sees the sun rise through a crack in the buildings, turning everything, for a moment, the colour of gold.

She paces in her cabin, her trunk lying open on the floor by her narrow bed. Through a tiny round window she can see the dark water and the faint light reflected on its surface. She hears a low groaning noise rising from the bowels of the boat, and she feels light-headed.

For the first time, Siu Sang is really alone.

She has spent her whole life surrounded by her family, by her brothers and sisters, servants, the people on the street right outside her home. She shared her bedroom, walked to school with her sisters, went to the café with her friends. On rainy days she sat in her favourite spot by the window and dreamed while her mother hovered and wondered what her daughter could possibly be thinking about.

Here, the window offers nothing except shades of grey and blue, alternating textures of dark and light. She has no telephone, and has spent her first four meals on this boat alone. She thinks she is perhaps not pretty enough for the other young people on board and does not try to approach anyone. The pattern of the tablecloths in the dining room is burned forever on her brain.

She picks up her old novel and begins to read. She knows so much of it by heart that, two hours later, she finds herself looking at the last page and wondering what else she could possibly do. She sighs and stands up to open her cabin door.

She steps out into the hallway and sees another girl popping her head out of the door directly opposite. The girl looks up at Siu Sang and smiles, her grin more like a monkey's than a person's. She steps out and offers her hand.

"What's your name?"

"Leung Siu Sang. And you?"

"My Western name is Susie. My mother said I have to start introducing myself that way so that I'll be used to it by the time I arrive in Canada. Are you going to be married too?"

"How did you know?"

Susie laughs knowingly. "Oh, so many girls from my class at school were getting ready to go to Canada. There are a lot of boys there, you know, and no women at all, except old ones. But I think it'll be a great adventure, really exciting. I heard they have eight-foot bears there. What do you think?"

"I don't know. I don't know anything about bears." Siu Sang is confused.

"Me neither, but that's the fun part. Do you want to get a soda with me? They have snacks in the dining room between meals."

They walk together to the dining room, Siu Sang listening while Susie talks. After their snack, Susie wonders if they can trick the other passengers and crew into thinking they are twins. Siu Sang thinks this is impossible and says, "But I am much taller, and our faces are completely different."

Susie laughs again. "Don't you see? That's the challenge. There's no fun in doing something if it's too easy."

Siu Sang doesn't see.

Together, they walk around the deck, engaging in conversation with as many people as possible. Susie, Siu Sang soon learns, has been taking English lessons in preparation for her marriage and is eager to use it.

"We're twins, born at the same time. We are going to Canada to marry two brothers. We look alike, yes?" Most people simply nod and agree. Siu Sang stands to the side, chewing on her fingers, hoping that no one will figure out this lie and punish them somehow.

The captain, a British man from Brighton, calls them Sue and Susie. "Like two peas in a pod," he says. "You can't even tell them apart."

———

The motion of the boat now seems a part of Siu Sang's body, the gentle rocking like the pulse of her blood. When she sleeps, she floats through her dreams fluidly, down and then up again, where she wakes, gasping for air.

In between visits with Susie (although they are hardly visits, more like explorations during which Susie inevitably drags her to an obscure corner of the ship, where they are chased out by men who seem not quite angry but not quite happy, either), Siu Sang has had a lot of time to think. This trip is like an extended twilight, the in-between time after leaving and before arriving. An afterlife that isn't quite death.

Her mother frightened her with cryptic warnings, and her voice never quite leaves Siu Sang's head. Her mother-in-law, a woman she has never met, never written a letter to, never even seen a photograph of, looms like a giant in her mind. Although her older sister is now married, she has said little about her own mother-in-law, who still lives in a small village in China. Siu Sang will be living with her future husband's parents and does not have the comfort of distance to help her.

She thinks little of her husband, and when she does, she drifts off, her mind repeating, over and over again, the image of his face in the photos they sent and the nice things he wrote in his letters. "You are very beautiful," he wrote, "and I miss you before I have even met you."

When she has been thinking too much (as her mother always told her she did), she tries to tell herself that she is only making herself more frightened than she needs to be. Her husband's family are only human, after all, and cannot do anything that bad to her. She convinces herself of this for a couple of hours, maybe an entire afternoon, but that creeping, almost-dark feeling always returns, and she is left exactly where she started.

Sometimes, she feels like a pawn. There have always been other people who decided what she should do or where she should go. She thinks she should resent this, but does not. It is easier this way, and less trouble for everyone.

On the second-to-last day of their trip, Susie trims her toenails at the foot of Siu Sang's bed, cursing as she tries to steady her hands against the sway of the ocean. It's no use; unlike Siu Sang, she's a round girl, built solid, with stiff, heavy-footed legs. She is unable to throw her body into the movement of the waves. Susie tosses the clippers aside and picks up a nail file instead.

Siu Sang has the covers pulled up to her small nose, her knees drawn up to her chest underneath. A driving rain has forced most of the passengers to stay in their rooms. The men play cards in the dining room. The women are mostly unseen. Last week, the captain told Susie to watch out for the rain, a sure sign that Vancouver isn't far away. "I don't know how the people who live there can survive. They must be a city of water rats," he said as he strode away on the deck.

Siu Sang turns the idea over in her mind—a city teeming with dripping rats, moving like one furry ocean across sidewalks and concrete, through puddles whose muddy, opaque water splashes up and clings to their fur. She shakes her head and feels the warmth of the blankets around her like the heat of Hong Kong—slightly musty, humid, pervasive.

She hears Susie whisper.

"Susie, did you say something?" Siu Sang sits up and sees Susie hunched over her knees, her head hidden.

"I'm scared."

"Don't be scared. It's just a little storm. Remember what the captain said? It'll be over tomorrow." Siu Sang gingerly pats Susie on the back.

Susie looks up, her eyes painfully dry. "No, I'm scared. About being married. About Canada. About maybe never seeing my parents again."

Her nostrils flare and she shuts her eyes, rubbing them with her fists. Siu Sang watches her body ready itself for crying— deep breathing, mouth open—but no tears come. She thinks that this dryness, this feeling of wanting to explode but not being able to, must hurt far more than the crying itself.

"I'm scared too, Susie."

Susie looks at her, the redness in her face turning dark, deep. "Is that it? We're just two scared girls and there's nothing else to say? I might never see you again either. Can you say anything about that?"

Siu Sang doesn't know what Susie wants, doesn't know how to say everything will be all right; even if she did, she knows and Susie knows that everything might be awful. Those comforting words would mean nothing. And it's all true: there is nothing they can do if things do not turn out well, if their husbands begin to beat them, if they are deathly allergic to the Canadian air. They will have to stay, no matter what.

She moves over and puts her arm around Susie's shoulder, changing her breathing pattern to match hers, breath for breath. Siu Sang, without looking out her porthole, knows that the sky and water are dark and that they are hurtling forward through no effort of their own.

Early morning on the boat, and she leans over the rail on deck, wind slicing through the perfectly permed curves and dips of her hair. Her eyes are fixed on the ocean, blue like she's never seen, somehow glittering hot and impossibly cool at the same time. She closes her eyes and imagines a city perched on the edge of the ocean, rounded and organic as if it has risen, fully formed, from the blue surrounding it. Sunlight beats down on the seaweed green of buildings and houses. A sea-village, cool and warming at the same time.

She arrives and cannot believe that this (a thousand and one shades of grey, hunched beneath a sky so heavy and dark that the city seems beaten into submission, seagulls its only release) is real.

Cranes move slowly through the skyline, loading and unloading among piles of bright yellow sulphur. Boats, gulls, cars. Each noise is indiscernible from the last—a constant high whine broken only by the sound of the ocean, like glass cracking slowly in the cold.

A lock of hair falls in her face. She presses her right palm against her forehead, her leather trunk between her knees. She looks around the dock and sees Susie stepping into a blue car. Her small eyes scan the dozens of faces for her older sister. The crowd looks back at her coldly, like a monster with hundreds of eyes.

She steps off, and her sister and brother-in-law materialize to pull Siu Sang to a taxi waiting at the foot of Burrard Street. She looks back and sees nothing except a sea of heads and the ocean beyond. She turns to Yen Mei, hoping that her sister will reach out and hold her hand or place an arm around her shoulder, but Yen Mei only looks forward, with her hands in her lap, and lets her husband do all the talking.

When Siu Sang is ready to meet Pon Man, it is at her sister's apartment in Chinatown. The windows face an alley where seagulls pick at the rotting produce and shit on the fire escape. Siu Sang walks gingerly over the floors, trying to keep the ancient grime and mildew from touching her feet. If she weren't so nervous, she would laugh at how different this place is from the sophisticated suite Yen Mei described in her letters to the family in Hong Kong.

She has spent the last two hours deciding which of her five silk dresses to wear and parting her hair from the left to the right and back again. She is sitting now, in her pale green dress with the gold leaves, on the frayed corduroy couch in the corner. Her sister, fat with her first pregnancy and bustling, hurries from the stove to the table, setting out tea and pastries. Her brother-in-law waits outside.

Siu Sang closes her eyes, sees the photo of Pon Man, which she has kept in her head all this time. She imagines them dancing in one of those supper clubs Yen Mei keeps talking about, their hands smelling of spaghetti and clams, his jaw smelling of aftershave. Through her daydream, she can hear people arriving, the commotion of coats and shoes and voices. She is afraid to open her eyes.

As her eyes adjust to the daylight, she sees that the room is full, that her sister is perched awkwardly on the arm of the couch beside her. There he is, his black hair shining and smooth. She stares at his lips. Pon Man looks carefully at his shoes.

His mother begins to talk, asking all the necessary questions: when will the wedding be, where can we have a suitable banquet, what else must be provided? She looks carefully at Siu Sang, judging the set of her mouth, the width of her hips, the white smoothness of a rich girl's hands.

His father is smiling helplessly at her.

Pon Man stands up and hands a thick red envelope to Siu Sang's brother-in-law, who nods in understanding. Siu Sang looks over at the money; Yen Mei whispers, pig-like, "The dowry." Pon Man looks over at Siu Sang and smiles, saying nothing.

As they are leaving, Pon Man's father grasps her hand quickly.

"My daughter."

Siu Sang sniffs her hand afterward (an odour she cannot place and soon forgets, supposing that all old men smell this way) and hopes that Pon Man does not smell the same.

The newly married couple stands in the photographer's studio, smiling. Siu Sang fidgets. The lace on the back of her wedding dress is beginning to itch. Yen Mei, watching from the side with her hands on her round belly, shakes her head and mouths the words, "Don't move." Siu Sang winces and looks straight ahead.

Pon Man says something funny, and the photographer laughs. Siu Sang wishes she could understand and giggles along until she realizes that Pon Man knows very well she hasn't learned English and can therefore see through her trick. She purses her lips.

At the reception, Siu Sang doesn't think she has ever seen so many old men. They are bunched in corners, wandering around with whiskies in their hands, pumping Pon Man's fist up and down. Seid Quan stands in the middle of it all, listening patiently to the other men's stories of shy brides and wedding night heroics. When Siu Sang asks Yen Mei who all these people are, she replies, "Your father-in-law is a big man here, you know. Everyone in Chinatown knows him." Siu Sang looks across at Shew Lin, who is sitting with a group of older ladies.

"What about her?" She nods in her mother-in-law's direction.

"I don't know much about her," says Yen Mei. "Only that she is supposed to be a very good cook."

Siu Sang drops her eyes before anyone in her new family can catch her watching them. She looks instead at her bouquet—fake red roses with drooping plastic ferns and baby's breath. "Fake is more expensive," Yen Mei had whispered while they dressed, "and it lasts forever." Siu Sang wonders what she is going to do with this indestructible bouquet, whether she is bound to it for the rest of her life. She sighs.

"Speech!"

Siu Sang turns her head and sees Seid Quan stand up at the front of the room by the head table, nodding at the men cheering him on. The room hushes. As he opens his mouth to speak, Siu Sang pushes herself into a corner.

It is well past midnight, and the party has ended. Siu Sang kneels awkwardly on the floor, rummaging through her trunk for her nightgown. Her wedding dress is puffed out over her knees and rumpled. She is visibly upset.

Pon Man emerges from the washroom wearing only an undershirt and his tuxedo pants. He is rubbing the back of his neck with his hand and looks tired. He sighs and sits on the bed. "What are you looking for?"

"I can't find my nightgown. It's not here." Siu Sang looks up, her arm buried elbow-deep in silk and cotton. "It was here this morning!"

Pon Man laughs, his slim body vibrating like a guitar string. He kneels down on the floor with his new wife. "What do you need the nightgown for?"

three

downtown

The phone rings. I look up from the careers section of the newspaper and reach over to the side table.

"Sam? It's me, Matt."

I pull the phone closer to my face, as if the extra inch will make this conversation more private. My mother stands in the doorway to the kitchen, tongs in her hand. I can hear the ginger sizzling in the hot oil.

"Why are you phoning me?"

"I need to know. You're never coming back?"

"I can't. I'm here alone with my mom. I've quit school. There's no way I could come back."

I don't tell him that I am afraid, that the years stretch ahead of me, seemingly empty, that I have no idea how I will fill in the time. All I really know is that I cannot leave.

He pauses, and the miles of air between us crackle. "What if I came to Vancouver? I could find a job. Maybe I could help out with your mother—you know, drive her to buy groceries and stuff."

It's as if the walls of my mother's house have started to cave in, and drywall and flakes of paint are raining down on my head. I cover my mouth with my free hand and say nothing.

"Hello? Sam? Are you still there?"

I place the phone carefully back in its cradle because only disconnecting will stop that roaring in my ears. My mother calls me in for dinner.

The kitchen is cold and dark. She never turns on a light or the heat unless we have company, or unless I complain that my eyes hurt from reading in the gloom. It is seven in the evening, and outside a cold spring rain clatters against the tiny window above the sink. I look over at my mother, and she chews so deliberately that I decide it's best if I don't speak at all. After we eat, she washes dishes. I wipe and put away.

Steam rises from the hot, soapy water. My mother's hands are red and chapped.

Suddenly, she starts with the drain in the bathtub. "You leave all this hair in the tub, and you never clean it out. You can't just come back here and treat my house like a hotel."

"I just forgot," I mumble.

"Forgot? Forgot? When's the last time you forgot to read one of your precious books? You just think housework is dirty, below you. You think I'm no better than a servant, that I'm stupid because I'm no good at English." She points a soapy finger at me. "You think you're better than me, I know it. What good is all your reading if you can't even heat up a can of soup, if you can't find a job? It's because you're useless. Go ahead, tell me you're useless."

With her sharply filed nail pointing at me and her angry Chinese words throwing themselves through the air, I want to turn around and run. I look behind me at the dark hallway and living room and realize that leaving right now will only make things worse. I put my head down and open the drawer closest to the sink to put the cutlery away.

I nick my mother's hip with the corner of the drawer and turn around to apologize. Instead of standing at the sink, glaring at me behind her thick glasses, she collapses on the floor, one wet hand clasping the spot on her hip I have just bumped. Her eyes are tightly closed and she is motionless.

In a deep, flat voice, she says, "You've just killed me. Go ahead, do whatever you want now. Dance on my grave; I know you want to."

I almost laugh. There she is, lying in a pool of dishwater, one hand on her chest, the other on the fatal wound I dealt her, pretending to be dead yet speaking all the same. The light from the fluorescent bulb above the sink has turned her skin bluish-green. She half-opens one eye to see how I'm taking it.

"I died without the love of my ungrateful daughters. It's too easy to forget the pain of a mother's labour. Killed by a useless, unloving child."

A dark, thick bubbling bursts from my stomach and into my head. *Useless.* I can hear nothing else.

I pick her up by the shoulders, not at all surprised that she pretends to be limp. Crouching down, with my mother's upper body in my hands, I begin to shake her. Her eyes pop open and her teeth start to rattle together. I stare at her face, the smugness of fake death replaced by fear.

"I'm not useless," I hiss at her in English, and I know she understands. I shake her again. "And you're not fucking dead!"

I let go and she falls backward, hitting her head with a thump on the brown linoleum. This time, her eyes are closed because she is scared, because she is trying to catch her breath, because, for the first time, I've said what I think and she knows it is right.

I walk out of the kitchen, through the hall, down the stairs and out the front door. The coolness of the night hurts my lungs; the driving rain hits my face like thousands of needles intent on piercing my skin so that they can get to the bottom of this mess. I walk toward Hastings Street and the industrial stretch of waterfront that hugs the East Side on its northern border.

I can hear the water echoing in my ears. I cross Hastings, then Dundas, and just keep going. I walk past warehouses, fish-processing factories and the barbed-wired fences protecting it all. I know the ocean is there somewhere, and even though I am wet, soaked through with so much rain that it begins to come out of my eyes, I don't care. I just keep going.

Finally, I come to a thin sliver of rocky beach. The mist in the air meets the water, and it is all grey—beach, ocean, sky. I could be on the moon. Down the beach, I see something flickering in the almost-dark. I walk to it, thinking that perhaps this is what I have come for, that this shiny, glinting thing could be the answer to everything.

There it is: a glass ball the size of a basketball—hollow, perfectly round, faintly green. I pick the seaweed off it and hold it to my stomach, staring at the bubbles in its surface, at its seeming fragility. I wonder how far it has travelled to wash up on this beach. Water streams off my nose and onto the glass.

I look around at all the water—in the ocean, collecting in puddles, soaked into my jeans—and realize there is nowhere else to go. I think I might drown. I fish in my pocket for a quarter, walk across the thin strip of sand to a phone booth across the street and dial the number for my best friend from high school.

"Hi, it's me, Sammy. Listen, I'm kind of stuck. Would you mind picking me up?"

When I hang up, I see that I am still holding the glass ball in my left hand. I step out onto the road and roll it gently down the middle of the street. It isn't long before a car turns the corner and knocks it to the side, where it smashes against the curb, leaving nothing but tiny pieces of glass that catch the light off the street lamps. I sit on the sidewalk, hoping my friend will bring me a towel and a change of clothes.

We are all eating dinner together—my sisters, my parents, my grandfather, my older sisters' boyfriends. I am almost bursting with something I really want to say, something that burns my six-year-old throat from being kept in too long, something that is really, really important. Every time I open my mouth to let it out, someone else starts speaking, makes a joke or spills something on the floor. I squirm in my seat. My face is red with frustration, and I stop eating altogether in protest.

Finally, when everyone else is chattering and the noise in the room just can't be any louder, I stand up and yell, "You're all mean, just mean!" Everyone stops. A pair of chopsticks clatters on the floor.

My mother pulls me out of my chair and drags me to the back door. I look in her eyes (fleetingly, surreptitiously, for it would never do to have her catch me staring) and immediately see that the fire behind her glasses will only consume me faster and more ferociously if I try to stop it. I let my body go limp.

As she shoves me through the doorway and onto the porch, she hisses, "See how you like it outside all on your own. I bet an old, scary lady will come and take you away, so you'd better watch out."

She turns around and closes the door.

I creep to the window, press my ear to the two-inch crack my mother has opened to air out the steam that collected during dinner. I can hear everyone, still eating, laughing at me. "She's just a shrimp," someone says. "Watch out, she's going to turn out wild," says another. My grandfather makes a clucking noise with his throat. "She's just angry," he says quietly. "Your grandmother used to say things before she thought all the time, just like that." I hear my mother let out her derisive, cruel laugh, and the conversation falls silent.

I walk to the edge of the porch and peer down at the cement driveway and vegetable garden below me, now covered in frost. The alley is dark. Garbage cans stand in the dim— short and squat like demonic little leprechauns, waiting for just the right moment to spring on me and search my pockets for hidden gold with their precise, skinny fingers. To the east, illuminated by the dull yellow of the street lamp, a long-haired grey cat stands, staring. It blinks before running off, its paws skittering on the loose gravel. I pull my turtleneck over my nose and inch backward until I can feel the cool stucco of the house through my sweater.

An old lady, I think. I shiver as I remember that I don't know any old ladies. One of my grandmothers lives in Hong Kong, where, my mother once told me, she is slowly going blind and getting fatter and fatter. The other grandmother, my father's mother, died the day I was born, a story my sisters like to tell when they want to scare me. I know nothing about old ladies, only that they like to steal children and, perhaps, simmer them for soup. It occurs to me suddenly that those dried brown things in the herbalist's shop look suspiciously like little baby toes. I whimper into my sleeves.

I can hear my father and sisters laughing in the house. I imagine that they are planning all the things they will do now that I'm no longer living with them. *Penny*, I think, *is going to watch all the music videos she wants all day long.* Wendy might even move her fiancé in when they get married, to luxuriate in all the extra room. I resolve to return when I am all grown up and give them a piece of my mind. *See if I help them out then.*

I slump down and wrap my arms around my knees. The wind is cold and blows through my sweater and corduroys. *At least*, I think, *a soup pot would be warm.* I close my eyes and lean my head against the house. As I start to fall asleep, the cold disappears. I dream of an old woman, her face lined and brown, leaning toward me, her hands held out to warm my cold cheeks. She squats and pushes my chin up, breathes her hot breath on my ears.

A warm gust of wind smelling of mothballs, wet wool and soap blows against my face, pushing against my eyelids and tickling my nose. My eyes snap open, but there is nothing to see, only the same old dark. When I stand to look up and down the alley, I think I see, out of the corner of my eye, a small figure scurrying to the west, its head obscured by a knitted cap. As soon as I turn my head to look more closely, it's gone, leaving behind only a faint trace of its comforting, old lady smell.

When I turn around, Daisy is holding open the back door and gesturing for me to hurry up and come inside. "Grandmother always used to let us in when we were small. Come on, then, before Mom sees." I run, careful to tread lightly. I follow Daisy to the basement, where she hides me until our mother goes to bed.

The club is dark and steamy, and the beat of the music seems to go on forever, an undercurrent that never changes, song after song after song. You could whisper your most hidden desires to the person right next to you and be sure he would never hear it. I stand by the only exposed window, trying to breathe the damp, urine-scented air outside rather than the sweat-scented air inside, which moves slowly and thickly.

After I dried off and put on borrowed clothes, my friends and I headed to this place, a rickety old downtown building surrounded by the kind of people my mother always warned me against. "Don't get too close—you don't know what they might have."

I figure I must have an aura of despair hanging on me like a big wool sweater. One by one, my friends have all managed to pick up guys (toothy and gelled, all of them) and I am still, two hours later, hunched over in a corner by myself, drinking one Long Island iced tea after another.

Outside, a raggedy man has fallen into the Dumpster. He pulls himself out, clutching a plastic bag—dripping with dirty water—as if it contained gold.

I tell my friends that I'm leaving and walk outside to hail a cab. As we approach my mother's house, I ask the driver to let me out at the convenience store so I can buy cigarettes. I walk the rest of the way home.

The rain clouds have blown away and the streets are silent, the kind of silence that makes me walk faster. The cool breeze brushes my skin; I think of ghosts floating past me, trying to regain a sense of life by latching on to my body. I can see my house from two blocks away—its dark windows, the shadows from the drooping branches of the Japanese maple beside the front door. *There's nothing I can do. I always have to come back.*

As I walk up, keys in hand, someone steps forward, emerging from the shadows smoothly, silently, like he's floating. I stop moving and think, somehow, that if I remain motionless, he won't see me and will disappear, melt back into the darkness. As he moves forward, I see the dull glow of his red hair, the ice of his pale skin. The bartender from Penny's wedding.

"I had a feeling that you'd need some company tonight," he says, holding out his hand to me.

It's like seeing a vampire and knowing that he can enter your house only if you let him in. You know that, if you do, bad things will happen, blood will flow, and he will consume you. Yet something tempts you—death, rebirth, immortality, sex. Who really knows? The decision is harder than it seems.

I take his hand.

"Always there when I need you, even if I don't know that I do." I know he will hurt me, make me feel as if my body is splitting in two. He will challenge me, physically turn me inside out, and I will like it; the only thing I own is my body, and it will do whatever I say, even if it knows that the wisest decision is to do the opposite. I unlock the door and lead him to my bedroom; he's a demon enclosed by my four white walls. His eyes burn, blue-hot.

integration

Siu Sang has been at Woodward's for two hours and cannot find what she wants.

Earlier that morning, she had complained to her husband that she needed money to go shopping, to buy new clothes for the coming winter. He handed her twenty dollars and gave her brief directions to the Woodward's department store downtown.

She did not tell him that she did not want to go alone.

She walks by the snack counter and looks curiously at the menu posted up near the ceiling. She puzzles over the malts and hot dogs until a woman asks her if she would like anything. "We have some nice egg salad, dear, if you're watching your weight."

Confused and silent, Siu Sang hurries away.

She guesses that the women's clothes are upstairs, but cannot find an elevator to take her there. She walks around the displays of garden spades and light bulbs, turning her head to look at a wrench or storm lantern whenever someone walks past.

An older woman stops. "Do you need help? You look lost." Siu Sang only smiles tightly and shakes her head, unsure of what this woman has just said.

She tries to remember something from her lessons; every evening, after he finishes his accounting homework from night school, her husband helps her, taking her over the same words: *bus, tree, walk, store,* but her mind does not take it in. She has not gotten any farther than the alphabet, but she nods and pretends to understand when he asks. Now, only half-formed words tumble around in her head—even she knows they are nonsensical sounds.

She finds the washroom, sits on a toilet in a stall and stares at the white door in front of her. She feels abominably big, as if her ignorance has blown her up to ten times her normal size. Everyone must know how stupid she is, how she cannot even point or gesture to tell people what she wants. Pon Man once told her that he, too, had to learn the language and that the only way to do it was to just jump in. She had smiled sweetly and continued repeating the phrases he spoke to her.

"I am lost."

"Where is the washroom, please?"

"I would like the chicken."

I'm too slow, she thinks, *like a dumb turtle.* The harsh light from the ceiling makes her hands look green, and she rubs her eyes, tears pricking the inside corners.

When she arrives home, her husband is studying his accounting textbook again. She walks closer to him and can smell the oil from the restaurant in his hair. She imagines she can even smell all the dishes he has cooked that day: Reuben on rye, eggs Benedict, chicken stew with biscuits. Her eyes swim as she looks at the rows of numbers in front of him, the pluses and minuses that mean someone must know how much money there really is in the world. He looks up at her and smiles. "How was your shopping trip?"

Siu Sang pauses.

"Well, where are your new clothes?"

She breathes in. "There just wasn't anything I liked."

On her wedding night, Siu Sang slept in her husband's arms, her body curved into his like a baby's. He had touched her all over, stroked her body from head to toe. When everything had come together and it seemed as if they couldn't have been any closer, her body stretched out as far as it could and then snapped back together, forcing her to open her eyes and look Pon Man in the face.

Every night for one week, he had held her like this. She found herself reaching for him long after they had fallen asleep, crying for him when he did not wake up as soon as she did. During the day, she wondered if this was shameful, if her mother or, worse, her mother-in-law, would condemn her as a woman with strange and unnatural tastes. But as nighttime crept through the windows and into the house, she ceased to care. *Let them think whatever they want,* she thought, breathless at her own daring. *I will do as my body says.*

As soon as the second week began, Pon Man awoke at five o'clock, put on his cook's uniform and left, taking the bus to English Bay to work breakfast and lunch at the Sylvia Hotel. Siu Sang watched him dress with one eye open, sleep still weighing down her body. When he came home, he opened up his accounting textbooks and studied until dinnertime. Siu Sang floated about, afraid of disturbing him but wanting to touch him all the same. After dinner, at exactly six thirty, he boarded another bus to attend his classes at the college. Siu Sang stayed in her bedroom, reading her novel or rearranging her jewellery in its rosewood box. He arrived home at ten thirty, walked straight into the bathroom and climbed into bed at eleven. The first night, Siu Sang leaned into him, put her hand on his neck, but he was already asleep and rolled away from her, grunting.

Tonight, she watches him, his still-damp hair around his head like a shadow, but a living one. She puts a finger on his ear, feels his pulse even there. He snorts, and swats her hand away.

She turns finally and reaches for her nail polish, hidden in a drawer in the bedside table (Siu Sang is afraid her mother-in-law will pronounce this a silly extravagance and confiscate it, scolding her as she dumps the ruby red bottle in the garbage). She carefully paints her toes, reminding herself that she must wear covered slippers and socks all the next day so that Shew Lin doesn't see. She blows on them, points her breath away from her husband so that he does not breathe in the heavy fumes.

Staring at her feet, she imagines how they would look in gold, open-toed pumps, the lacquered red peeking out like a surreptitious wink. She could wear a short black cocktail dress, perhaps with a draped, low back, and Pon Man might wear a tuxedo with the bow tie undone and hanging around his neck in a careless, rakish way. They would smoke Lucky Strike cigarettes, hers in a gold and green holder. They would dance, but only when the crooning singer onstage would personally ask them to, saying into his microphone, "Everybody, please give a warm round of applause for my favourite couple, Mr. and Mrs. Pon Man Chan."

And the smoke would swirl around their heads, the breeze gently lifting Siu Sang's perfect curls. Pon Man would laugh at the crooner's jokes and repeat the punch lines in a whisper close to her ear. As they rode home in their yellow and black taxi, Pon Man would kiss her on the mouth and slip his hand up her skirt.

Siu Sang falls asleep, her cotton nightgown bunched around her knees, her hands between her legs, holding herself as if she is afraid she might break.

She cowers in a corner of her bedroom, listening for the sounds of her mother-in-law approaching. She has been married for two months and has proven to be completely useless.

Shew Lin opens the door slowly and pokes her broad head around the frame. Siu Sang can feel her eyes scanning the room, resting, for a moment, on the very chair Siu Sang is hiding behind. Shew Lin shakes her head and mutters, "Useless girl." She retreats into the hallway and slams the door. Siu Sang, her head covered by her hands, allows herself to cry.

She listens for the sounds of her mother-in-law in the kitchen, the sounds that mean she has returned to chopping and stirring, all those chores Siu Sang cannot do. She creeps out of her bedroom and crouches in a corner of the hallway where she can watch Shew Lin attacking a head of bok choy, unseen. The window in the kitchen is steamed over and, despite the fact that it is four o'clock in the afternoon, the house is surrounded by fog and is almost completely dark. There are several pots bubbling on the stove, and the entire house smells of pork and soup.

Siu Sang knows exactly what Shew Lin is thinking (for even though she cannot learn English or stir-fry chicken, she understands daydreams like no one else). She watches Shew Lin look out the window at the vegetable garden in the back; Siu Sang knows she is thinking about what she will do with the surplus zucchini and beans she will pick this week. Siu Sang sees Shew Lin's flying knife slow down slightly, and she can hear her mother-in-law thinking about this tall house and how full it will be with grandchildren running through the halls and down the stairs. The chopping stops altogether, and Shew Lin smiles. *Thinking about her first grandson,* Siu Sang thinks. *How typical.*

Siu Sang stands up and walks into the kitchen, knowing that this is where Shew Lin wants her to be. She sits down at the kitchen table, her eyes red and her nose swollen. She picks at some pastries, dropping the crumbs all over the vinyl tablecloth, and does not look up.

Shew Lin chops viciously, each drop of the knife like the cracking of bones. Siu Sang winces every time the knife hits the wooden board, imagining that it is her fingers her mother-in-law is cutting off, one by one.

"This house is mine."

Siu Sang turns her head. "Did you say something, Mother?"

Shew Lin looks surprised. "No, nothing. You must be hearing things."

She grabs a head of garlic and smashes it, sending cloves into every corner.

Pon Man buttons up his new grey suit, looks at himself in the mirror on the closet door. Siu Sang can see her own face behind him, watery in the warped glass.

"What do you think? Good enough for tomorrow?"

She nods, sits down on the bed. "I think it looks very professional. Just what a young accountant would wear."

He laughs. "I hope so. This suit cost more than all my other clothes combined."

"But you'll be making so much more now. I didn't like to think of you working so hard for so little at the hotel."

He begins to unbutton his jacket. "I didn't like to think of it either. But I just couldn't work for my father anymore. I'm sure you understand how it is. I couldn't be an individual then, you know?"

Siu Sang does not know and does not understand (why would anyone want to stand out in real life when that only means others will notice you and see you for all the wrong things you are or could be), but she nods, thinking that an accountant's wife should be smart and understanding, the kind of wife who can swap chicken recipes with other wives.

"I'll be home much more now, think of that. No more night school, no more getting up at five just so I can fry eggs and pancakes for fat tourists. Our evenings will be ours, just you and me, I promise." He sits down beside her, naked but for his shorts.

When he touches her again for the first time in three months, she responds to him so quickly that she makes him laugh, his lean body pulsating against hers. She throws her arms around him, wants their bodies to touch all over so that she will disappear into him, so that they can be a new creature together.

After it is over, Siu Sang drifts in and out of sleep, her feet tangled in the sheets and with his. He pushes his head up against hers and whispers, "We should have a baby soon. My mother keeps talking about it. A baby will make us as happy as it will make her."

Siu Sang opens her eyes and stares at her husband, his flushed cheeks, the blackness of his eyes. She wonders if the decision to have a baby has already been made without her, if her husband and his mother have determined that now is the time. She has always known, of course, that she must have a baby eventually, but she never supposed that it would have to be so soon. *How stupid of me,* she thinks. *He makes love to me once we have enough money to support a child. Of course.* Her body feels as if it is shrinking.

"Of course, a baby."

He looks at her, his eyes travelling over her hair, her eyes, her mouth. "I love you," he says.

This is the first time he has said this, and Siu Sang is unbelieving at first. *How could he say he loves me?* she thinks. But then, she sees that he must mean it, for he is smiling at her as if she were the only thing in this entire world that he would go to war for.

"I love you too," she says and immediately buries her head in the pillow.

He falls asleep long before she does, but she does not mind, only watches the thickening dark through the window, the fall of nighttime rain.

Late in her first pregnancy, Siu Sang perches on the edge of her bed, staring at her reflection in the mirror. For the last few weeks, she has been seeing nothing but flesh. She is overwhelmed by the very solidity of her body, the hunger that seems to chew a hole right through her, the earthy textures of the fat and muscle underneath her skin. She cannot think of anything but her growing self—it doesn't matter where she is or what she is doing, all she sees are the layers of fat encasing her fingers, her neck, her knees. If she was ever pretty, she can no longer see it—she cannot even imagine it. Yet she eats and eats, even as tears of disgust pool inside her eyes. Siu Sang never lets those tears fall, for she can never tell who might be watching.

A baby. A son. The reason she is here. And she keeps on feeding it.

She creeps into the kitchen after breakfast for a snack and finds that all the cookies, pastries and cakes have disappeared. She stands, dumbfounded. Her mother-in-law pokes her head around the corner and says, "Missing something?"

Later, her husband smuggles in a tin of biscuits, which she hides in her chest of drawers. Soft biscuits, the kind that crumble in her mouth like cake and call out for coffee. The kind that coat her belly with pillowy fluffiness.

As Siu Sang is licking cookie crumbs from her swollen fingers, Shew Lin appears in her bedroom door holding a tray with a bowl of steaming soup. Siu Sang throws a blanket over the biscuit tin and swallows quickly. "Something medicinal, to help my grandson grow strong," Shew Lin says.

As Siu Sang holds the hot bowl (her fingertips feel as if they might burn clean off, but no one cares about that), she feels like a fugitive and a bad, deceitful person for hating her mother-in-law as she does, but what else is left for her? It is either silence or fighting.

I can eat only when she says I can. She makes fun of how fat I am. I heard her say yesterday to Pon Man that I would be a useless wife without her. She wants me to be a bad daughter so that she can say, "Aha—I told you so!"

She finishes her soup and lies down, moving her biscuits to the back of the drawer. She touches her belly through her dress (like an enormous umbrella, patterned with English roses and violets, all the better to make Siu Sang look even more like a hilly pasture), feels the baby pushing against her ribs. She shifts, and the baby shifts with her, a movement at once both dependent and independent. If she could, she would reach into her uterus right now and rip this baby out, pass it to her mother-in-law and never look at it again. *After all,* she thinks, *she's the one who wants it the most anyway.*

Angry, she pushes herself off the bed, fits her fat feet into her quilted slippers. *I cannot stay here. This place will kill me.* She imagines herself dying of cruelty after giving birth to a still-born baby, lying wanly on a white bed with white mosquito netting as Shew Lin weeps wildly in remorse. Siu Sang smiles. *At least,* she thinks, *there is one scenario that might go my way.*

She leaves her bedroom, stands at the top of the stairs, her feet balanced on the edge and her hands placed protectively on her belly. Her eyes close and she feels the weight of her body tilting downward. The danger hits her like an odour and her eyes snap open, wide.

She lives in a house with thirty-two steps.

She walks down slowly, her right hand holding the banister, her left hand on her belly. Her head spins; she sees her hands, the stairs, the pictures on the walls swirling around her, her own pregnant stomach the centre of it all. She is nauseated.

This baby feels like a lead weight tied to her body. She has had dreams in which it is born with her mother-in-law's head, complete with knitted cap and yellowing teeth. Yet she is never surprised, only mildly annoyed that she should have such an ugly child. By the time she wakes up, she has torn the head off the baby and no one but her seems to notice.

This may be your house, old woman, but this is my child.

The sun is beginning to set outside and the hospital room has turned golden. Siu Sang looks at her daughter sleeping and watches the breath move in and out of her, her little chest rising and her fists clenched. In the fading light, the shadows are sharp and half of the baby's face is dark, a line dividing it neatly in half.

The flowers her husband brought from the garden are on the side table in a blue plastic jug, hanging over the edge, top-heavy, like women with their heads down. Yen Mei visited this morning, dragging along her eighteen-month-old son, a bug-eyed toddler who sucked his thumb and stared at Siu Sang unblinkingly. She left the baby a stuffed koala bear with a pink ribbon around its neck. It sits, bug-eyed as well, on the windowsill.

The hospital is quiet at this time in the evenings. She can hear the soft-soled steps of the nurses pushing the dinner carts, the muffled cries of other babies in other rooms, the sick ones in the nursery. The rooms and hallway are all painted pink, and both she and the baby are wrapped in soft flannels that smell like bleach and talcum powder. An older nurse who speaks Chinese has been helping her, teaching her how to change diapers, feed the baby without choking her. Last night, just before her shift was over, she tucked Siu Sang into her bed.

"Are you warm enough, my dear?"

Siu Sang hardly remembers how long she's been here.

She walks into the washroom to take a bath and stays in the big tub for a half-hour. She watches the steam rise from the water and swirl upward, disappearing into a vent in the ceiling. Her body appears pale and deflated under the water, lifeless. Tiny wrinkles run up and down her stomach. She traces the white stretch marks with her finger, the dark brown line that runs from her breasts to her pelvis. *I look used up,* she thinks.

When she steps into her room again, her face flushed and pink, her hair dripping water on the floor, her husband and his parents are waiting for her. Shew Lin has the baby in her arms.

"Mother and I talked last night," says Pon Man, "and we agree that we should give the baby a Western name so there won't be any confusion when she grows up. If I had a nickel for every time someone called me Pat or Paul, I'd be a rich man. What do you think of the name Wendy, like in the Peter Pan story?"

"Wendy?" asks Siu Sang, wrapping her bathrobe tighter around her body. "Peter Pan?"

"Right. How would you know that story? Well, I think it's going to be Wendy—easy to say for the old folks."

"Wendy," Seid Quan repeats, nodding.

"The doctor told us you can leave tonight," Pon Man says. "Isn't that great?"

Seid Quan nods again in agreement, his hands behind his back.

Pon Man continues, "I packed all your things while we were waiting, so all you have to do is get dressed."

Shew Lin looks up and takes in Siu Sang's wet hair, bare feet and damp robe. "Didn't your mother ever tell you that you shouldn't wash your hair for a month after the baby's born? You'll have dampness in your bones when you get old if you're not careful." She turns away and holds the baby to the fading light. Siu Sang stares, thinks, *Wendy for such a wrinkled, wormy thing?*

In the new car (purchased exactly one month ago so that the baby would have some way of moving through the city besides a taxi), Shew Lin holds the baby all the way home. Siu Sang's hair sticks to the back of the vinyl car seat. Her wool skirt scratches the backs of her thighs. The smell of gasoline drifts in through the open windows and she breathes it in, letting the burn spread through her lungs.

———

Shew Lin sits in the living room, knitting something bright safety orange. Seid Quan listens to the radio and chuckles. The baby is asleep, and Pon Man skims over the evening newspaper in his bedroom while Siu Sang naps. All is quiet.

It begins as a slight wailing—a quiet, high-pitched buzzing. Pon Man turns around, searches the room with his eyes. He stands up to go to the door. Siu Sang cries out louder, and he looks back and sees that the noise is coming from her.

She is curled up in a ball on the bed, whimpering, her hands tucked between her legs as if she is trying to make herself as small as possible to minimize her pain.

"Do you have a fever? Is it because we just had a baby? Tell me." He stares into her wild eyes, but she says nothing, looks through him as if he is a window into another, evil, painful place. He places his hands on her shoulders and shakes her.

She knows he is looking at her, that she is confusing and frightening. She can sense her mother-in-law in her knitted cap crouching outside the closed bedroom door, her ear pressed up against the wood. But she doesn't care. If she did not cry, wail like a lost child, she would explode, and pieces of her would be everywhere, ruining the furniture, staining the walls.

It's like a splinter, this feeling that she hates the baby so much that she would rather reach into its face and pull out its brains than take care of it for one more day. This hatred started days ago, and she thought she could hide it, control it by ignoring it and letting it fade on its own. But then it grew, attracting all the other evil feelings she has ever had about this house, this family, this country, even her own husband. Tonight, as she rocked the baby to sleep (its hands like talons, nothing like the chubby baby hands she had expected and heard about), she could feel the bitterness like a tornado in her belly. The swirling, mad mass forced its way up through her esophagus, exploded into her lungs and, finally, spilled out of her mouth. She couldn't stop it and didn't want to, for as painful as it was now, it would hurt much, much more to keep it in.

She can see it in his face, the little thought that is now taking shape: *My wife is insane.*

He won't want to believe it, she thinks loudly, trying to form thoughts above the roaring in her ears. *But he will soon enough.* She opens her mouth, intending to remind him of all the nights they spent whispering and giggling and touching, but instead, she wails even louder, and Pon Man sits back from the force of it all. He reaches out to touch her, and Siu Sang thinks that if he makes contact with her skin (her raw, raw skin, like a body turned inside out), she will have to kill him. She rolls away.

"You're going to wake the baby if you keep this up."

She stares at it, at the wrinkled face, the tiny pursed lips. *It sleeps so peacefully,* she thinks. *This is hardly fair.* If the baby wakes up, she will have to tend to it, feed its smacking mouth, change its shitty diaper. She would rather plunge her hand into boiling water than feed it one more time, so she closes her mouth and swallows.

Siu Sang quiets down to a whimper, a high-pitched whisper of a scream like the squeak of wet fingers on glass. She lets Pon Man cover her with a blanket before he sits down in the armchair by the window. After an hour and a half, Siu Sang is fast asleep—dried tears dotting the line of her eyelashes—and the baby starts to cry.

Yen Mei stands by the window in Siu Sang's bedroom and looks out at the schoolyard across the street. "Well, it's not so bad, is it? The house is pretty nice, much bigger than the one we bought."

Siu Sang wants to laugh. "That's because Ken's parents don't live with you. If we had a house that was any smaller, I'd have to share a room with my mother-in-law." They giggle, but quietly, their hands covering their mouths.

Yen Mei sits down and rests her hands on her pregnant belly. "I don't believe how big I am already. The second one sure shows a lot faster."

The second one. Siu Sang swallows her fear and looks at the blanket on the floor where Wendy is shaking a rattle. "I can't take it anymore."

"Take what?" asks Yen Mei.

"Take this. I don't love the baby. I think I might be going insane."

Yen Mei laughs. "That's funny."

"No, really. Didn't you ever feel like you wanted to just run away, leave everything behind?"

"I don't know." Yen Mei looks confused. "I didn't love the baby at first either. I mean, I was just so tired, and he wouldn't let me sleep. But by the time he was Wendy's age, that had all passed."

Siu Sang wonders if she should press on, if she should tell her sister what she has really been thinking (about the glorious *crunch* the baby would make on the sidewalk if Siu Sang were to drop her out a window, about how she wants to pour boiling water on her mother-in-law's head as she sleeps, about the silence she longs for and wants to find, perhaps somewhere in the mountains, where she could sleep and dream and never come back) or if she should forget it, knowing that Yen Mei, chatty, gossiping Yen Mei, has never helped anyone.

After Yen Mei leaves, Siu Sang sits down at the desk in her room and pulls a blank piece of paper toward her. She wants to write to her mother, tell her everything, but her pen will not move. In the end, Siu Sang knows, her mother will only urge her to stay.

Instead, she writes a letter to Susie, filling the paper with densely packed words, back and front. When she is finished, she reads it over and then realizes that she has no idea where Susie lives. She holds the letter in her hands for one more moment, then tears it into little pieces.

She tries to cry, but the sobs die in her throat and she chokes. Mucus collects in the back of her mouth until she cannot make any more noise.

Siu Sang wakes up, her whole body jerking like a marionette. She looks at the clock beside her bed. Five thirty and she hasn't even helped with dinner yet. She stares at the baby in her crib—wide awake and trying to shove her fist into her mouth. She takes her into the living room and props her up with pillows on the couch, where she can see her from the kitchen. Siu Sang ties on her flowered apron and stands by the stove, waiting for Shew Lin to tell her what to do.

Her mind is still sluggish from the nap, and she has been feeling slow all week. Her feet feel like lead. Every morning, her daughter cries at seven and Siu Sang is forced to get up, her eyelids heavy with sleep. By the time Pon Man returns home,

Siu Sang has just finished changing out of her pyjamas and combing her hair.

Shew Lin has been spending most evenings remarking loudly on how lazy wives raise lazy children who grow up to ignore their parents and leave them to die.

Shew Lin pushes past her to get to the fridge and mutters under her breath, "If you can't be any help, at least get out of my way."

Siu Sang steps back into the corner and watches her mother-in-law move quickly from sink to stove to fridge, stick her fingers in boiling water and toss vegetables in hot oil. She feels overheated suddenly. She crouches down and rests her head on her knees.

"What's the matter with you now? Don't tell me you have your period again." Shew Lin stands over Siu Sang, her left hand still holding her long cooking chopsticks.

"I think I just need to lie down." Siu Sang stands up, sways and steadies herself with one hand on the wall. "Can you look after the baby?"

In her room, she crawls under the blankets and pulls them over her head. She wants to be buried underneath the darkness, feel the weight of it on her chest, become flattened by it. She can see, in her mind, the white crib in the corner. *It ruins everything,* she thinks. *How can it be totally dark with that white thing glowing like that?* Frustrated, she cries, the cocoon of the blankets muffling the noises and hiding her from the rest of the house.

She hears Pon Man creep into the room. His touch on her hip feels like a hundred tiny needles piercing her skin.

"Don't touch me."

Pon Man backs up and looks at her with confused eyes. She glares at him.

"I'm not an animal. Stop looking at me like that. Why don't you get out and whine to your mother?"

Siu Sang turns away from him and buries her face deeper into the pillow. Even now, she can feel her husband's eyes in their dark room watching her, the whites glowing steadily like neon lights in the street.

"I'm taking you out for dinner tonight, so you'd better get dressed." Pon Man stands in the hall, his hands on his hips, smiling.

"What do you mean? What's this all about? Wait—who's going to look after the baby?"

"Mother will take care of her. I have a surprise for you tonight, but I have to take you out for dinner first. Go—we have twenty minutes before we have to leave."

Siu Sang hurries into the bedroom and pulls her green dress off its hanger. She rushes through her makeup, polishes her black pumps with the bed skirt and runs to the car, where Pon Man is waiting in his chocolate brown suit.

"Where are we going?" she asks, rifling through her purse to see if she's forgotten anything.

"The Palomar Supper Club, you lucky woman."

Siu Sang claps. "I'm so excited! Will we see any famous people? Maybe Frank Sinatra?"

Pon Man laughs. "I think Frank is a little busy somewhere else. There'll be other singers and dancers, though."

When Siu Sang walks into the club, her arm casually draped through her husband's, she holds her breath (if she lets it out, who knows what she might say). She stares at the velvet curtains on the stage, the candles on every table, the twinkling lights hanging from the ceiling. Women smoke, holding their cigarettes delicately, their elbows resting on the white linens. Men laugh, swirl caramel-coloured drinks in crystal tumblers. *I'm not dreaming,* she thinks. *I'm really here.*

As the hostess leads them to their table, Pon Man whispers into her ear, "And here's your surprise."

Siu Sang looks through the dim and sees a young couple. As she tries to make out their faces, the woman cries out, "It really is you!"

"Susie?"

Susie wears a black satin cocktail dress and pearl-grey gloves. Beside her, her husband grins madly, pumps Pon Man's arm up and down. Susie runs to Siu Sang and hugs her.

"It's just the most amazing luck! Jerry here went into your father-in-law's shop to get his hair cut, and Pon Man was there, and they started talking and figured out who their wives are and look! Here we are. Sit down. Let's get you a drink."

Pon Man lights a cigarette and leans over. "You didn't see this coming, did you?"

Siu Sang shakes her head and tries to laugh. She feels a thick dampness in her throat making its way upward, where she is sure it will explode on the air like a tiny bomb. She stands up again and looks around wildly. "Where is the ladies' room?"

"I'll take you there." Susie grabs her hand and leads her through the tables and into a narrow hallway. As they walk in, Siu Sang drops Susie's hand and hurries to a stall.

"I tell you, that husband of mine is full of surprises." Susie shouts at Siu Sang through the door. "He's a little short, of course. He reminds me of those toads. You know, the big warty ones."

Siu Sang, the full skirt of her dress puffed around her knees, cries silently. Shreds of damp tissue stick to her fingers.

"But all in all, he's not so bad. He didn't want me to go out and work, but I grew so tired of sitting around all day, watching the dust collect just so I could wipe it off. Until we have children, I don't want anything to do with being a mopey housewife."

Siu Sang pulls on the toilet paper, and the roll falls to the floor, disappearing underneath the edge of the door.

"So I got a job at the sausage factory, you know, that one on Keefer? It's not so bad, and I meet a lot of nice girls. Maybe I should have them all over for mah-jong and invite you, too. Look at that—did you drop the toilet paper? I'll just pass it through the gap here. Siu Sang? Wait—are you crying?" Susie rattles the latch on the door. "Let me in. Are you hurt?"

Susie bursts in. Siu Sang weeps into a wadded ball of tissue. The makeup around her eyes has run all over her face. She gulps.

"Do you need to tell me something? What's the matter?"

And Siu Sang starts to talk. She tells Susie of the letter she once wrote to her, not knowing where to send it. She thinks that her words will never end, that her list of complaints is infinitely long and that she will die long before she gets it all out. But when it's all over, she looks at the clock on the wall and sees, shockingly, that only eight minutes have passed. *Even the clock knows that I am nothing but a complainer, that my problems are really so few that they don't even fill a half-hour.*

"I never knew it was like that. I'm so glad I have no children yet."

"I'll die if I have to live like this anymore."

"I know."

"What's going to happen to me?"

Susie thinks for a moment, screws her eyelids up. "You need to do something, honey. I know you're not used to doing things for yourself, but you have to change your life if you're unhappy."

"What do you mean?"

"Oh, I don't really know. I just think that you have to get out of the house or find something to do, you know? Your mother-in-law does everything, so you feel like you don't own anything, not even your own daughter. Maybe if you had something else to do, you wouldn't hate the baby so much. You could take a class, or learn how to manage the house on your own. Just take it slow—one thing at a time."

Siu Sang sighs, dabs at her eyes. "I think I need to fix my makeup."

Susie laughs. "Yes, and we need to go back to our table, or else our husbands will think we've run away together."

When they walk back, a woman has started singing, her silver gown pooling on the floor around her feet. She sings an old, old song about a girl who dreams about her prince. Siu Sang closes her eyes and follows the sound of her voice as it rises and falls, floats through the air and settles over the well-dressed, cool-as-vodka crowd.

In the mornings, Siu Sang, in capri pants and a light jacket, walks to the park with Wendy in a stroller. When she returns home, she eats a lunch that her mother-in-law has cooked and sits in the living room that her mother-in-law has furnished.

As Susie told her, *one thing at a time.*

Siu Sang has had a lot of practice at being quiet, at going unnoticed. It's easy for her to creep around the house and watch her mother-in-law as she bustles through her day. When Shew Lin is in the living room, dusting the mantle and beating the furniture, Siu Sang sits on the stairs, half-hidden by shadows.

When Shew Lin is cooking, Siu Sang plays with the baby at the kitchen table, feeding her mashed-up fruit.

There are perfect, invisible reasons for her to be anywhere, anytime.

The house is all angles, with windows recessed deep in darkly papered walls. Dark corners are everywhere, in every room, even during the day.

Siu Sang sticks close to the walls.

At first, she watches her mother-in-law to make sure she isn't reading Siu Sang's mail or hiding food, but then she begins to see the cooking and cleaning, receipts and groceries, hundreds of small tasks, each an equal component in the running of a family. Shew Lin talks loudly, moves with hurricane-like energy. Everything she does is meant to be noticed and the centre of attention. And so it is.

Opportunity never comes to those who are impatient.

One day, Shew Lin drops one of the grocery bags on the front steps. Siu Sang emerges from the corner and picks it up, gathering the spilled fruit. She carries the bag into the kitchen and puts the food away.

Siu Sang pools all her energy, sleeps through the night like she never could before (strained and pulled tight like a violin string on the verge of snapping, she had spent most of each night immersed in her fantasies or, lately, crying into the sheets balled up in her hands). Pon Man seems relieved at the relative quiet and has not said anything about the change in her behaviour, likely afraid that any word will disturb the thin, fragile peace. She is glad for his silence.

Another day, Siu Sang heats up some leftovers for dinner when Shew Lin is late coming home from the dentist.

She visits Susie in the afternoons after her shift at the

sausage factory. Siu Sang walks briskly down the sidewalk with the stroller, thirty minutes there and thirty minutes back. Susie teaches her cooking shortcuts, how to knit and read a pattern, the right way to plant beans in a garden. Siu Sang asks her where she learned all these things.

"I don't know. Some of it from my mother, I guess, and some of it I just learned from watching people or reading things." Susie shrugs and goes back to beating the egg whites for her basic sponge cake.

Little by little, Shew Lin's work is whittled away. One task. A second. Soon enough, entire sections of the house are Siu Sang's to manage—the bathroom, the front deck, the upstairs hallway. Siu Sang can see her mother-in-law's confusion: Should she be happy, afraid, suspicious?

I've got her off-balance, Siu Sang thinks. *It won't be long now.*

the morning

The pain is bad. It's not the pain of a paper cut or a sprained ankle, or even of a cramp from swimming just after you eat. It's a deep, inner pain, the pain you think of when someone says, *My guts are twisted.* If you could close your eyes and forget the dimensions of your body, it feels like it's coming from your very core, a hot place miles away from the surface, where only the deepest pain is felt. It's almost good.

I look over at my bedroom door, where I've stuffed old sweaters in the crack by the floor. I put my hand over his mouth, hoping that my mother won't hear us in her room down the hall.

In the dark, he moves like a white eel in deep water—fluidly, easily, with a faint, electric glow. My body disappears in the dim and he is alone, moving around the room in a narcissistic dance, like a restless sleeper. He reflects what little light there is (the red hair burns in the night); I absorb it.

He's beautiful, and my eyes ache with it. His skin is perfect. His body is tall, broad-shouldered. He is in control of his muscles, the integrated movements of his arms, legs and torso. And the rippling of bad intentions under the surface, somewhere beneath his smooth, cool skin, only makes him sexier. A black light shining behind a white curtain.

My legs ache from being over his shoulders and, from where I'm lying, they look like the legs of a mannequin—stiff, detached, not really human. Everything seems ugly now, and the pain is just pain. I feel like something inside of me has been shaken loose and is rattling around. A lost organ in a hollow body.

His eyes are closed, and he has forgotten, for the moment, that I'm watching him.

When it's over, I stay in bed while he creeps down the hall to pee. "There's no mistaking the sound of a man pissing in a quiet house," he says, "so I hope your mother is still asleep." He lets himself out, and I can hear his car start and then drive away. I wait until I can no longer hear it before I close my eyes. If I can't see anything, then perhaps I'll forget that I even have a body.

My sleep is shallow, and I feel thick, like I'm stuck, trying to run through mud. I open my eyes slowly, feeling sick with bad sleep but not wanting to wake up either. Through the window, a faint light. Five in the morning. Dawn.

I breathe in; his smell (beer, hair gel, acid sweat) sits heavy in my room even now, four hours later. I get up to pee, feeling that there's something I need to be rid of. I stand up for a second, sway and fall down. My knees hit the floor and I wince. I put my hands on the bed to lift myself up again, and I feel something wet, a little colder than lukewarm, and thick. I look, and there's blood, a pool of it in the middle of the mattress, streaks of it on the quilt, drops of it on floor.

Whose blood is that?

It's coming from me, and it's still coming, inevitable and steady. The blood on my thighs is still warm, and I put my hands between my legs to try to stop it or hold it in. It comes out anyway, through my fingers, hot. I stand up again, and my feet slide on the slick puddle I've left on the floor. Something twists inside me and I start to fall again. I steady myself on the dresser. I leave a red handprint that starts to drip as I walk down the hall to the bathroom. *Water,* I think, *all I need is a little water.* The bathroom is mercifully cool.

"Mom?" I call out. "I need you."

judgment

The second baby arrives. Another girl.

Shew Lin wants to laugh, cackle loudly at the way fate is playing her daughter-in-law. When Pon Man arrives home from the hospital late on a foggy November night (the smell of apples and burning leaves in the air, a smell, Shew Lin often thinks, that is nothing like the mangoes and dust of the village), he seems afraid to mention the baby at all. Shew Lin carefully looks grim, nods slowly when he recounts the baby's weight, the dimples already in her knuckles.

"Daisy," Pon Man says, washing his hands at the kitchen sink. "Like the flower. You know, the white one with the petals and the yellow heart."

Seid Quan nods, smiles uncertainly and congratulates his son with a handshake. Pon Man looks disappointed that he has already washed his hands.

When the baby and Siu Sang return home, Shew Lin's heart secretly jumps at the pain of wanting to hold the little girl all the time, of loving her so hard that her entire body shakes with it. But her broad face never changes from the same stony look she has always had, the one that falls away only when Siu Sang leaves the room. Still, she knows that a grandson will somehow fix things, give Seid Quan and Pon Man a miniature version of themselves (amalgamated, an unbreakable hybrid of him and him, a living example of how they could live together without the silence that bats down spoken words).

She must fear me, she thinks as she watches Siu Sang leave the living room, *or the family will fall apart. Without fear, she will never do as I want.* She looks over at her husband and son, reading newspapers at opposite ends of the long, narrow room, facing each other yet almost totally obscured.

It wasn't so long ago that she first stepped off the boat, saw the two of them together for the first time. She arrived, her loose dress hiding all the accumulated flesh of childbirth and old age she acquired in those lonely years. She was the family's connection between the small village in China where she was born, and had once expected to die, and a port city in Canada where she knew no one except these two men, both, in different ways, products of her body.

She was unsure which old man standing on the dock was her husband. The other wives, all in their fifties and sixties, were standing behind her, murmuring their confusion. These men were thin, ghostly figures in the mist, no more tangible than the cloudy blue mountains in the distance. *A whole army of phantoms,* she thought as she scanned the crowd for something, anything that looked familiar. Perhaps a cough, a cologne, a thin hand raised in greeting. Anything.

Pon Man stepped forward, the only young man there, and held his hands out to his mother.

In her hurry to reach her son, she forgot to look for her husband. She held Pon Man's face in her hands, making sure he was as flawless as he had been when he left her.

"So tall," she said, "so handsome. Must be the cold Canadian air."

It was only then that she saw Seid Quan, wearing a suit stiff with newness. His Adam's apple poked out above his collar, and his face, finally in full colour, was crooked, wrong somehow, and old. This was not the face she remembered from his last visit home, the visit during which they conceived their son.

But then he reached out and touched her hand and she remembered. The surprising softness of a hand that knows almost nothing but hard work.

She walks back to the kitchen, intending to look into the garbage can to see if Siu Sang—who, since she returned from the hospital, has remained remarkably silent—has thrown out any food that could still be eaten. *I did not work so hard to keep my husband and son together just to have her come in and disturb it all*, she thinks. *I am the glue and spine of this house, and she will have to remember that.*

On the kitchen counter is a small porcelain figurine, a tiny ballerina with one perfect foot pointed in the air. Shew Lin picks it up, stares at its white face and black arched eyebrows. She remembers seeing this in Siu Sang's room, and now that silly girl has carelessly left it in the kitchen, probably after washing it in the sink. *Well, who knows what could happen to such fragile things in a house with children?* Shew Lin hurls it against the wall, watches the ballerina's head split into two, her slippered feet splinter into jagged, sharp pieces. She turns around and walks out, leaving the mess for her daughter-in-law to find.

———

All day, every day, the house is silent. Sometimes, when the weather is bad, a draft whistles through the hall, front to back, carrying the sounds of outside in. When Shew Lin opens the door to collect the mail, she can hear the traffic two blocks away on Broadway, the shouts of the children at the school across the street, the hammering at the new house being built around the corner. When she shuts the door again, the only thing she hears is her own slippers on the parquet floor.

"I can see you are unhappy from your letters, daughter, even if you never really say so. When I was young, I had many fights with your father's family. They did not hesitate to make me feel stupid."

Shew Lin has steamed open a letter to her daughter-in-law from the girl's mother. She has been looking for signs that Siu Sang has been complaining about her and the way she has been treating her. *She's a crazy girl,* Shew Lin thinks, *crying like that all the time and then becoming silent, like she is made of stone. She will pass on her insanity to my grandchildren.*

But here is evidence.

"If you are having problems with your husband's family, your husband should never know it. It is a terrible thing to choose between your parents and your wife."

Shew Lin laughs. *Weak advice from one rich woman to another,* she thinks. *So then we are both keeping secrets.* She glues the envelope back together. She tiptoes outside again and places the letter back into the mailbox.

Ten minutes later, Siu Sang walks through the door, the letter in her hand. She pushes the double stroller into the hall and hurries into her bedroom, leaving both girls strapped down, still wearing their overcoats and woollen hats. Shew Lin watches as the babies begin to whimper, and then listens as Siu

Sang begins to cry for the first time in months, her weeping masked by the simultaneous cries of her daughters.

Shew Lin thrusts her hands into the stroller and strokes the girls' cheeks, wondering how long the babies will have to stay in the hall like this (for she cannot take them out, bound as she is by her own rules of fear and control), if Pon Man will have to arrive before they are taken out of their seats. Shew Lin sits on the floor in front of them, lets them pull on her worn, brown hands.

In her head, she retreats into the continuous thought that runs like a loop through all of her waking hours. *Grandsongrandsongrandson.*

I should have kept my mouth shut, she thinks. *It's only when you finally get what you want that you realize it's no good.* Even when she is not in the room, Siu Sang creeps into her thoughts, a cleaning hurricane that displaces all of the other things in Shew Lin's head. *She's useful now, but does that mean that I am not?*

Siu Sang has suddenly turned into the daughter-in-law that Shew Lin had always wanted.

Siu Sang wakes up at six o'clock, has the children clothed and fed by seven thirty, and begins cleaning at eight. Mondays, it's the living room and hall. Tuesdays, the kitchen, bathrooms and closets. If she finishes before the week is over, she starts all over again, scrubbing invisible dirt, batting away invisible dust.

"Don't you think you should rest? It hasn't been long since Daisy was born." Shew Lin approaches her carefully one morning, measuring her words so that she sounds firm, distrustful.

"Rest? Dust comes into the house whether I rest or not." And she walks off, the toilet brush tucked into the waistband of her checked apron.

Later, Shew Lin checks on the children. The older one rips paper into strips. The baby sucks her thumb and stares out the window, big eyes following the cars that drive past, the birds that swoop down from the power lines. Shew Lin only rarely touches them, does not even play with them and usually only peeks into their room before she sneaks off to her worn brown brocade chair, the only dusty thing left in the house.

In the evenings, she has taken to listening outside her son and Siu Sang's bedroom door. Tonight, she puts her ear to the keyhole and, when she's sure no one is watching, down to the crack by the floor. But it's as if Siu Sang knows when Shew Lin is crouching just outside, and not a sound escapes, not the scraping of a chair against the floor, not even the regular breathing of two people asleep. *Closed tight,* she thinks, *room and mind.* For so long, she was used to the sounds of her daughter-in-law weeping—the wounded animal, the rawness of a throat being torn into shreds by overuse. As Shew Lin listens to the quiet, she can feel the house slipping away from her, the family spinning counter-clockwise in a fury of dirt and suds and rags. She pulls her head back from the closed door and sits on the floor, her thick legs poking stiffly out the bottom of her wool skirt.

When I came here, she thinks, rubbing the sore joints in her knees, *I didn't know what kind of family I would have. After all those years of dreaming about finally living with my husband, there I was.*

At first, shortly after her arrival, it was a little dance. They were carefully treating each other like mutual guests in a hotel, moving out of each other's way in the hall. He knocked when she was in their bedroom, and they slept with a thin sliver of space between them.

Their memories of each other hung in the air like a dividing curtain. They had expected certain things and were afraid to see if those things could really be.

One night, Seid Quan walked to the closed door of his bedroom and heard his wife undressing for bed—the swish of her dress as it fell to the floor, the slap of her bare feet on the wood floor. He walked in silently.

Naked, she was clearly an older woman. Flesh sat on her hips softly, in layers. Her breasts were flat, and the bones on her shoulders and neck stuck out, sharp like knives. She looked at him and her eyes flickered—once for embarrassment, twice for longing.

"Come in," she said. "It's cold out in the hall."

That night, he touched her, his own body like a wire hanger, all angles, long and thin. She wanted to laugh at the way they looked, she the dumpling, he the celery stalk. But nights were short, and they had already waited long enough.

Hours later, Seid Quan's face was buried in the back of Shew Lin's neck, his arm around her waist. The curtains of the window above their bed swayed in the draft. He ran his hand down her shoulder, her arm, felt the rough spot on her elbow.

"What are you thinking?" she asked, as she brushed the iron-grey hair out of her eyes.

She could feel the struggle, the words forming in his throat and creeping up to his mouth, but he could not speak, could only push his face deeper into her body as if he were hiding and wished to cover himself in her skin.

"Do you remember the little house in the village? The garden with the winter melon?" His head nodded against her shoulder, and he inhaled, as if ready to speak.

"I know," she whispered. "You don't have to tell me."

The cold of the hardwood floor seeps through her layers of skirt and stockings, interrupting the flow of memory. She remembers that she is supposed to be eavesdropping, not day-dreaming, and soon sees that Seid Quan has snuck up behind her and stands motionless, his hands clasped behind his back. She sighs.

"No, I didn't fall," she says, holding up her hands so he can pull her to a standing position. "Don't worry." She pats him on the arm. "Why don't we have some tea?"

The third girl. She is underweight and hairy, and has been jaundiced since Siu Sang delivered her. Shew Lin knows there is nothing to save this baby from the disappointment. Siu Sang returns from the hospital with her lips pressed even harder together and new lines around the corners from the effort of not smiling. It is not until the baby has been at home for one week that Pon Man decides on a name.

"Jackie," he says finally. "Sounds rich, doesn't it?"

This is the only thing that Shew Lin can hold on to any-more. How good can a daughter-in-law be when she delivers only girls? Never mind that Shew Lin loves the babies and tells her friends in Chinatown about their cuteness and intelligence, and never mind that Shew Lin herself gave birth to only one son after two daughters. She can call her daughter-in-law use-less if she still has not done what they brought her out to do, if her husband and son still stare through each other whenever they meet. If the grandson who she knows will fix everything still eludes them.

Wendy is now attending kindergarten and is away all morning. Siu Sang has not taken any time to recover from this delivery and has been cleaning again, ignoring her still-big belly and stiff back. While she's busy, Daisy and Jackie are in the playpen, sometimes for two or three hours at a time, always until they make a fuss, which isn't often. Daisy has been trained to feed the little one by tipping the bottle with both hands into her sister's mouth.

Shew Lin occasionally walks by and picks up the girls and tries to soothe them, especially the baby, who is crankier than the others but still never receives any attention until Pon Man comes home. She has done this only a few times, though, because as soon as she does, Siu Sang stops what she's doing and watches her closely. *Treating me like I'm a stranger, like I would hurt the babies. The nerve.* Yet these thoughts never become words. Once, Siu Sang was afraid of her. Now, Shew Lin is afraid of Siu Sang, and she leaves the children alone.

When she looks Siu Sang in the eyes, she can see the chaos behind them. Others may confuse this for blankness, for the stare of a woman who is dim and unthinking, but Shew Lin knows better. She can see the swirl of children and house and expectations (the opaque mess that seems flat but is really just a murky combination, a fetid soup), and knows that the tasks Siu Sang sets for herself are the only things standing between her and utter madness. *It is lucky she found housework when she did,* Shew Lin thinks, *for she could not go on any longer as she was.* But even now, Shew Lin has braced herself for the next outburst, the moment when Siu Sang will no longer be able to sustain it all, when she finally, cathartically, implodes.

She is lulled by the sounds of the night—the sighs of her husband, the creak of the mattress when he moves. Shew Lin is a light sleeper, and when she wakes, it is these sounds that comfort her and pull her into the warmth of her sheets and the darkness of a good sleep.

Tonight, she lies awake, stiffly moving her head to better hear the strange sound that is cutting through the usual grumblings of nighttime. It is not until her hands and feet grow cold with apprehension that she realizes the sound is coming from the back garden. She slowly stands up and steps into her slippers, careful to be as quiet as possible. Seid Quan, sleeping on his stomach, does not stir.

As she pads through the long, narrow hallway, she wonders (with the paranoia that only disrupted sleep can bring) if Siu Sang has murdered one of the children and is digging a shallow grave by moonlight under the zucchini bed. Shew Lin shivers and pulls the thin sleeves of her nightgown over her clenched fists. "That girl will ruin us," she mutters to herself.

She steps out onto the back deck and squints into the darkness. Someone is crouched in the corner of the garden, pulling at the dirt with bare hands. She takes another step forward and knocks a small pot over the railing. It lands on the stairs below and smashes. Pon Man turns around, stands up straight and looks directly at his mother from his spot in the corner.

Shew Lin hurries forward, ignoring the dampness from the grass that seeps through her cloth slippers. *It is Pon Man who is digging the grave,* she thinks. *He's killed her at last.* She looks up at the sky and wonders how much time they have to hide the body before sunrise.

When she reaches him, she sees that he is standing beside a small pile of weeds. His hands and the knees of his pyjamas are covered in dirt. Shew Lin stops suddenly and stares.

"I woke up a while ago," he says, "and remembered that I hadn't weeded the garden like I was supposed to. And I thought

I might as well do it now, because there's never any time. Siu Sang will want me to do something tomorrow, I'm sure, and Father wants to go over the bills and accounts again with me. And you," he looks her in the eyes, "will follow me around the house all day, asking me questions I don't want to answer."

She takes his cold, mud-caked hands and rubs them in hers. He speaks so quietly that she is unsure if she is meant to hear him or not, so she remains silent. He pulls his hands away and wipes them on his chest. When she reaches for them again, he pushes her away.

"I have to finish, Mother. What will happen if I don't do everything I'm supposed to? Well, even you can't answer that, can you? Go back to bed."

Pon Man turns back to the flower bed and crouches down, using his hands to feel around the plants. Shew Lin opens her mouth to say something, to assure him that everything will be just fine, even if the garden is a mess of weeds and bugs, but he holds his back so stiffly that she simply stands, mute. She wants to run back to the house and forget this ever happened, perhaps remember it as a baffling dream, but she is afraid to leave him alone, squatting in the dirt and scrabbling at weeds. *If he talks some more,* she thinks, *I must be here to listen.* She sniffs—her nose has begun to run from the cold.

Slowly, she walks backward toward the house, rubbing her nose with the back of her sleeve. Her toes, encased in damp and clammy slippers, are numb. She keeps her eyes on her son and backs up the stairs and into the kitchen. There, she sits on a chair by the window, tucking her feet underneath her. Pon Man moves slowly from one bed to the next. She closes her eyes, thinking that one second will make no difference, and rests her head against the cool glass.

It is only when Siu Sang taps her on the shoulder that she realizes she has slept through the rest of the night. Shew Lin blinks at the grey dawn and sees that the garden is meticulously weeded, but her son is nowhere in sight.

Shew Lin knows something is going on. Her son and husband, two men who have barely said a dozen words to each other in the last year, have been conferring in English every night for a week. She is comforted by the fact that Siu Sang cannot understand them either.

One Saturday afternoon, Siu Sang and Pon Man walk out to the car, both dressed for business—he in a suit, she in a sombre skirt and cardigan. They leave the girls at home. Shew Lin watches them drive away through the living-room window. She turns around to ask her husband if he knows where they're going, but just as she is about to speak, Seid Quan pushes himself out of his chair and walks down the hall. The door to their bedroom closes.

The next week, at dinner, Pon Man looks at his mother and says, "Siu Sang and I have put an offer on a house."

Shew Lin looks blank. "A house? What do you mean? There's plenty of room here."

Pon Man shifts in his chair. He looks at his father. *When was the last time they looked at each other?* Shew Lin wonders.

"Actually, I have agreed to sell this house so that Pon Man will have a respectable down payment for the new one. I thought that, since it will only be the two of us, we could rent an apartment in that new complex they're building in Chinatown." Seid Quan laughs nervously. "After all, it would be silly for us to live in this big house all by ourselves."

There is no way that Shew Lin will show her anger and

disappointment; that would be giving her daughter-in-law exactly what she wants. She glances at Siu Sang and sees that she is smiling, lips together as if she is thinking of something naughty to say but does not dare say it. Shew Lin feels everyone is disappearing, travelling somewhere without her, and she is only holding on to them by a rapidly thinning thread that unravels and grows taut in her worn hands. Holding on as tight as she can will only hurt her, pull her stiff arms out of their old sockets. But she cannot prepare herself for the letting go.

She remembers this lost and dizzy feeling from once before; the day she brought Pon Man to the boat that would take him to his father. She held on to a rail, needing, for the first time, physical support. Shew Lin watched Pon Man's small body as it was swallowed up instantly by the crowd of men and boys marching deliberately to a boat that seemed even more than black as it sat on the thick brown water of the Pearl River. *How could a boy so small possibly be big enough to leave his mother?* she thought, waving at his shrinking body. She felt she might throw up, and almost wished she could, because then she would have an excuse for feeling this unbalanced, this forlorn. If he turned back to wave, she didn't see.

But this, the loss of her home, of her family dream, is much worse, for no one will understand. She will be the cranky grandmother, the one who cannot loosen her steel grip on her son and his wife. She had better shut up.

Seid Quan says, "Don't you agree that this is the best plan?"

Grasping her hand, Pon Man whispers, "I'm sorry, Mother. We just need our own space."

She nods and says, "Yes, very sensible." She stares at her

bowl of rice, counting each grain so that no one will be able to see her eyes.

One month after Shew Lin and Seid Quan move into their new apartment (right in the heart of Chinatown, facing Gore Street, where children, always poor, usually wearing shoes with loose soles, play in the street, dodging the slippery remains of rotting bananas and napa cabbage; where Shew Lin can smell the cooking of the woman on the second floor, even when there is no cooking going on), Siu Sang gives birth to another daughter. Unlucky number four.

On the phone, Pon Man sounds more tired than he has ever sounded before, and Shew Lin resists the urge to ask him if his wife is wearing him down to his bones. Instead, she asks when she can visit and bring them black vinegar and hot ginger soup to restore their energy.

"Whenever, Mother. It doesn't matter to me." She hears him sigh. "I shouldn't be so short with you. I'm just a little worn out. Why don't you come on Saturday? I'll pick up some ice cream."

Just before he hangs up, he says, "Right. I almost forgot. We named her Penny, like the one-cent coin, you know? Lucky Penny. Tell Father, will you?"

Shew Lin practises saying all the girls' names in a row: "Wendy-Daisy-Jackie-Penny." She does not like that they all sound so much the same, for she is afraid she will never be able to say them well enough for people to know whom she is talking about. "Wendy. Daisy. Jackie. Penny." If she breathes in between, it sounds much better.

Seid Quan walks into the living room. "Any news?"

"A girl. They've named her Penny."

"Penny," he repeats, and nods. "Sounds good."

"Aren't you going to say anything else?"

"What do you mean?"

Shew Lin and Seid Quan are at opposite ends of their small living room. The balcony door is open, and a slow breeze thickly moves the stiff curtains. Seid Quan reaches up and wipes the sweat off his high, lined forehead. Shew Lin scowls, thinks, *The face of a man who never speaks.* She knows that Seid Quan would say that he only speaks when necessary.

"There's no boy, Seid Quan. What is the point of all this?"

He stares at her blankly.

"Why do we sacrifice for them when she can't even birth a boy? This whole nonsense is your fault. We wouldn't be sitting here right now if you hadn't said yes to everything they asked."

Seid Quan looks out the balcony door at the mountains almost hidden by a low yellow haze. Around their heads, the smells of Chinatown are coming through the windows, and the slow wind does nothing to help; it only stirs the odour of rotting produce around, like a thick soup. From here, the shouts of the vendors hawking their goods sound a lot like Shew Lin's voice: tinny, high, straining through distance.

"We know she's crazy. We've done everything for them, and I just bet they will never come to see us. This dirty little apartment will be too much for the fine Hong Kong lady. They won't want to be reminded of the hole they put us in."

Seid Quan looks up at the ceiling and studies the stain from the water damage. She can hear him thinking that he meant to talk to the landlord yesterday, but his memory is not what it used to be. She wants to tell him that perhaps he should start writing these things down.

"I'm tired, do you understand? Tired of always living in places chosen by other people, tired of waiting for someone else to do things for me—you, Pon Man, anyone. I used to do things for myself, but now we have no home, so what good have all your decisions done for us? You and I, we've had only one home together, and now we don't even have that. Didn't I work hard enough? Didn't we deserve it?"

He hears the break in her voice and looks over. She is bent forward and is rubbing her forehead with both hands, rubbing as if she has a stain on her face that she cannot get rid of.

"You never say anything. It's because you blame me too. No one believes I am a good woman. Everything I've done and said is for the family. Everything. I'm old now—how can I apologize? No one would believe I was trying to be nice, anyway."

She knows he is thinking of all the things he has heard her say, the bitter things that came out when she did not have the time to stop them. She has never asked for his help, so she supposes he must be forgiven for never thinking she wanted it.

He walks over to her chair and kneels down in front of her, his joints creaking. He holds her face in both his hands and leans his forehead against hers. They sit like this for a few minutes, taking turns breathing: one in, the other one in, one out, the other one out. She can feel how papery their skin is, how, even when pressed together, there is no oil left, just the dry outer layer, leached by wind and sun and age.

She gently pulls his hands away from her face and releases them so that they dangle from his arms, like mittens on a string. She cannot look him in the eyes anymore, cannot keep running along at this high emotional pitch where everything is at the surface. It's just too much.

"I'm going to lie down in the bedroom," she says, "where I can hear myself think."

It has been many years since Shew Lin was a little girl, and it seems like it has been even longer since she came to Canada and tried to adjust to life here. The weather, with its incessant drizzle, the days of sunshine that hurt her because she knew they could never last. Cold blue mountains that blocked her in, a cold blue ocean that sparkled at her wickedly, strange children saying things to her she could not understand but knew were bad, a heavy sky seen from a foggy window.

She misses the dust and red clay mud.

The part of her that used to dream happily seems to have left her, and she feels disconnected, like a balloon that has been let go and is left to float above the treetops, going one way and then another.

When she tries to remember what she was like as a young girl, she sees nothing. She can remember helping her mother kill and pluck chickens, the coolness of the water from the well in the middle of summer, the ache of her bones at the end of a hard day as she tried to fall asleep. But she cannot picture her own face, the one that must have looked out at her from the little hand mirror she kept by her sleeping mat. And she cannot remember the things she must have thought.

It is a hard business, growing old.

Yet she cannot quite shake the feeling that it is not simply her old age that is obstructing her memory. Nor is it the distance between Canada and China. It is something more insidious and quiet. Something with a snake-like progress, slowly winding itself around her mind and chest, over and over again, squeezing the memories out through every orifice, squeezing her lungs (*how is it that it became so hard to breathe?*) and wringing the air so that there is nothing left for her to inhale, even if she could.

Shew Lin is no fool, yet she ignores the slow disintegration of her body and mind, the slow leaching into the land she stands on. After all, she would rather die than ever admit that she has grown weak or is somehow less than she used to be. *It's this place,* she finally remembers. *It's here that is erasing my memory. It may as well kill me, then.*

At first, nobody noticed anything. It was only Shew Lin who knew, who adjusted her walks so that she could avoid the big hills, who sat down at the kitchen table to chop her vegetables instead of standing like she used to.

But then, little by little, more things began to change. One day, Seid Quan found her in the washroom, sitting on the edge of the tub, her feet still in the now-cold bathwater. She smiled and brushed him off after he helped her up. "I just got so tired trying to get out that I needed a little rest. We are all getting old, aren't we?" And she walked slowly to the bedroom, where she lay down, still damp, on top of the covers.

Pon Man became alarmed when she cancelled their weekly family dinner, the only chance she ever had these days to cook all the good things she prepared so well. When he asked her why, she sighed and laughed. "Oh, there was nothing good to buy at the markets today. No one values freshness anymore."

And by then, she was fooling no one.

When Seid Quan begged her to see a doctor, she refused. Instead, she sent him to every herbalist in Chinatown with a list of her pains, then brewed the soup they gave him in a little clay pot, filling the air with the thick smell of reconstituted roots and ground plants. "No doctors," she told him. "I've lived almost eighty years without ever seeing one, and I'm not going to start now."

Yesterday, Seid Quan slipped while carrying her to the bathroom. They both fell to the floor. Seid Quan bandaged the cut on Shew Lin's head by himself before he called his son. In five minutes, everything was settled. They would go live with Pon Man and his family for the time being.

Slowly, Pon Man lifts his mother out of the car and carries her into his house. Her head rests on his shoulder, and the top of her knitted cap tickles the side of his neck. Seid Quan follows behind, carrying two suitcases. He looks at her feet dangling from his son's left arm and whispers, "Like a doll made of cloth, stuffed with cotton."

Shew Lin cranes her neck so that she can look at her husband over Pon Man's shoulder. "You should know better than that. I was never a lady, so how could I be a doll?"

Pon Man laughs, and Seid Quan says, "You'll never lose your hearing, at least."

Pon Man gently lays Shew Lin down on a bed in his small spare bedroom. He draws the blankets up to her chin and begins to tuck her in, but Seid Quan steps forward, puts his hand on his son's shoulder and says, "I'll do that." Pon Man nods and steps backward, out of the room and into the hall.

Seid Quan sits on the bed beside her, not touching her, not moving. "All that work, and now dying," he murmurs.

Shew Lin opens her watery, red eyes; she likes to keep them closed because the air hitting her eyeballs stings, like water on a wound. "You shouldn't whisper like that and think you can get away with it." She sighs. "Too old to learn new tricks."

She closes her eyes again, lets the familiar smell of her husband fill her head, displace the unfamiliar scent of her daughter-in-law's detergents and perfumes. Six months ago, she would have preferred to sleep in the streets rather than in this house, but there isn't much point in thinking such things now. Shew Lin can even think kind thoughts about Siu Sang, who, at thirty-eight, is pregnant once again, likely for the last time. Shew Lin allows herself to feel optimistic about the chances of Siu Sang having a boy. *The last one*, she thinks. *The lucky one, the one who takes care of the old. If it is not a boy, then it will be a different sort of daughter.*

She smiles at the thought and falls asleep, her head cushioned on Seid Quan's hand.

Shew Lin has been dreaming again. Before she came to Canada, her dreams were merely extensions of her daily life. Cooking, cleaning, writing letters, braiding her daughters' hair—a mirror held up to the events of her day.

Since then, as the nights wore on through the rain and fog, her dreams have started to build like the movies from Hong Kong her son and his wife go to see. Tragedy, vengeance, a noble death both inevitable and surprising.

Last night, she stood over her dead son, his body pinned underneath a city bus. She could see nothing but his face and that undeniable look of death—eyes and mouth open, a stiff jaw, grey skin. He looked small again, the way he looked when he left for Canada, except that, in this dream, he was terribly, terribly thin, the way beggars in Guangzhou looked after the war.

Through crooked dream logic, she knew that his death was his wife's fault, and she went looking for her. Shew Lin travelled the world searching for this spoiled girl on the run. She beat back a cobra in the jungle, flew a helicopter through the

Grand Canyon, escaped a fire in a Thai whorehouse. And yet the girl still eluded her.

Finally, she returned to the narrow house she used to live in with her husband and son, her body drooping with defeat, her knees sore from running. The tall house creaked as she walked up the front steps and through the door.

And there she was, calmly sitting on the living-room sofa. She was wearing a black silk dress (extravagant, even in mourning), and a thin veil covered her face, although Shew Lin could still see that her eyes glittered darkly in that poor, dusky light.

"We waited so long, but finally we had to bury him without you. What were you doing? Having fun?"

In a single, glorious movement, Shew Lin reached for her sword and cut off Siu Sang's head, not even wincing as the girl's head fell to the floor.

And in the end, she poured gasoline all over the house, set it on fire and sat in the kitchen, waiting for the hot, hot flames to lick her face. She had finally saved this family, allowed it to start all over again, cleanly.

A perfect, white silence. Then a rumbling, slow at first, then gaining speed.

Shew Lin's body has started to shake uncontrollably. Her eyes are tightly closed, and she can feel them starting to roll back in their sockets. She tries to grab the sheets, the side of the bed, anything, but her fingers are immovable, heavy. She hears her husband calling for their son, can feel his hands holding her down by the shoulders. Pon Man runs in, holds her ankles, one in each hand. The sheets are damp with her sweat.

Suddenly, she opens her eyes and stares at her husband and son, their heads close together, both of their foreheads lined in concern. Above them, the bedroom light shines weakly. *Only forty watts,* she thinks, *how typical.*

The shaking subsides, and Shew Lin turns her head to the side, her mouth open in exhaustion. She can tell that it's sunset from the light coming in through the window. The walls are pink and orange, the colours shifting, there and not there. She doesn't move, feels light as a snowflake bouncing through the air in the night. White on black.

She hears Pon Man and Seid Quan whispering, about her, of course. *So,* she thinks, *it really doesn't matter, does it? Because they love each other but have travelled in parallel lines, same speed, same places, but never meeting. Maybe after this, without me, they'll do better.*

Pon Man leans down and puts his head beside hers so that they are touching, ear on ear.

"The baby came this morning, Mother. The girls have named her Samantha. Sammy for short, like a boy." He laughs quietly.

Shew Lin reaches out and holds his hand. "Sammy. Does she look like you?"

"Just like, actually. The only one."

She sighs. "Yes, that's the right thing. She will do just as well. You must hold her as I would, as I held you."

Seid Quan looks at his wife's face. "What was that, my dear? Did you say something?"

Shew Lin shakes her head, knowing that neither of them will understand the myriad things that go into keeping a family intact, the things that are both inevitable and illogical. But Shew Lin knows that the illogical sometimes makes the most sense.

She closes her eyes, feels the light on her face. Someone slips a hand, warm and dry, into hers. She drifts off, dreaming of a gentle ocean, her son's face when it was unlined and untroubled, a warm rain and a long-ago wedding.

She balks at the smell of his skin, the smell of sweat and burning wood, the same smells she spent hours scrubbing from her body. He does not look at her directly but smiles shyly at her feet. He has not yet lifted her wedding veil.

Is he clean?

They sit side by side on a low, hard bed, and Shew Lin thinks that the silence will render her deaf; it fills her head and swirls slowly around the room—viscous and heavy. Under the bottom edge of her veil, all she sees is a thin rug covering a hard-packed dirt floor and her own feet, large and clumsy, ironically encased in delicate silk slippers. Absent-mindedly, she begins to pick at a callus on the palm of her hand with her thumb.

Seid Quan turns toward her slowly, his body moving inch by inch. He takes her hand and holds it to his face. He finds her callus and touches it lightly.

"So much hard work," he says and gently places her hand back on her lap.

She is shocked that this boy, so peasant-smelling, has touched her so quietly. She expected a man wild from his years in Canada, a man with white habits and brutal manners. She can still feel the pressure from his hand, and her face grows hot.

"Give it to her, big brother! Give us some action!"

There is shuffling in the hall outside their bedroom door, and Shew Lin hears a crowd of boys giggling and making cat noises. Seid Quan has made no move.

Tired and cranky, she turns and pulls the veil from her face in one long rip.

four

the hospital

On the way to the hospital, my mother starts to pray.

As far as I know, my mother never went to any kind of church, never said anything about God. But here, in the back seat of a taxi, with my head on her lap, her eyes are closed and she's muttering something in Chinese to someone about me, about how she can't lose another person, about how I'm the last one, the child of her old age, and the most precious of all her daughters. She whispers that she will try harder and be a different kind of mother. Her hand on the side of my head is warm and dry, like a warm quilt by the fire during a rainstorm.

As we drive through the city, I watch the sun come up, turning the buildings pink and then yellow. The streets are empty, no homeless people, not even a street cleaner. The concrete looks more human at dawn, and the city makes me want to cry.

I push my head into my mother's stomach, feel the softness of her belly skin (grown large and then small, stretched and then contracted so many times). I'm hurting her. *This* is hurting her.

"Mom?"

"Yes? Is it getting worse?"

"No, I just want to ask you something."

"What's that?"

"Will you promise not to tell Wendy or Daisy or anyone else? I just don't want them to worry, I guess."

"Whatever you want, Sammy. Just close your eyes. We'll be there soon."

The waiting room at the hospital is strangely empty. Except for the nurses and one bored-looking security guard, we are the only ones here. They assign me a bed right away, and my mother stays in the waiting room, sitting in the corner in a plastic bucket chair, her back straight, her hands folded in her lap. I wave at her as they lead me into the back, and she smiles, her mouth tight at the corners. She's still wearing her pyjamas. I half-expect her to wail, to fling herself at me and weep as if I am being led to the electric chair, but she only sits and nods to me reassuringly. *When,* I think, *did my mother become so stoic?*

A thin curtain separates me from an old man who calls for something in a language I don't recognize. The nurse asks me a few questions, mentions that if something happened that I didn't consent to, it's perfectly safe to tell her. I shake my head and turn to the wall. There are many things I could talk to her about (how my body is so angry with me I feel as if my skin is burning from the inside out, how I know this has to be the last time, but I'm scared that it won't be), but I don't, because that would mean opening my mouth, and if I do that, there might be no stopping the flood of words that pours out. I put my finger in a tiny hole in the concrete and scratch at the mint-green paint. It flakes away and falls to the floor like dry skin, feathery. In this fluorescent light, you can see every little flaw in every surface.

The doctor apologizes three times while he examines me and keeps asking if this hurts. Of course it does, but I don't say anything. Perhaps if he thinks I don't speak English, this will go faster.

"Well, you've stopped bleeding now, so we won't have to keep you or give you a transfusion. I'll send a blood sample to the lab, just to make sure everything's okay. I think it would be all right if you went home."

I look up at his face. He's very young. "Why was I bleeding?"

He frowns. "The abrasions in your vagina and on your cervix are pretty superficial. Sometimes women bleed a lot once and it never happens again. Sometimes it means something serious, sometimes it doesn't. There isn't any point in keeping you here any longer if you feel better. If something out of the ordinary happens or you start bleeding again like this, come back and we'll do some more tests. But let me ask you: are you sure this was, you know, consensual? Because if it wasn't, that would explain a lot."

To him and to the nurse, this is no more complicated than a girl lying because her mother is in the next room. "Yes, of course it was consensual." I sigh and try not to think. There really doesn't seem to be any point.

When I walk out to meet my mother, she looks scared to ask me anything. I tell her what the doctor said and leave out the sex part, hoping that the explanation that's not really an explanation will satisfy her. She doesn't say much, just guides me out the door to wait for a taxi.

———

The afternoon light in the vegetable garden is pink and orange. My father bends over his cucumbers, making sure they aren't too wet or too dry. I sit on the fence, my legs swinging as I nibble on a carrot he has just unearthed for me.

My mother steps out onto the porch wearing her fancy clothes. "All right," she says, "I'm going to the banquet now. Make sure you feed her something healthy." She disappears inside again, and I can hear the clicking of her heels as she walks through the kitchen and living room and slams the front door. The smell of hairspray wafts out on the warm summer air.

My father stands up, eyes twinkling. "What do you think? Dairy Queen or McDonald's?"

The sun is sinking as we drive home. My body is turned sideways so that I can look straight out the passenger window, my face still sticky from the Peanut Buster Parfait. My hair whips around my face as we drive down Main Street, and the sunset turns everything a goldy-yellow, like the colour of the giant squash that grows in the garden at home. I wish that we could just drive like this forever, watching the dry cleaners and discount furniture stores flicker past like scenes in a movie.

"We're almost home, Shrimp. Better roll up your window." I look over at my father. A flap of skin on his neck (*Had I ever seen that before? Where did it come from?*) sways in the wind, making him look like a rooster. He frowns, and the lines on either side of his mouth are deep and scary. I shiver.

"Cold?" he asks me, but he doesn't even look.

When we arrive home, I run to the garden and peek to see if anything has grown since we left. My father stands beside me. "These plants just keep growing and growing," he says, his hand resting on the top of my head. "Even if we wanted to stop it, we couldn't." He bends over the zucchini and points at the orange blossom. "See that? It just grows that itself. No one tells the plant what to do; it just does it. Perfect, isn't it?"

"I guess. I like the eating part best."

He laughs. "You're all stomach, Sammy Shrimp. I'd better run a bath for you—you're covered in chocolate."

As he walks into the house, I stay outside, run my hands over the creeping string beans, bend down to smell the onion scent wafting up from the chives. I kick at a big kabocha squash and watch two earthworms wriggle their way up from underneath. I imagine them blinking in the fading daylight— their wormy eyes heavy-lidded and wrinkled—as they reluctantly pull their long, stretchy bodies out into the open, forced, as it were, to come to life.

"Sammy," my father says to me, "you're like your grandmother: saying all the wrong things, meaning something else." He coughs and reaches into the sheets for a tissue.

I shift in my seat, trying to act like I don't notice that he's sick, that his face and odour spell out *I have been in this hospital for so long I am part of it*. Through the open door to the hallway, an orderly piles white towels soiled with old blood and food onto a rolling cart. I turn back to my father and nod.

"You're not listening." He turns onto his side, rolling on top of the tubes that snake from his arm to somewhere I can't see under the sheets. "Your grandmother, all she wanted was to see us all succeed. We always had to be together. If we were apart, she thought bad things would happen." He laughs. "I only ever wanted to run away."

I look my father in the eyes for the first time in months. They are watery and slightly glazed, but still, he holds my gaze. "I try to remember things to tell you girls, but sometimes the memories come when no one is here and then they disappear. Now that you're sitting with me, I want to tell you everything that's in my head right now, even if the stories make no sense." He grins. "I'm sorry to bore you."

How does he always know what I'm thinking? "What did grandmother say that was all wrong?"

"Oh, so many things. She was hard on your mother, but only because she wanted the best for me. She wanted me to have a perfect wife and, you know, no one's perfect." He shakes his head. "She always said what was on her mind, especially if it was something mean. Like you."

"I don't do that!"

"Sure you do. Remember when you called Penny your Pig Sister?"

I frown. "She eats all the chips. And her clothes smell bad."

"You see? Just like your grandmother." He sighs. "I miss her soup sometimes."

After a few minutes, my father falls asleep, still on his side. I pull the blankets over his shoulders and sit on the windowsill, waiting for Jackie to return from the cafeteria. A nurse comes in and pulls the tubes out from under his sleeping body. She smiles at me.

"Aren't you a good girl to be sitting with your dad like this? It's nice to see kids who value their families."

I look out the window, wishing that what this nurse seems to think of me was true. I could be a good daughter, filled with compassion and sympathy and kind thoughts, instead of the raging, sullen, hard girl I really am. I could run and run, but even I doubt that I could ever escape myself.

Jackie walks in, holding two muffins and a coffee. I am so relieved that I stand up immediately to give her my chair. In the hallway, I breathe deeply and eat my muffin while sitting on the floor.

Bleach. Vomit. The smell of the hospital clings to me; I know from experience that it is almost impossible to wash off (I remember scrubbing my skin raw after every visit to my father's room, but it was never any use). I step out of the taxi and onto our front lawn, glad, for once, that I am coming home.

After changing my sheets and wiping down the floor in my bedroom, my mother sits on the edge of my bed while I drink the hot soup she's made. It's like dishwater, and just bland enough to make me feel better. She hands me a little packet of crackers, which she probably stole the last time she ordered soup at a restaurant.

"Are you sure you're feeling better?" She puts her hand on my stomach.

"I'm okay. The doctor gave me some pills for the cramps."

She looks out the window, and I can see the reflection of the trees outside in her glasses. She blinks, and the miniature trees sway. She looks back at me, and now it's only her eyes I see.

"Are you sure you're telling me everything the doctor said? There's nothing else?"

I don't know what she suspects. I become sweaty.

"Did that white boy do this to you? The redheaded one, from the wedding? Or is there another one? Your Aunt Susie is always telling me that the boys are worse these days, expecting things from their girlfriends."

I look at her hair, her nose, her mouth, anywhere but her eyes. "There is no white boy, Mom. Not anymore. I've told you everything."

I know she doesn't believe me, but she stops asking. She gives me a hot water bottle and stays with me until I close my eyes. In my sleep, I can feel her moving around the house, the unmistakable noises of her presence (shuffling slippers, throaty coughs). Instead of waking me, they lull me into a deeper sleep, where I lie dreamless, caught in a world where I don't hear or see or feel. When I wake up hours later, I can hear her singing in the kitchen; the bang of her pots and pans accompanies her in a wild, rhythmless way. "*Que sera, sera,*" she sings, doing her best Doris Day impression. Somehow, not knowing what will be is a comforting thought.

I sit up, rub my eyes and walk to the kitchen, following the sound of my mother's voice. She stands in the middle of the room, holding a Bundt pan with her oven mitts. She nods at me, smiling. "You want some? It's still warm."

She slices me a piece of apple cake, the first apple cake I remember her baking for twelve years. She smiles widely at me, passes me a plate and sits down, watching as I eat.

"It's good, Mom."

"Isn't it? Do you know, your Aunt Susie gave me this recipe in 1964."

She leans back in her chair, places her hands over her stomach. I look at her, suddenly aware that she sits like a mouse, all bones and skin and nerves. Where has her stomach gone, her fearsome bulk? I blink and look again. In the living room, the curtains are open, and music is playing from the radio.

Years ago, when it was all over, when the house fell silent and my sisters had gone back to their everyday lives (back to their real homes, or back to work, where they could teeter in high heels and pretend that they were independent and business-like, hard as lacquered red nails), my mother wrapped herself in layers—knitted vests, fleece sweatshirts, elastic-waisted sweatpants—and burrowed herself into the living-room sofa.

My body—twelve years old and so, so angry—pushed itself into uncomfortable new directions, and I slinked about the house with greasy hair and hunched shoulders. Through my stringy bangs, I peered at her (wet, pink eyes, tissue clamped in her left hand, the other resting on the bony shelf of her clavicles).

The only times she moved off her spot were for dinner and, sometimes, for bed. She cooked and we ate, sometimes leaving chunks of food in our bowls—our silent, hungry protest. Sometimes she cried, silent tears that rolled quickly down her cheeks and disappeared in the folds of her turtleneck. There were a lot of leftovers. I don't know if she ever really slept.

I grew some more, my unnoticed body taking on a leaner, harder edge. Some nights I didn't come home, and when I did, everything about me smelled like beer or pot or cigarettes or all three. Still she sat, nodded at my staggering self as if I were coming home from a Bible study. By then, I was used to it. By then, anything else would have been alarming.

I shake my head, stare at her face, wonder if that could truly be satisfaction over apple cake she is feeling.

"Are you feeling okay, Mom?" Somehow, this isn't right. She sits there, flour smudged on the tip of her nose, head tilted to the side as if she is trying to see me in the right light.

"Oh, I'm just fine. How are *you* doing? You need to rest, you know, after what happened at the hospital."

"All I've done today is rest."

"Yes, but . . ." she folds her hands in her lap. "You haven't been the same since you came back. What happened in Montreal?

I mean, you never seemed to like it there that much, but you seem sad now."

"Sad?" I'm confused. The sweet cake fills my mouth, and my head swims. "How do you know I'm sad?"

"I just noticed. You're not working or in school. You stay at home all the time."

"But you never notice anything. I can't remember the last time you asked me how I was doing." I put my fork down, swallow the last crumb.

She picks a napkin up, folds it down the middle, pushing on the crease with the palm of her hand. "Well, you know. It's hard sometimes, keeping track of what all you girls are doing. You see, we're alone now, so I have more time for you." She leans forward. "I don't know why you were so sick, and maybe I don't need to know, but I want you to tell me what is really going on with you."

She's trying, I think. *How is this possible?*

"You feel sorry for me," I say quietly.

She blinks hard. "Yes, I do. I know what it's like to be sad."

"This is different."

"No, it's not. How? I moped around the house, didn't talk to anyone—same as you. I'm trying to change things now, don't you understand?"

I shake my head. She leans back again, holds her hands in front of her chest as if she is trying to prevent her body from cracking in two. "I want you to do something. I want you to stop looking at me like that. I want you to try, too. Will you at least think about what I'm saying?"

I push my chair away from the table. "Thanks for the cake, Mom." I place my dish in the sink (quietly, for any noise would ruin the moment, and then we might be back where we started) and walk briskly toward my room through the living room, drawing the heavy curtains on the way. I turn to look back and see the piano—spotless, smooth, unplayed. I can never walk past without seeing it. My eyes can't skip over its solid, silent shape like they can with the silk flowers on the dining-room hutch or even, in the past, my mother sitting in the dark. Its noiselessness is not really noiseless at all. I step forward and run my hands over the dusty bench.

I can hear, still, the violent thumping of my hands playing scales. I sounded nothing at all like those children we saw in the news, the ones who won musical scholarships and the top awards at contests. Those girls (eleven years old, bespectacled, long, smooth braids) looked years younger than me, their imminent pubescence hidden by bibbed dresses and shiny Mary Janes.

I banged out my lessons, stormed my way through "Long, Long Ago." I wanted to fling myself at the piano, break through its dark wood frame, ruin its innards. My sweatshirt sagged at the collar, and as I watched my hands on the keys, I could keep track of my hangnails, the ragged edges of my cuticles.

When I quit, I simply stopped. I said nothing. My mother said nothing. The piano stood between us, its cover growing a fine layer of undisturbed dust. I didn't touch it, and my mother didn't ask me to. I waited and waited for her to say something, until the waiting became the past. The piano itself disappeared under mismatched doilies, china figurines and Christmas cards from relatives in Oakland, Toronto, Perth.

All those things that belong nowhere else are now marooned on the piano. There is no escaping that I disappoint her, that the piano remains so that she can remind me of my failure. Although, perhaps, it reminds her of something too.

I head to my bedroom, knowing that, underneath it all, it's still just a piano.

When I wake up on sunny mornings, the first things I see are the mountains. They're painfully sharp in the morning light, reassuringly real and yet unreal at the same time. I want to reach out my hand and touch them, yet I know if I did, all I would get is air. My love for them is no less for this.

The ocean is different. It exists separately and does not enter into the daily workings of my life, except for the western breeze that blows across the city, that moves my curtains from left to right. It is not so much mysterious as all-knowing and silent. There is a lot it could say if it chose. A silent partner in this landscape I was born to.

I've driven through Vancouver with my mother, my sisters and, in the past, my father; so many things happen as we drive, watching the streets go by, the quality of the light changing as we travel from east to west, or east again on our way home. It is really the East Side that is Vancouver for me—the netless basketball hoops stranded in their concrete courts, the stained stucco on the sides of squat apartment buildings, the spit-crossed sidewalks that seem to lead everywhere you'd ever want to go until you realize that they can only end in ocean or mountain or trees. The smell of the city comes in through the windows, and it's easy to forget the purpose of the drive, the lives we've left at home, the ugly days when it rains and we have to take the bus.

At home, the portraits on the wall are of the departed, and I can't walk to the kitchen without seeing old images of my father, my grandfather and my grandmother. All in a three-quarter portrait pose, all smiling, all without a body.

They hang there, three in a row, suspended on the dark wood panelling, fading a little more every year. But it seems my mother has come to life lately—bustling, grasping my wrist when I need it, even before I ask. Surely, this is life, even in the presence of the past.

I walk this city every day, sidestep the garbage, hold my breath through the alleys. But even in the dirtiest of places, where the sidewalk is covered with gum and the hum of traffic and city noise is so loud that you can't even hear your own footsteps, you can always look north and see the mountains. And there's always a breeze, faintly salt-scented, that touches your face as you turn to look west.

death

Pon Man shakes off the shreds of his dream (in which his mother follows him through his daily life like a shadow, disappearing when he turns his head, reappearing in his peripheral vision) and sits up, aware that he is alone in bed. Down the hall, he hears a low keening, the kind of sound he imagines lambs being led to the slaughter might make. He swings his feet over the side of the bed and into his slippers. He wonders if one of the girls is sick and Siu Sang has gone to help her.

He knocks on the bathroom door, listens at the crack in the door frame. He can see the light spilling out into the hall from the gap by the floor.

"Hello? Is anyone in there?"

And then another low cry—choking, wet, wordless. Pon Man reaches for the knob and turns.

Siu Sang lies on the linoleum floor, her pyjamas around her knees. There is blood coursing thickly from between her legs; there is blood on the floor, blood on the walls, blood all over the toilet and spattered on the mirror. She cries, her mouth an open hole amidst all the blood so that it seems to be streaming from her face as well.

Pon Man breathes through his mouth, knowing that, otherwise, he will gag.

He wraps her in three towels and carries her through the house to the car outside. Wendy opens her bedroom door and peers out at him. "I'm taking your mother to the hospital," he whispers. "You'll have to clean the bathroom." He wonders if he should warn her about the blood, but decides there's no time. He leaves quietly, as if he is absorbed by the night.

As they drive through the streets (empty and black and wet—not even a cat), Siu Sang begins to talk, her words a damp babble at first. But then she repeats herself, her voice slowly forming each syllable as if she can remember only the individual sounds and words themselves have lost their meaning.

"It's a curse. She laid a curse on me."

Pon Man does not dare take his eyes off the road. He squirms. "Who? Who are you talking about?"

"This is my punishment for hating her, for birthing only girls. I knew I was sick as soon as Sammy came out. I could feel the blood pooling inside."

"Who put a curse on you?"

Siu Sang reaches up from the back seat, where she is lying, and grabs his shoulder. Later, he will see the thick red handprint on his jacket, like the devil's mark. "Your mother, of course. Now that she's dead, she has nothing better to do than torture me."

Pon Man is afraid to speak. He hopes she will forget these words in her pain (he wonders if she is perhaps right, but then shakes his head, burying *curse* and *torture* and *mother* beneath the unordered clutter in his brain) and that he will be free to drive the rest of the way in silence. At the next red light, he turns to look at her. She is asleep. He is so thankful he could cry.

Later, as he sits in the waiting room while doctors remove Siu Sang's uterus, he relives, over and over again, the sight of his wife lying, her eyes wide open, in her own blood. He could smell the fear in the air—his or hers, he doesn't know—the sickening combination of flesh and blood and terror. He rubs his face with the heels of his hands. *As if,* he thinks, *there hasn't been enough sickness already.*

Shew Lin's funeral was only two weeks ago. That afternoon, the warm air smelled like berries and mulch to him as he rubbed his hands, red and sore from the casket handles. The funeral went well—lots of people, a touching service. He arranged everything himself, not knowing exactly what his mother would have wanted because, like many superstitious old ladies, she refused to talk about her death. So, as he made his way from funeral home to cemetery, he could only guess, imagine her voice in his head one last time, saying *yes* to this or *no* to that. As Shew Lin was the first to say, only her boy could know her so well.

When Pon Man walks into the recovery room to see his wife, she lies with her face to the wall, her back stiff and perfectly straight so that he knows she isn't sleeping. Her whole body blames him, makes him feel like a foolish little boy whose selfishness has ruined everything. He can hear her thinking, *Your children did this to me. It is your mother who wishes me to suffer.* He reaches into his pocket for his cigarettes and steps away from her, walks into the hall, where, under the fluorescent lights, his skin looks not quite there, in the process of disappearing.

When Pon Man brings her home, she doesn't speak. The girls creep about the house silently, their eyes moving from left to right as if they are looking for hidden dangers that might leap out of dusty corners. Seid Quan carefully moves in the last of his things from his apartment in Chinatown, making sure not to bump the walls with his boxes, afraid, perhaps, that the vibrations will travel through the drywall and into Siu Sang's bedroom.

Pon Man brings her hot water with lemon, ties on her apron so that he can cook the meals (meat pies and pork chops and casseroles made with canned cream of mushroom soup). He is silent as well, for if she begins to speak again in response to him, there is no telling what she might say. "I have children to think of," Pon Man says to himself. "And if her madness comes back, I don't want them to know."

He lets himself wonder what she must be thinking. Does she want to hold Sammy? Does being a mother make her crazy? What does she want—really, really want? The answer could not possibly be as simple as a genuine pearl necklace or a fig tree for the backyard. He searches his brain for the things she loves and can come up with nothing, not even the taste of watermelon on a hot day, or that movie where the girl is discovered and becomes a Hollywood star.

Picking up things that he knows she has touched, he wanders through the house, hoping that one of these objects will tell him that essential thing about his wife he needs to know. He touches them all: the feather duster, a white leather glove, the case she keeps her glasses in. Pon Man stares at each one, turns it over as if something might be hidden on the underside. Nothing. He even finds his old sketchbook, the last pages filled with drawings of Siu Sang, but these say more about him as a young, impatient artist than they do about her.

He rummages through the old boxes in the garage, hears the mice skittering away and climbing the insides of the walls. He plunges his hands into her forgotten things, pushes aside the red silk pillows her mother insisted she bring to Canada. He is sure that he will know what he is looking for when he finds it.

Pon Man lifts the lid of Siu Sang's trunk, the one she brought with her from Hong Kong when she first arrived. In a pocket in the lining, he finds an old book, a romance novel with a picture of a young, open-faced girl on the cover. He wipes it off with his sleeve and lets out a tense breath.

"So this is it," he whispers. The pictured girl is poised, ready for misfortune but knowing that the real happiness, the romantic ending, is a sure thing. He realizes it is the promise of the perfect life that Siu Sang lives for—a life of martinis and glamour and perfectly behaved, beautiful children. The kind of life this fictional girl on the cover of a book fully expects.

He thinks of Siu Sang's middle-aged body: the unmistakable scars of motherhood and age, the thin snakes of stretch marks on her stomach and thighs and breasts. Even when she is naked, he can almost see the rose-coloured cardigan she wears every chilly day floating like a ghost above her damp skin, the cork-soled slippers on her feet and the tissue tucked into her sleeve.

He pushes the book back into its pocket and lifts the trunk back onto its shelf. Standing beside the station wagon, he squints at the cobwebs in the corners, the window slicked over in layers of grease and dust. He listens for the sounds of life behind the door to his house, but hears nothing, not even the breathing of his family. From in here, he could pretend there was no one home at all.

Wendy stands in the middle of the room, a damp dishcloth in her hand. Pon Man can see the tears starting behind her eyes, although her face remains still, the muscles held tight beneath her skin. He wants to run to her, pick her up and carry her and her sisters away—somewhere far, through the Rocky Mountains, out, perhaps, to the open prairie, where Siu Sang would never think to look. Wendy blinks, and one tear rolls down her cheek and off the point of her long chin.

Siu Sang is systematically running her finger over every dish her daughters have just washed. If her finger is covered in soap, food or grease, she throws the dish through the air to smash against the pantry door. *Her eyes,* Pon Man thinks. *I cannot hide them from the children.* The other four girls are huddled in a bunch in the hall. Sammy crouches behind Jackie's legs, her chubby hands clutching the thick blue denim.

"What is the point of having daughters if they cannot even wash a plate?" Siu Sang speaks in a low growl. "I teach them and teach them and still, here they are staring at me like there are no brains in their heads. Tell me, Wendy," she turns to her oldest daughter, "do you have a brain? Do your sisters?"

Wendy doesn't move. Her voice comes out in a croak. "I think we all do."

"You think, do you? Isn't that funny?" She holds a ceramic soup spoon in her hands, examines it thoughtfully, then tosses it toward the back door.

Pon Man looks around him, his mouth opening and closing, soundless. He wants to speak, he wants to run, but he stands instead, his silent mouth gaping, his feet glued to the carpet. *What kind of father am I? What kind of husband?*

He feels a shadow behind him, a faint breathing on the back of his neck. He turns and sees Seid Quan. "I thought I would see what all the commotion is about," he says softly.

Siu Sang spins, sees Seid Quan watching her. "You. I'm so tired of looking after you and cooking your disgusting meals. I feel nothing but pity for you, you sad, musty old man."

Pon Man steps forward, grabs Siu Sang by the wrist. "That is enough. Do you see how you're scaring the children?"

She laughs. "They're not scared. Look at them. Not a brain between the five of them. How could they be scared?"

Pon Man sees that his father is hustling the girls downstairs into the basement. "We'll leave you if you keep this up. You have to stop."

Siu Sang stands still. "What do you mean, leave me?"

"I mean that I will take the girls and move away."

"You would really leave me?"

"If you don't stop this nonsense."

Siu Sang pulls a paper towel off the roll, dabs at her eyes. "You don't know how hard it is, how hard I work to cook three meals a day for all these mouths. The girls don't appreciate me. You don't appreciate me. It's just as well, I suppose. You can find another wife who won't complain."

Through the window, Pon Man's flowers sway in the breeze. *How nice it would be to sleep among the blooms, feel the dew gather on my body as I sleep.* He feels the guilt inflate his chest, push on his liver and lungs. *I'm not perfect either.* He puts his arms around her waist.

"I won't leave. It'll be all right. It will all be forgotten tomorrow."

Siu Sang collapses into his arms, cries out to him. "I'm so tired. So tired."

He leads her to the bedroom, where he tucks her in. She looks up at him one more time. "Do you know how it is? It will kill me."

He pushes her hair off her forehead. "Yes, I know. We'll all do better. I promise."

Pon Man opens the door to their bedroom; all five of his daughters stand in the hallway, waiting for a sign. "Get in here," he whispers, holding the door open.

Siu Sang does not look at the girls, speak or even grunt as Pon Man orders them into a line at the foot of the bed. He steps back and clears his throat.

Wendy goes first. "Mom, I'm sorry."

Daisy: "I'm sorry."

Jackie: "I'm sorry too."

Penny: "Sorry, Mom."

And then Sammy, squirming under Pon Man's tight grip. "I'm sorry too, Mom."

Pon Man marches them out again and sits, alone, in the living room, staring at the rubber plant in the corner. He can hear his daughters loudly whispering in the kitchen, talking about their mother's insanity.

"Maybe Dad will commit her to a hospital this time."

"I don't care. I wish she was dead."

"She's a fake."

"She just wants attention."

He watches the dust float through a shaft of light that somehow snuck its way through a wayward crack in the curtains.

He imagines the motes as tiny circus clowns tumbling through a big top from a tightrope, or shooting through the air from a cannon.

Pon Man wanders the streets of Chinatown on a Saturday morning, killing time as he waits for his father. Seid Quan is stepping down from his position as chair of the clan association and is overseeing the election to replace him. He had asked Pon Man if he would like to attend. "You could vote. I paid your membership fee last year." Pon Man almost said no, had the word balanced on his tongue. Somehow, though, it never left his mouth, and he drove with his father to Chinatown and walked into the offices beside him. He tried to ignore the surprise on the other men's faces.

It's funny, he thinks, *how hard I have tried to get out.*

He cast his vote (for an old classmate of his, the son of Seid Quan's roommate from the house on Princess Street) and immediately left, turning as he walked through the door. "I'll be in the car," he said, and Seid Quan nodded, his eyes focused on the ballot box.

He walks for twenty minutes, circling the junk shops on Pender, full to the ceilings with paper lanterns, plastic Buddhas and paper fans printed with poorly reproduced bamboo and apple blossoms. He peers through the algae-green water at the live fish who don't bother to swim but instead float in the murky water as if resigned to their fates (steamed whole in cast iron woks, drizzled with hot oil scented with green onion and ginger). At Main and Hastings, he stands for a moment, watching the addicts lurch down the stairs leading to the public underground washrooms. *This neighbourhood has declined.* As soon as he thinks this, though, he knows that it is only partly true; Chinatown was never a respectable place (he remembers the days when the streets were dotted with nightclubs and gambling dens, when burlesque dancers stood in the alleys, half-naked, so they could finish their cigarettes in peace). It is only that, now, the problems have no fine veneer of entertainment or respectability covering them up; rather, they have bubbled to the surface, raw sores on an already scarred and rough skin.

He walks back to the car and slides into the front seat. *Perhaps from here,* he thinks as he wipes off a streak of dust on the dashboard, *no one will see me.*

Pon Man reflects that it is uneasy, the relationship between the Chinese and the single-room hotel dwellers. It is as if they never see each other—although they must, for they are always careful to keep their distance. They have more in common, though, than they think. The goal for everyone is, of course, escape.

He shifts in his seat again, picks up the newspaper lying beside him. "Chinese-Canadians Calling for Head Tax Redress." Pon Man looks closer at the headline and squints as if he does not quite believe what he has just read. Some important members of the Chinese-Canadian community have banded together to demand that the money their grandfathers and great-grandfathers paid to enter Canada be returned with interest. Pon Man laughs.

"How silly that anyone should think we will ever get that money back," he says to himself. "I don't want it, anyway. It's just blood money—pure and simple." He lights a cigarette and hangs the tip out the window.

And he wants to forget. The years between his father's arrival and his own were not happy ones; they were filled with awkwardness, anger and loneliness, physical and otherwise. He remembers wishing he could come to Canada to be with his father, and he remembers that as soon as he set foot on Canadian soil and saw Seid Quan's thin shadow he wanted to go right back. *They will drag everyone's suffering into the open—and ours, too.* He will have to explain the ugliness of the family's past to his daughters (the anger he feels, muffled by years of suppression but still there, churning through his stomach, pushing at his insides, making him feel nauseated every time he hears or smells his father coming, the lost opportunities, always the lost opportunities), and he is not quite ready for that yet.

He sees Seid Quan walking down the street toward him, leaning, as always, to the right to accommodate his shorter leg. Pon Man breathes faster, feels the buildings of Chinatown begin to close in on his car as if they are toppling over and will bury him in their misery-soaked bricks. He leans over and pushes the passenger door open.

They drive away, speeding along the Georgia Viaduct as fast as the car can take them. Pon Man turns his head to his father. "Everything go well?"

"Yes. Peter got in."

Pon Man nods, steers the car toward Venables. "Good. I voted for him."

"They were surprised you came. They said you should come more often, maybe sit on the board next time."

Pon Man says nothing. As he breathes, he can smell Seid Quan's tweedy scent, the faintness of his aftershave, the same brand he used in the barbershop. Pon Man's stomach flips.

"I'm busy enough, I think. The children, you know, and the wife."

Seid Quan nods. "Of course. That's what I told them."

Pon Man knows his father is thinking it is all an excuse, that time could be made if Pon Man wanted, but he cannot go back there, immerse himself in the workings of Chinatown, the place he knows so intimately. Even now, he is sure that, if he were blindfolded, he could find his way among the alleys and streets just by his sense of smell, by the dips of the pavement under his feet. He is no longer a Chinatown boy—he is an accountant with a house on the East Side. He tends a flower garden. He loves his car.

He looks at Seid Quan, at his lined face held still and set, the short hairs around his ears waving in the breeze from the open window. Pon Man's own face hardens, and he lets his body grow cold. If he begins to feel pity, he might just do everything his father wants.

The office is silent, and the cleaning lady has come and gone. Pon Man punches numbers into his adding machine. Outside, it is raining, and the highway is dark and slick. He checks his watch. Six o'clock. He leans back in his chair and stares at his ghostly reflection in the window.

Ed from down the hall pokes his head into Pon Man's office. "Pon, aren't you going home to your lovely wife and daughters soon?"

Pon Man smiles. "Ed, would you want to go back to a house full of women angry at you for being late?"

Ed snorts. "Good point. I guess I'll see you in the morning. Don't sleep at your desk—it'll ruin your neck." He walks down the hall, whistling.

Pon Man takes a sip from his cup of coffee. As he turns to organize his briefcase, he begins to cough. *Went down the wrong way,* he thinks. He closes his eyes and coughs into his fist. He can hear Ed jingling his keys in the reception area. He keeps coughing until tears start to form around the corners of his eyes, until his ribs start to ache from the violence. His chest heaves in and out. His hands shake as he cups his side.

"Pon, are you all right?"

Pon Man opens his eyes and sees Ed standing over him, a full glass of fresh water in his hand. He takes a deep breath, forces the cough to settle in his throat. "I'm fine."

Ed looks doubtful, but hands him the glass of water anyway. As Pon Man reaches for the glass, Ed breathes in sharply. "What's that all over your hand?"

Pon Man looks at the hand he had used to cover his mouth. Splattered all over the skin is new blood, slightly pink and mixed with mucus. He stares at it, then lowers his arm and hides his fist in his lap.

"Too many smokes, I guess. Listen, thanks for the water. I'll see you tomorrow."

Pon Man stands up and hurries down the hall and out the door, not even waiting to see if Ed is behind him. He bursts into the parking lot, running with so much momentum that he feels as if he is being pushed by a giant, invisible breath.

"Cancer." The doctor turns to Pon Man, sitting alone in a white plastic chair.

He swallows. "What are we going to do about it?"

"I'm going to refer you to the cancer centre, and they'll help determine your treatment, but I imagine there will be some surgery and then some follow-up radiation. After that, they'll assess the situation to see if you need anything further."

"Anything further?"

"Chemotherapy. But I doubt you'll need it. You're in pretty good shape. Just remember to stay off those cigarettes."

On the drive home, he thinks of all the ways he can tell his wife, and of all the ways she could react. He fears her screaming and crying, the way she might run to the bedroom and bury herself in the blankets for days. How will he tell his daughters? Wendy is married and out of the house now, and Daisy and Jackie are almost finished school, so he is not as worried about them. It is the younger two, Penny and Samantha—Penny, such an angry teenager, and Sammy, a little girl just getting ready for braces, her limbs just starting to grow out like gangly spider legs—who he fears will grow up crooked somehow, as they try to bend their still-pliable bodies to avoid the sickness.

He turns and stops his car on the gravel shoulder. He rests his head on the steering wheel and cries until his head feels simultaneously swollen and empty.

It is not as bad as he feared. Siu Sang sits on the edge of their bed and listens carefully, nodding at the doctor's instructions for eating and exercise. Pon Man sees a flicker across her face and wonders if she is thinking of being alone with the girls, of having to keep up this house and family on her own. But it is only a flicker and, soon after, Siu Sang writes notes on her calendar so she can remember the dates and times of his appointments. She reaches into his nightstand and pulls out his cigarettes.

"No more of these," she says and takes them outside to throw in the garbage.

He hears Wendy arriving for her weekly dinner at home. The girls chatter in the living room, their voices like the rising and falling calls of swallows. He steps into the living room and sits down.

"Cancer?" Jackie looks blank.

"That's what he said, dummy." Penny sighs heavily.

Wendy sits up straight. "When do you start treatment? I'll go with you to all the appointments and drive you home. You can't drive yourself."

Daisy whispers in Jackie's ear. "Do you think I can still move to Hong Kong?"

Pon Man looks at the two youngest, at Penny staring morosely at her ripped jeans, at Sammy fidgeting in her seat. He leans down. "Do you have anything to say?"

Sammy squirms and shakes her head. She looks over at her older sisters and slumps farther into the couch.

Pon Man stands up, relieved that it is all over. As he turns to walk into the kitchen, he sees that Seid Quan's bedroom door is open. He pauses and wonders if there is any way he can avoid this conversation. Perhaps his father will not notice that Pon Man is not at work. Perhaps the girls will manage to keep it a secret.

He shakes his head and walks slowly to his father's room, pokes his head around the door frame. Seid Quan sits at his small desk, reading *National Geographic*. He turns a page, clicking his tongue at the pictures.

"Father? Can I speak to you for a moment?"

Seid Quan looks up and smiles. Pon Man feels guilty, for he knows that his father hopes this will be a real conversation, that Pon Man will finally reveal himself and Seid Quan will, after all these years, understand the boy who has remained a mystery to him.

Pon Man sits heavily on the bed. "I have just been to the doctor, and it seems that I have cancer. I will be off work for a while, getting treatments. I might end up being very sick." Finally, he has the courage to look up into his father's face.

Seid Quan's shoulders slump forward so slightly that no one who is not his son would ever see it. His father's jaw, usually so firm, has fallen slack. Pon Man's eyes roam the room, rest on a framed photograph of his mother standing in the snow, her head covered by a scarf.

"I don't know what else to tell you. I know very little myself right now. I've been telling the girls not to be afraid."

Seid Quan nods, twists his wrinkled hands together.

"I'll keep you posted. And I'll call Min Lai and Yun Wo tonight to let them know."

Pon Man sees that his father has closed his eyes.

"It'll be all right. I'm not scared." This, he knows, is a lie, but he says it anyway. Pon Man stands up. "Well, I guess I'll go help Siu Sang cut up that chicken. She hates carving."

He leaves the bedroom and tells himself not to look back.

He has fallen into the deepest sleep he has ever had, one from which he is sure he will never emerge, one that will pull him down even deeper if he tries to climb out. But he finds that he doesn't care, that this darkness, punctuated by fuzzy dreams and unknown shapes, isn't really so bad, after all. *Preferable,* he thinks, *to some of the days I spend at the office.*

Pon Man's mind shifts, and he is walking on the crest of a snow-covered mountain. He carefully avoids the sharp rocks and clings to the face with his bare hands, which, he now sees, are tinged blue and peeling. He looks up at the crisp sun, the shadows that seem to tear the light in half, that are nihilistic opposites to the tall peaks he is meant to climb. Something pierces his foot, and he realizes he is wearing no shoes, only a pair of thin khakis and a yellow polo shirt. He shivers.

As he makes his way along the ice and rock, he feels a tug

at his waist. He reaches down and pulls hard on the rope tied through the belt loops of his pants. "What am I dragging?" he says out loud, then shudders at the echo that calls back to him.

Attached to his rope are all five of his daughters, each struggling to keep pace with him. Wendy's nose and eyes are red. Daisy cries openly. Jackie holds Samantha's hand in hers, and Penny stomps like a soldier, sending icy fragments spinning into the air.

"Where are we going?" he asks Wendy.

She looks surprised. "Don't you know? This was all your idea."

And he knows she is right. He must keep going, no matter what, even if he is lost.

They reach the peak, their breathing laboured and shallow. Sammy vomits on his feet, but he can hardly feel it through the numbness.

His mother stands at the peak with a flag. She looks as if she has been waiting for a long time. "I'm so glad you're all here," she says. "Now, we only need to wait for Seid Quan to arrive before we can raise the flagpole."

The girls are delighted and spring forward to put on the fur coats Shew Lin holds out for them. But Pon Man, his feet now encased in thermal boots, looks worriedly out at the setting sun. "How will Father make it in the dark?"

Shew Lin smiles. "There's no need to worry about him. He's stronger than you think."

"No, but he isn't. He really feels the cold."

She waves her hand dismissively. "I've never worried about him, and I don't think we should start now." She turns to the girls. "Come and I'll show you the ice rink. It shines just like a mirror."

Pon Man stares down at the jagged mountain below him, searching the snow for an indication that Seid Quan is on his way. The sun drops, disappears behind another far-off peak, leaving Pon Man standing in a sudden darkness. He can hear the girls snoring and his mother softly singing a lullaby. Still, no Seid Quan. Pon Man peers through the dark, noticing, for the first time, the endless shades of black on black.

He wakes in the middle of the night, moves his head to the side until the sharp pain slices through his throat. *Right,* Pon Man thinks. *I've just had surgery. Such strange dreams, though.*

He squints into the gloom and sees that someone has left the curtains open. Through the window, he can see the overcast night sky, the moonlight reflected on the silvery undersides of clouds. He suspects that, if he could stand up and look down, he would have a view of the hospital parking lot, but as it is, from where he's lying, it all looks painfully pretty.

Siu Sang sleeps on the chair beside him, wrapped in her rose cardigan. Her mouth has fallen open over her small teeth; her glasses sit on top of her head like rakishly placed aviator goggles. He wonders if he should wake her, then remembers that the doctors warned him not to speak for a few days after the operation. He reaches out and pats her arm instead. She doesn't stir.

The door opens and Seid Quan walks in, his hands around a steaming Styrofoam cup of coffee. "You are awake, I see."

Pon Man nods slightly.

"How about I just sit here with you, then, quietly. You should not talk, so I will not tempt you." Seid Quan sits on the windowsill and sips his coffee.

Pon Man feels his eyelids growing heavy again, and the sleep creeps from his toes all the way up his body until the warmth envelops his head. He falls asleep, this time dreamlessly.

A hot summer sky. A thin layer of smog smeared across the sun. He wipes his forehead with the top of his golf cap, then puts it on again. *Remission.* He has been running the word through his mind all day, whenever he has a free moment. *Remission.* He touches his throat with his long fingers.

The colours and noises of the Exhibition swirl around him—spinning lights, the shouts of boys in game booths who brandish three-foot-tall stuffed toys. Pon Man wonders if he will ever succeed in expelling the hot dog smell from his nose. He looks behind him at the Ferris wheel, where four of his daughters are caught in its slow loop. He wonders if Daisy can buy cotton candy where she lives in Hong Kong. Their two carts stop at the very top for just one moment; a breeze sways them gently, and Pon Man's heart jumps as he reaches out his hand. But then, the wheel turns again and they float downward, out of sight.

It was only yesterday that the doctor told him he was cancer-free. He had cried in the office like a woman, a wad of tissue balled up in his hands. Wendy, sitting beside him, laughed and then rested her head on his shoulder.

At home, Siu Sang cooked furiously, pulling together every dish Pon Man had ever said he liked, yelling at the girls to step up and help her before everything went rancid. During the surgery, recovery and radiation, there had been no noise, as if his family were afraid to speak lest they wake the cancer up. He hadn't known how much he missed the racket of banging pots, squeals from his daughters, even his wife's complaints.

When Seid Quan heard the news, he smiled and nodded, placed his lean, spotted hand on Pon Man's shoulder for just one second before he took it away again. As his father walked down the hall to his bedroom, Pon Man shouted to his family, "We should celebrate! How about the Exhibition tomorrow?"

In the blazing sunlight, his daughters stand in line for the roller coaster, eating candy, jostling each other for room. Sammy head-butts Penny in the stomach. Wendy and Jackie giggle, hold their bags of mini-donuts and cotton candy above their heads until the wrestling subsides. Pon Man walks toward Siu Sang and Wendy's young husband, both of whom sit at a picnic table, eating pretzels with mustard. As he sits beside them, his son-in-law, beads of sweat dotting his forehead, gestures to the lineup. "Can you believe it? You couldn't get me on that roller coaster for all the money in the world. I would throw up for sure."

Pon Man watches as his daughters climb into their car— two in front, two behind. When he turns to Siu Sang, she is picking at a large grain of salt caught in her back teeth. "Suicide," she mutters, casting an accusatory glance at everyone in general.

For the very first time, Pon Man wonders what it would be like if his wife died, if she simply expired quickly and quietly, leaving nothing behind. He looks at the lines on her face, her tightly pursed lips, the suspicion in her gaze as she stares at every person who walks by. He closes his eyes against the brightness of the sun and garish colours of the booths around them and tries to remember the young, scared girl he married, the girl who needed him so badly she cried out in the night.

When he opens his eyes again, he sees his daughters' green car rounding a corner and beginning its ascent. From this distance, he can't tell if any of them are scared.

Siu Sang stands up. "Oh," she says, clutching at her purse, holding it in front of her stomach like a shield. "There they go. Pon Man, they're going."

Wendy's husband hurries to stand beside Siu Sang, his upper lip shiny with more sweat. "Come on, Dad. Come see this."

Pon Man stands up just as the car tips over the big fall and begins to speed up. All the girls have their mouths open. Their hair pulls backward, away from their faces. Wendy, her head thrown back in laughter, flings her hands up in the air.

As they reach the bottom, Siu Sang lets out a big breath and collapses on the picnic bench. "I was so scared for a minute," she says. "Such a big fall." Her voice shakes.

Pon Man places a hand on the top of her head, feels the wiry ends of her curly hair on his palm. She looks up at him, her eyes wet and pink, the residual fear lingering in the looseness of her mouth and jaw.

"Did you see that? Oh man, I just about peed myself watching it." Their son-in-law's young face has gone pale and slack.

Pon Man slaps him on the back, and Siu Sang laughs, coughing into her hand. Tears form at the corners of their eyes as they try to hold it all in. She throws her arms around Pon Man's waist and leans into him, pushing him so hard that he holds himself as straight as he can to support them both.

He stares at himself in the small mirror lit from above by a tube of fluorescent lighting. He swallows, feels a slight burning in his throat. Opening his mouth wide, he pushes his tongue to the side, wonders if there is anything to see and, if so, whether he wants to see it. The smell of the urinals (sharp, masked by ammonia) reminds him that he is in the office washroom and that, at any moment, one of his colleagues might arrive and see him standing at the sink, making faces in the mirror.

When Pon Man sits back down at his desk, he pulls his cup of hot tea closer to him. He hasn't felt like eating or gardening or anything other than sleeping. The numbers in the open ledger in front of him seem impossibly small. How had he ever been able to read them?

"I'm fine. We'll be fine," he says to himself. He turns to look at the cars parked in the gravel lot outside, at the trucks rumbling past on the highway in the distance. "I'm in remission. There's nothing the matter with me."

Pon Man cups his hands around the mug, feels the warmth spreading through his arms. He likes the sensation of boiling hot liquid travelling down his throat as if, somehow, he could keep the sickness away with steam.

Pon Man lies hotly in a hospital bed that has been set up in his bedroom. The chemotherapy has sapped everything out of him, and it is all he can do to lie down and watch the hair falling off his body. The house is deathly quiet.

Siu Sang walks into the room, wiping her hands on her sweatshirt. "We have to bathe you today," she says. "The water is ready." Jackie peers around the door, waiting for her mother to tell her it is all right to come in.

His wife and daughter watch as he pushes himself to a sitting position on the edge of the bed. Breathing heavily, he reaches out with both arms and says, "You'll have to help me to the bathroom. My feet are swollen." He stares down at his own thin lap, unable to look Siu Sang or Jackie in the eye.

It is easier, somehow, to pretend he is someone else, that these two women are not his wife and daughter, that he was never the man who used to pay the mortgage and teach the girls how to ride their bikes. He feels their cool hands on his arms and back as they walk down the hall. When they lower him into the bathtub, he closes his eyes so that he is spared the sight of his own naked body.

"Jackie, you don't want to mix the towels. He has his own over here." Siu Sang's voice cuts through the air, and Pon Man opens his eyes. As soon as she sees him looking, she turns away and begins to arrange the soap on the counter.

"You don't want everybody else's things to touch me," he says quietly.

Siu Sang looks confused. "No. I mean—I don't know." Jackie inches backward until she is up against the door.

"Do you think the cancer is contagious?"

"Of course not. I'm not some village idiot."

"Then what?"

She pushes her hair to the side. "It's bad luck, isn't it?"

Pon Man leans his head against the cool tile. "What's bad luck? Do you mean me?"

"Yes, of course." Siu Sang smacks her fist against the counter. "You've been sick and better and then sick again. What kind of luck is that? What if the girls get sick? What if I do?"

He grips the sides of the tub. "Leave. I will bathe myself." Jackie takes a step forward and opens her mouth, but Pon Man waves her off. "Get out. Both of you. I don't need you."

Siu Sang pushes past Jackie into the hall, then turns around and pulls on her arm. They shut the door, and Pon Man hears them whispering, waiting for him to call out, or for the sound of him falling in the tub. He grunts and reaches for the soap.

Twenty minutes later, while drying himself off with as many of the family towels as he can reach, he slips and falls, crashing into the bottom of the emptying tub. Jackie and Siu Sang rush in, and he holds on to them with all the strength he has left. He wishes that this day had never started, that he could just lie in a pit by himself, in a darkness no one can penetrate, where he could live or die—whatever he ends up wanting. There is no choice in this moment, this real life.

As his wife tucks him into bed, he whispers into her ear, "I guess I do need you, after all. I'm sorry."

If she hears him, he cannot tell.

The doctor walks into the bedroom and stares at Pon Man, his eyes sweeping the entire length of his body. Pon Man holds his breath while the home care nurse adjusts his IV.

"Can you walk?" The doctor lifts up the sheet and looks at his swelling feet.

"I can, to the bathroom and kitchen. I don't jog around the block, though." Pon Man laughs, and then stops when he sees that neither the nurse nor the doctor is laughing with him.

"How does it feel when you eat?"

"It hurts my throat, and I've been throwing up." If there was any way to lie, Pon Man would do it.

"I'm going to call an ambulance now. We're taking you back to the hospital. I'm sorry, but you need more monitoring than this." The doctor looks sadly at Pon Man's thin face. "It will be better for your wife, you know—less work. And better for your daughters, too."

Pon Man nods, knowing that this is true. He wonders what happened to the optimism his doctor once had. "Can't we wait until tomorrow? I hate to leave so suddenly. I have phone calls I should make."

The doctor shakes his head. "No, I think we'd better go now. I'd like to get you under observation as soon as possible."

Siu Sang whispers to Jackie, who is standing in the doorway, and they immediately begin packing up Pon Man's clothes, books and medications into recycled shopping bags.

"One more thing: I think we're going to stop the chemotherapy injections. Honestly, they're not doing you any good anymore—they only make you feel sick. We'll keep up the painkillers to make you comfortable."

So certain, this thing, this death, he thinks.

One week later, he lies still in the hospital room, his breath moving deliberately in and out of his body. He feels as if he has been in this small room forever, that his home life is a blurry dream he cannot really remember. He moves his feet in circles, first the left, then the right. Their swelling has not stopped, and he knows that soon he will be unable to move them at all.

It is not often that he can think clearly anymore, and he takes this opportunity to look, really look, out the window. The sunlight is thin and the early morning clouds are strangely motionless. There is no wind today.

Pon Man has long given up worrying about what will happen to his wife and daughters. They are stronger than they appear, stronger even than him. A part of him knows that this, his illness and death, will become part of their mythology, an episode by which they will measure their growth. They will say, in years to come, that watching him die made them stronger, that grieving during those dark after-years only prepared them for newer things. He will become a flawless version of himself in their memories—a righteous man, a gentle victim of disease. He wonders if they will eventually forget the bulk of him, if he will one day be a memory no more substantial than a touching anecdote. He sighs. There's no point in thinking of things he can never control.

He thinks, perversely, of his father. The shaking hands that cut his hair until his treatments caused no more hair to grow. The way he over-salts his food. The care he takes in wearing his suit and fedora to simply drink coffee in the Hong Kong Café with his friends. How disappointed his mother was that they were never the close, whispering-in-ears family she had once imagined.

The way Pon Man never looks his father in the eye.

I've almost forgotten now. Pon Man sifts through the layers in his mind, dusty from morphine and sickness. He knows there is something there, a hint as to why he could not talk to his father without a sneer, why he ignored him so persistently that his daughters learned to ignore their grandfather as well.

He breathes out.

And he wants to cry because his mind has become glue and sludge and because he knows he needs to be forgiven for something, but what? What will he ask for, and how can he when he can hardly speak anymore?

Siu Sang walks in holding a muffin and a cup of coffee. As soon as she approaches the bed, Pon Man grabs her arm. She drops the muffin on the floor.

"What is it? What did I forget?" He asks, pulling her to him so that she feels his hot breath, hears the rasping deep inside his throat. "Can't you tell me?"

Siu Sang tries to pull herself upright, but Pon Man's grip is strong, stronger than it has been in months. She carefully puts the coffee on the side table and looks straight into his eyes. Open wide, searching. Wild. She puts her free hand on his shoulder and tries to push him away. Pon Man grabs her hair.

"You know what it is. You just won't tell me. I wish you were dead." He shakes her and her glasses fall off, onto his chest. Siu Sang screams.

Three nurses run in. One of them pulls Siu Sang off, and the other two hold Pon Man while they tie his arms and legs down with white cotton straps. He struggles, his back arching and his head tilted back, like a baby bird demanding to be fed. Siu Sang slumps in the corner, pulls her cardigan over her shoulders and looks out the window.

After the nurses check her for injuries, Pon Man whispers, "Please let me go. Untie me, please." He can feel sleep dragging him down; he knows he has to fight it if he has any chance of remembering anything. He cries out one last time before he falls, dreaming.

The early morning sunshine casts a pale yellow light on everything—the sheets, the pillows, his wife's hair. Six o'clock and the house is quiet, for once. Pon Man watches his wife's back as she sleeps, the ripple in her muscles as she breathes. He smells her hair, that familiar scent of musk and soap. She turns over, opens her eyes. Smiles.

It is so easy sometimes to say the wrong thing, to open your mouth and ruin a perfect moment. Pon Man can almost feel the stillness on his skin. Outside, he hears the thump of the morning paper as it lands on their front step. The girls will be awake in an hour.

He kisses her, his lips held gently against hers. She giggles softly. Their feet touch under the blankets. *We've been together so long,* he thinks, *and I can still make her laugh.*

five

the garden

I walk out into the sunshine, blink hard at the transition from dark to light. I put my briefcase down to check that my resumé is tucked safely away, unwrinkled. I adjust my suit jacket and stand up straight, trying to look like the sort of young woman who could cheerfully answer phones and photocopy memos. When I start to walk down our front path again, my skirt catches on a pile of thorny rose branches.

"Good morning." My mother waves at me, her hands covered in thick gardening gloves, her head obscured by a wide-brimmed cotton hat. "Watch your step."

I pull my skirt free and stand up straight as my eyes scan the front garden. She has trimmed the roses and planted delphiniums, peonies and pansies, filling up the narrow strip of dirt with a riot of spring blooms. She comes to stand beside me.

"I don't think I've ever done any gardening," she laughs. "Here I am, though, doing my best. The Italian lady next door helped me out."

Without uttering a word, I walk around the side of the house to the back garden. Tomato plants sit on the side, waiting to be planted. The lattice for creeping beans has been dragged out of the garage, where it had been sitting for twelve years, ever since my father died. A pitchfork leans against the fence beside the tall weeds.

When I was a child, our garden was beautiful, a mass of green and red and yellow and orange. Flowers burst open every spring and summer morning, and the vegetables grew fat and glossy. I ran through the sprinkler while my father bent over his plants in his rubber boots.

By the time everything was all over and my father was dead, the garden had turned brown and weedy, its flowers and vegetables buried under the uninvited dandelions and thorny, invasive blackberries. My sisters, who had promised to keep everything growing, forgot (the garden was easy to ignore, surrounded by rocks and fencing; the browner it got, the more it blended into the house itself), and my mother, never a gardener to begin with, retreated into her dark, dusty hole on the couch.

When I return to the front, she is digging a place for the hydrangea bush sitting on the lawn. "Did you see the tomatoes? I'm going to plant those as soon as I'm finished out here. They might die, but it's better to try, isn't it?"

"It looks nice." I pick up my case.

She straightens up. "Yes, it does. I'm very pleased."

I shift my weight from foot to foot, feeling as if I should be saying something (*I'm sorry* or *If I stay here, what will happen?*), so I mutter, "I'd better go. I don't want to be late for my interview." I hurry to the bus stop, my nose filled with the smells of damp earth and freshly cut grass.

———

My father died. People had to be informed. A funeral needed planning. My sisters and I stared at one another for two whole days, and then we got to work.

Daisy flew back home, arriving in Vancouver just twenty-one hours after the doctor's call (I answered and silently passed the phone to my mother, who cried out, tearing the air around us with the sound). Wendy drove to the funeral home, bringing with her the brand new suit she had bought for the body when we knew there couldn't be any more time. Jackie gathered his belongings from the hospital room into paper shopping bags and carried them close to her chest as she moved them from room to car to house. Penny and I stayed home, heating up can after can of soup for our mother and frying bacon and eggs for our grandfather, who didn't eat. He let his plate grow cold, his eyes cast down as if he was patiently waiting for the slow solidification of yolk and pork fat.

I remember my sisters talking bloodlessly about money. The life insurance could pay down the remainder of the mortgage, and Wendy and Jackie would support Penny and me while we were still in school. They would reinvest our father's savings so that our mother would always have something to live on. Daisy decided to move back to Vancouver. Our mother was spared the details. Numbers were nothing more to her than figures on a piece of a paper, presided over by someone else. That someone else became my sisters and, later, me.

Aunt Susie stayed with my mother in her room, emerging only to collect food and tissues. We barely saw them.

When the day of the funeral arrived, five days after his death, we were dry from crying, achy from effort and blank from thinking. People flew and drove in from everywhere, stayed in our house, tried to hold our hands. We pushed them off and poured them tea instead.

We sat on the sofa, all five of us wearing the thin black veils Aunt Susie gave us. I stared at the makeshift memorial my father's sisters had erected on the fireplace. The smoke floated up from musky incense sticks and around my father's picture. Relatives stood around us, silent. I felt as if they were watching us, waiting for one of us to slash her wrists, throw herself down on the carpet and writhe in overwhelming grief. But we simply sat there, our eyelashes flicking against our veils whenever we blinked to keep from crying or looked down at our black, sensible shoes.

The door to my mother's bedroom opened, and she emerged, supported on one side by Aunt Susie and on the other by Aunt Yen Mei. Her head rolled from side to side. She carefully placed one foot in front of the other as if she had forgotten how to walk. I watched as the crowd of relatives swivelled their heads to witness her slow progress across the room.

She kneeled in front of my father's picture. It revealed nothing, and we were the only ones who knew that it had been taken only six months before his death, that the look of displeasure on his face was actually one of pain, that the shoulder pads in his suit masked the thirty-five pounds he had already lost. My mother, who chose this particular photo, always preferred to remember misfortune.

She beat her head against the floor and cried, chanted, screamed. The old ladies who had come to help stood off to the side, murmuring what sounded like approval. I remember feeling as though I was in a ghastly imitation of a poorly acted opera, that my mother was the long-suffering soprano, the old ladies were the myopic crowd in the dress circle, and my sisters and I were the rarely noticed chorus, the ones who kept up the resentful and low background singing.

Later, at the funeral home, my mother was all business, arranging things with the funeral director, who bowed to us like a proper Chinese houseboy—stiff, obsequious. We were seated in a curtained area, separate from the rest of the mourners, presumably so that no one could see us grieving. But back here, my mother was preternaturally calm and spent the hour criticizing, in a loud whisper, the way the pastor was leading the service. I stared at her tear-stained face and listened to her complaints. I wanted to shove her, pull her hair until she acted like a normal person. Instead, I pulled at the tissue in my lap, shredding it into thin strips that floated off into the warm, recycled air when I breathed.

When the casket was lowered into the ground at the cemetery, Aunt Susie instructed us to turn our backs and whispered some dire prediction of what would happen to us if we watched. We all turned and stood there in a line, five black-veiled girls, straight-backed, in the late afternoon sunshine. I remember looking at one of Daisy's friends, a tall and pretty girl with curly honey-coloured hair who was wearing a white dress that shone like a light in the middle of all the black. As the casket went down, I watched her hair float on the wind behind her and her white skirt drift like a ghost around and behind her ankles. She was like a dream within a nightmare.

"Okay," says the eye doctor. "On a scale from one to ten, one being the clearest and ten being the blurriest, how badly is your mother seeing?"

I turn around and look at my mother in her small vinyl chair. She looks expectantly at me, waiting for me to translate what the optometrist, who uses words she doesn't know, has just said. The fluorescent lights flicker, and it is as if I am watching a movie and can see the transition from frame to frame. I open my mouth, knowing that some concepts just don't translate.

I mumble something about numbers and blurriness, and my mother, frustrated, interrupts me in Chinese. "What are you talking about? One, ten, six? He didn't really say that, did he?"

I turn again and say to the doctor, "Seven. She says her blurriness is at seven."

"All right, then, let's turn off these lights and have a look." He spins on his stool and flips a switch, and the room is black except for a thin line of light coming in from the waiting area through the crack at the bottom of the door. I can hear clicking, a deep "Hmmmm" from the doctor and my mother tapping her feet on the floor.

He turns the lights back on. "Well, it looks like things are pretty good. No change from the last time, and if you're careful, your eyes will be great until you're a hundred." He chuckles.

"He says your eyes look good, Mom."

She looks at him and then quickly looks at me. "Is he sure? What about the spots, those black spots I keep seeing?"

I ask the doctor, and he says, "Everyone sees spots, Mrs. Chan, even me. It's nothing to be concerned about."

As I repeat this to my mother, her face changes to fear. If she's perfectly healthy, what will everyone expect of her? Will she have to learn better English or how to file her own tax returns? She brings her hands up to her eyes, touches her lids with her fingertips. I reach out to her and place my hand on her shoulder. I had always thought of her as surrounded by a thin but unbreakable layer of glass that my sisters and I couldn't penetrate, even when we wanted to. Right now, however, touching her, feeling her blood and pulse underneath her skin, I see that it can all be simple, but only if I make it so.

The optometrist says to me, "She's lucky to have you." This I don't bother to translate; after all, she never believes what he says anyway.

That afternoon, after my mother has gone to bed for a nap, I wander around the house, touching furniture and Hong Kong magazines, tissue boxes and shoes. I pull my grandfather's old cigarette tin from my closet and sit down to look through the photographs again, but the air is so still that I leave the tin on the bed and begin to walk, stirring up old smells and older dust. I run downstairs, open the front door and step out into the yard.

The flowers my mother planted three days ago are already growing. Big round peony buds. Pansies that creep along the dirt, filling up space that was once empty. I pick up a stray branch of the clematis that my mother has been try-ing to train over the low brick fence. I loop it around a post, tucking the tendrils into the crumbly grout. I notice that the grass is growing in on the flower garden, so, on my knees, I begin to rip off the uneven blades.

Weeds have started to come back. The topsoil is lumpy. Aphids have begun to eat through the leaves of the new plants. I walk to the garage for gloves, a spade, shears and a bottle of pesticide. In the back, I pause to run my hands over the sprouting beans. "Even if we wanted to stop them from growing, we couldn't," I say to myself.

The soil feels like warm flesh in my hands, as if I am freeing a long-lost, living person from years and layers of

dirt. I pull out buttercups from around the base of the daf-
fodils my father once planted, which have, somehow, sur-
vived years of neglect to return every spring, their blossoms
bobbing in the wind, perennially cheerful even in rain or fog.

When I finish, I lie down on the lawn. Muddy water seeps
through my jeans and sweater, but it doesn't matter. I squint
into the sky, watch clouds floating in from the north. My eyes
close and I fall asleep, the spade in my hands.

In my grandfather's old cigarette tin full of photographs, I find
one in which my grandmother is standing beside a low bush
covered in snow in their front yard. She is wearing a scarf over
her hair and a thick, light-coloured coat. She has taken off her
glasses for this picture and is smiling shyly, coyly at the person
behind the camera. The date is January 1957.

My grandfather, looking through his camera (and at the
photo itself, years later, perhaps every day, perhaps to help him
forget the loneliness of living in a bedroom in a house full of
people who never wanted him in the first place), saw the same
thing I am seeing: a middle-aged woman who has become vain
in his presence, who has, suddenly, it seems, begun to care
about the curl of her hair and the proportions of her smile.

"Perhaps," she might have said, "I love you after all."

In later pictures, they are always close together, shoulders
and hands touching, their bodies finally, I think, talking. "We
are no longer beautiful," she might be saying, "but we are
something else in a different place now, and it is better."

I imagine that my grandfather, so long untouched, cries.

return

Crumpled into his brown brocade chair (once his wife's, with his wife's scent, but after all these years, it is only himself he smells), he cries into his hands, not caring that he will soon have to accompany his daughters and granddaughters to his son's funeral and look dignified and stately, not caring that his suit may be wet, not caring that he has never cried in his life, only now.

How could it be that it is the year 1988 and I am still alive? Seid Quan pounds his own head with his fists. *I should have died a long time ago.*

Outside his bedroom door, he can hear the wailing from his daughter-in-law, who is now, finally, able to weep and scream publicly. His daughters have flown in, Min Lai from Toronto and Yun Wo from Guangzhou. He can feel them hovering in the hall, waiting to hold him up should he collapse. Waiting to surround him and protect his ninety-three-year-old ears from the assault that is Siu Sang's grieving.

When a man has lived long enough to need protection, then he has lived too long.

He stands up, brushes the wrinkles out of his grey wool pants. He will stand as straight as he can, walk like a soldier to keep himself from stumbling blindly. His friends—the ones who are still alive—and their sons will be waiting for him. They will tell him how sorry they are and place their hands on his shoulder in sympathy. They will not be comfortable with an old, weeping man, and Seid Quan hasn't disappointed anyone yet.

He eats dinner with his son's family and does not speak to anyone, not even to his five granddaughters, who, one week after the funeral, are all still staying with their mother. They speak rapidly in English about money and the mortgage, and ignore Siu Sang, who chews slowly, placing one grain of rice in her mouth at a time. He steals a glance at her (sneakily, for, in his experience, direct eye contact does not end well), sees her blank eyes as she eats. Strangely, he misses the rage and fear he had once been so used to. *This emptiness,* he thinks as he pushes the food around in his bowl, *is much worse.* He wonders if he could help her—perhaps they could remember Pon Man together, maybe even Shew Lin as well. But as soon as the thought enters his head, he dismisses it. *She hates me, and I can be no comfort to her.* Afterward, Seid Quan carries his dishes to the sink and walks slowly back to his room, his eyes fixed on the orange-gold of the carpet so that he will not see Siu Sang picking up his plate as if she expects cockroaches to erupt from its surface.

He looks out his window and sees the wall of the house next door, his bedside light reflected as a perfect square of yellow on the white stucco. He turns back to the piles that surround him on his bed, pulls out a thin brown envelope, the address written in thick pencil. A letter from his son when he was still a child living in the village.

Seid Quan finds that he can only let his eyes float over the contents (he is afraid that he will cry again, and he is not sure his body can take it). Phrases jump out, appear like lighted matches before they vanish.

"The others say I look like a girl."

"Mother made dumplings."

"I am sticky from the heat."

"Do you miss us?"

He asked his son, six years ago, why he never talked, why he never looked him in the face. Pon Man turned red and said nothing, choosing, instead, to walk away from his father and leaving him with his questions and an image of his son retreating.

He wonders now if he could have returned permanently to the village, if he would have been a conquering hero or simply a finished man, one whose useful days were irrevocably over. *The village*, Seid Quan thinks. *It took me seven years, working day and night, to pay back the village.* He thinks of the word *slave*, then dismisses it from his mind. *I can't be that way, always a victim, always the one being put upon.*

He pushes the letter back into its envelope and drops it on the floor, where it settles into the carpet delicately, deliberately. He gathers up all the rest and carries them to an apple crate in his closet. Carefully, he stuffs the letters into spots that are seemingly too small for the papers that fill his arms, but Seid Quan is a patient man and, after a while, he has packed the crate so tightly that the lid almost doesn't fit. He pushes down until he hears that click—the click that means the parts of his past he can no longer look at are contained again. He does not remember what the crate hides anymore, can only guess at the contents that could be seventy years old. He is not quite sure if this pleases him or not, only that the hiding is necessary because he has lived this long and could live even longer.

Seid Quan stands up and walks to the kitchen, where his daughter-in-law is washing the dishes. He places the kettle on the stove, murmurs something about making tea and stands there, watching her hands move quickly through the soapy water.

As he opens his mouth to say something, she turns around and says, "Is there something you need? Because I'll just get it for you and then you can sit down and be out of my way."

He looks at her angry face, the tenseness of her neck and takes a step backwards. "Well," he says, "if you could just bring me that tea when it's ready." And he turns around and heads back to his bedroom, tripping on a stray shoe lying carelessly in the hall. He closes the door and leans against it, relieved.

Seid Quan strolls down Pender Street in Chinatown. The shopkeepers nod to him, although these are not the men with whom he played mah-jong or drank whisky. It is their sons now, young men in nice cars, young men whose families live in South Cambie, young men whose homes have a view of the downtown core, where tall buildings blot out Chinatown. He wonders what they pay in property tax, whether their fathers died in nursing homes.

He is now at the corner of Pender and Main. He stops and gazes at the large herbalist's store that used to be his barbershop. It is not so different, really; the exterior is the same red brick, and the same single-room apartment hotel is on the second and third floors. The old women still hustle up the street, sharp eyes examining the dried currants and beans as they walk by. The herbalist, a middle-aged hustler from Hong Kong, looks up briefly at Seid Quan and looks away again. *I suppose I am too old to even really be seen anymore.*

These streets are so familiar to him; his feet navigate every bump and turn automatically. He dreams of his beginnings here: his first coffee, his first meal, his first suit. He remembers the day when he and Pon Man explored the city together, the day when it seemed possible that Seid Quan could know his son. They strolled in Stanley Park, took pictures to send to Shew Lin. They posed for each other at the seawall, Pon Man laughing at his father's stiffness.

"No, Father, you look old. Move your head. Yes, Father, just like that."

When it was Seid Quan's turn, he looked through the viewfinder and was surprised that his son needed no direction, that his body knew just what the camera wanted. Seid Quan waved his hand to tell Pon Man not to move and snapped, knowing that this was a perfect shot.

They bought ice cream at English Bay (rum raisin for Seid Quan, mint chocolate chip for Pon Man) and sat on a bench together, quietly watching ladies and their dogs, young couples with their arms around each other. Seid Quan felt fortified, strong in his conviction to make his son love him and confident of his progress. They would buy a house, just in time for Shew Lin to come and decorate. Pon Man would take over the barbershop, maybe expand enough for a decent pension and to support his parents. There would be a daughter-in-law, grandsons galore and fresh meat and vegetables to be had for breakfast, lunch and dinner. Seid Quan would work in his study, practising calligraphy and listening to opera. No more cafés, no more one-room apartments, no more fourteen-hour days with hands immersed in other men's hair.

Seid Quan smiles, slows down slightly as he walks north on Pender. Somehow, as he walks through the late afternoon light, he cannot remember the bad parts, the times when he was eaten up by loneliness, or the times he thought he might die if he could not see his wife one more time. He sees only the light reflecting off the tall houses, the pigeons pecking at the remains of steamed buns littered over the ground. He thinks he would like to embrace his son just once.

He comes to and finds himself sitting on a bench in a small grassy spot just off Gore. A bus rattles past, and his right knee is sore. He watches the sun dip past the roofs of the shops, feels the evening breeze push through the grasses that graze his ankles. An old man, perhaps even as old as Seid Quan himself, walks across the street, guided by a young woman in jeans and sneakers. In his right hand, he carries a cane, although his hands shake so much, Seid Quan wonders why he bothers. As he totters closer, he looks up at the trees and smiles. Seid Quan realizes he has seen that smile before.

"Lim," he whispers. He holds out his hand, grabs the edge of the young woman's sleeve. She turns, frowning.

"Lim, is that you?" The old man raises his bushy white eyebrows, peers at Seid Quan's brown face. He starts to cough.

The young woman leans over. "I'm afraid he doesn't know his name anymore. Are you one of Uncle Lim's old friends?"

"Yes, yes." Seid Quan stands up straight, holds one of Lim's spotted hands in both of his. "Old friends, from the village. You are one of his relatives?"

She smiles. "No. I volunteer at the nursing home just up the street. Uncle Lim and I are good friends, aren't we?" Lim leans his head against her shoulder.

Seid Quan fishes in his pockets and pulls out a handful of bills. "Please, take these. In case Lim needs something extra. Maybe you could buy him new slippers. Take it." He shoves the money into her hand. "We were good friends once."

"I really shouldn't take this, but thank you. You should come visit. Uncle Lim likes the company."

Seid Quan watches them walk up the street, stares at Lim's hunched back and skinny legs. *Sammy will look like that girl when she grows older,* he thinks, then remembers that none of his grand-daughters would ever hold his arm as they walked down the street together. He tries to think of the last time he had a conversation with any of them, the last time he made eye contact. Nothing.

He knows he must move eventually, return to the house where his daughter-in-law stares at a blank television, but instead he stands in the slowly emptying street, reasoning that no one will miss him. When it is so cold that he feels the familiar stiffness in his joints, he leaves, but not before.

When Min Lai asks him if he would like to move to Toronto to live with her, he understands that it isn't really a question. There is nothing else to do. His son is dead. He is too old to live alone. There is nowhere else to go. His daughter says that, one day, he might come back to Vancouver, after Siu Sang pulls herself together, after things settle down. He wonders what that means.

His daughter and granddaughters pack all his necessary clothes and books and leave him to deal with his papers. He rifles through the top drawer of his dresser, wondering how much he'll need, knowing, of course, that policemen don't stop Chinese men on the street anymore and demand to see their documentation, but thinking that maybe he should bring it all anyway.

"Look at me, thinking like an immigrant," he says to himself.

He ignores the crate in the closet, packed full of his secrets. He briefly considers throwing it out, or burning it, but immediately decides he cannot. He wonders if he will feel lighter when the crate is thousands of miles away.

He leaves almost all of his official papers, neatly bound by rubber bands, folded up into airmail envelopes and stuffed into an old cigarette tin, and takes only his citizenship card and passport. His personal things, though, require more consideration.

On the back of an old takeout menu, he finds an inventory list, written quickly in pencil.

Straight-edged razors, box of 100

Barber's scissors, 4 sets

3 barber's chairs

4 stools on casters

Cash register, used

17 combs

3 jars of disinfectant

4-quart jar of shaving cream

7 tins of hair wax

Aftershave, variety of brands

He thinks of how a man can identify with his work, can say to people he meets, "I am a dentist," and know that it's complete and true. "I am a barber," he says to himself, trying to remember what it felt like. He feels nothing, thinks that perhaps *I am lonely* or *I am arthritic* might be closer to the truth. He leaves the list behind too.

He wakes up at four the next morning, unable to sleep even though his flight does not leave until the evening. He knows without looking that his one small suitcase is downstairs by the front door, that all he has to do is put in his dentures and get dressed. Really, what could be easier? Perhaps he will grow to love Toronto as he grew to love Vancouver. And maybe, this time, it won't take so long.

If someone were to ask Seid Quan about his dreams, he would say that he doesn't have them. All his life, when he woke up in the morning, a pleasant blackness blanketed the events of the night. He went through his days—working, reading, eating— unburdened.

Tonight, he is on an airplane for the first time, hurtling through the darkness. He sits upright, staring at the small reading light above his seat. Min Lai sits beside him, her mouth slightly open as she sleeps. She shifts in her seat, draws the thin airline blanket to her chin. The cabin is quiet (human noise dwarfed by the constant roar of the engine, the hiss of stale air circulating through vents) and his eyes close.

He runs his hands through Pon Man's hair, through the thick tuft at the top, the wispy hairs at the base of his neck. Seid Quan cannot see his son's face, only the black hair, his thin shoulders. He is unsure whether this is the young Pon Man, the small fifteen-year-old boy, or the older, sick Pon Man, the one who lost so much weight he was like a heron, all joints and bones. He decides that it doesn't much matter; as long as it truly is his son, he is happy.

As he trims the hair around the ears, he listens for the sounds of Pon Man's breathing. He can hear the snip of the scissors, even the plop of the damp hair when it hits the floor. But Pon Man remains perfectly still.

It is only now that Seid Quan realizes he is cutting the hair of a dead man; worse, his dead son. But he finds he cannot stop, and he goes on, his hands shaking as the hair drops on his wrists, sticks to his sleeves.

He hears Shew Lin. "It's over now. You can stop."

He looks for her but cannot see her. *How is it that I can see only my son and hear only my wife?* He turns around, and there is nothing but a deep darkness.

"Father? Wake up. They're serving breakfast now." Min Lai pats Seid Quan on the shoulder.

He rubs his eyes and stares blearily at the tray in front of him.

"We'll be home in an hour and a half," says Min Lai, peeling open the top of Seid Quan's apple juice. "And then you can have a really good sleep."

The windows across the street glow amber, the setting sun giving the otherwise expressionless houses an air of mystery, of kept-back knowledge. Seid Quan walks back to his daughter's house in Toronto after a day of walking around a different Chinatown.

Only five months since his son's death.

It was beyond him, then, to imagine the things he would want to say to his son, the kinds of things he would want to ask forgiveness for. Now, as he shivers in the sharp and dry autumn air, his mind will not stop. Even though his feet propel him slowly forward, his memories, the snapshots in his head, keep his thoughts circling endlessly. He walks through a pile of dead leaves and does not notice the crunch, the sound of withering, of dryness.

It was simple; he wanted his son to love him.

A father has a right to his own son.

He feels so far away, farther away than when he lived in Canada alone and could only return to the village every four or five years. Vancouver calls to him (he swears he can hear the ocean even from here, while he walks up and down Spadina, fingering the slippers and fans and lanterns), and his face is always turned west. Here, in this strange city, he has begun to forget what Shew Lin looked like; Min Lai has never had time to organize her photos, and they sit somewhere in her attic in an unmarked box. When he wants to remember, he shuts his eyes and remains perfectly still for several minutes. Even then, he can see only a shadowy outline, a fuzzy version of his wife, as if he is looking through a dirty window.

He is so frustrated that he could scream. But he does not.

He looks up and sees that he has walked two blocks out of his way. He turns around to retrace his steps, hoping that no one is looking out a window and feeling sorry for the addled old man wandering the streets.

Such small trees here, he thinks. *Like starved children.*

His daughter's house is brightly lit, and he can see the shadows of her family moving from room to room. Her sons are good boys and often drive him around the city, showing him the things they think he might be interested in: the CN Tower, Maple Leaf Gardens. They laugh loudly, slap each other on the shoulders, play cards at night in the basement. He is grateful for all the noise.

His son who had no sons himself.

As he walks in the door, his daughter peers out from the kitchen and smiles at him. "I'm so glad you're home," she says. "I've made your favourite dish."

Outside, the wind picks up the fallen leaves and throws them at the house. Seid Quan turns around. "Like dead fingers tapping on the window," he whispers.

Outside, the cars on Queen Street speed past, kicking up

fragments of dead leaves. Inside, Seid Quan lies in a hospital bed. He has had a ruptured brain aneurysm and is dying quickly and quietly. He is not conscious.

He hears the shuffling of his daughters, grandsons and nurses around him and their soft murmurings; it is as if they think that loud words will frighten him into death. He can see nothing except the differently coloured stars underneath his eyelids. He is dizzy. Faces spin, lopsided. He sees Lim slowly cracking in two, blood pouring from the split. He sees Shew Lin's brown, lined skin. Babies. Little girls. Heads of hair.

He wonders if that sound is breaking glass, or if it is simply the sound of his hearing splintering off before it stops working entirely.

He has not moved and has no wish to. There are many things he has outlived, and ninety-four is too old to want to remember. When he sleeps, he dreams as he never has before.

On the last day of his life, when, to everyone else, it seems that nothing has changed, Seid Quan sees his son as he was when he first arrived in Vancouver in 1951. His boyish face smiles; as he turns to walk away, Seid Quan's eyelids flutter and he goes to follow.

Seid Quan and Shew Lin walk together in a park not far from their house, taking a break from their son's growing and noisy family. As they hold each other's hands and look north toward the mountains, they both tuck the minutes away inside their minds. These are moments not to be forgotten.

It is so easy, she thinks, *to forget, to wake up in the morning and see nothing but the old man beside me.*

Those trees are so green, he thinks, *and the mountains so blue, the colour of truth, if we could but see it.*

chinatown

I don't often return to Chinatown. It's hard to look, really look, at the messy beginnings of our lives here, the bustling community whose backdrop consists of damp produce boxes and alleys criss-crossed with sagging power lines and trails of urine. It doesn't sound pretty, and it isn't. The beauty of these twelve square blocks is not why people stay—or are unable to leave.

I walk toward Gore and stop in the grassy area just in front of my grandparents' old apartment. I look down at my feet, firmly planted in the uneven lawn; I don't want to move. A bus drives by and the trees sway in the after-breeze.

In my head, I can hear my father complaining about having to come here. "It's dirty, and there are always street people hanging around."

It's easy to forget about Chinatown, bypass it altogether when you're moving through Vancouver. The tall buildings of the downtown core dwarf it, and there is really nothing here anymore that you can't buy somewhere else. But it remains an uncut diamond in the back of my mind—shining dully, its glow persistent and unflagging.

In this place, which is both familiar and anonymous, no one cares about the rest of the world, only about the price of gai lan today, or the freshness of the cocktail buns. I can become anything I want: the girl who is no longer afraid of herself or the one who spends her nights numbly trying to escape her own body. I have travelled here because I am looking for my mother.

Out of the corner of my eye, I see a familiar moving shape. I turn around and watch my mother struggle with five full grocery bags stuffed with food so she can fill the stomachs of my sisters, their husbands and their children, all heading home tonight for the first family dinner in a long time. She tries to make her way to the bus stop as I stare at the apparent emptiness of her body (the hollowness, as if there is nothing under the skin anymore; is she still unbreakable or even scary?). She looks small and worried, and I feel ashamed somehow. I take a step toward her. She sees me, and the lines drop from her face like a garment. I take her bags and we go home together.

acknowledgments

To Kendall Anderson for her incisiveness, diplomacy and vision.

To Louise Dennys, Diane Martin and Marion Garner for their enthusiasm and faith.

To Carolyn Swayze for knowing from the very beginning that this novel would find a home.

To Mary Novik and June Hutton of the SPiN Writing Group for ideas, solutions and unflagging good cheer.

To Andrew Gray and the Booming Ground Writers' Community for the opportunity.

To Thomas Wharton for knowing my novel could be something better and being the very first person to say so.

To Keith Maillard, the best teacher I ever had, for pulling my real voice out of the muck.

To Alden Habacon for shamelessly promoting me everywhere he goes and truly believing I can write no wrong.

To my sisters for recognizing the writer in me when I was seven.

And finally, to Troy, for everything.

JEN SOOKFONG LEE was born and raised in Vancouver's East Side, where she now lives with her husband. Her poetry, fiction and articles have appeared in a variety of magazines, including *The Antigonish Review,* *The Claremont Review,* *Horsefly* and *Jasmine.* She was a finalist in the Stephen Leacock Poetry Contest and was a Knopf Canada New Face of Fiction for *The End of East.*

Visit her Web site at www.sookfong.com.